Praise for *The Crows of Beara*

"As Johnson's wounded, good-hearted characters sort inner truths along the mystical Irish coast, the personal decisions and missteps they make have consequences that reach around the world. A captivating tale of our yearning to belong and the importance of following this ancient call." — Kathryn Craft, award-winning author of *The Far End of Happy* and *The Art of Falling*

"Like Ireland itself, *The Crows of Beara* pulls at something deep inside the reader and won't let go. In this captivating and thoughtful novel, the enchantment of Ireland heals two damaged souls and reminds all of us that no matter how dark life may be at times, there is always hope." — Kelli Estes, USA Today bestselling author of *The Girl Who Wrote in Silk*

"You don't have to love rain or Guinness or wild, windswept coasts to be seduced by the delicate intermingling of Irish mythology, environmentalism, and love that are entangled at the heart of this novel; the juxtaposition with darker, harder truths of grief and addiction create a rich and reflective resonance. From France to Ireland, across centuries and oceans ... where will this author take us next?" — Jenny Williams, author of *The Atlas of Forgotten Places*

"Haunting, hopeful, and transporting. You'll sink into this story of loss and redemption and be carried away from the very first page." — Kelly Simmons, author of *One More Day* and *The Fifth of July*

"*The Crows of Beara* takes the age-old question of whether a book's setting can be a character one step further by proving that it can be an emotion. Ireland is longing. Daniel is the lure. And Annie—well, she's something special. A sumptuous book through and through." — Scott Wilbanks, award-winning author of *The Lemoncholy Life of Annie Aster*

"Julie Christine Johnson swept me away from the first page ... I wanted to fly off to Ireland immediately and hike the Beara Way. Annie Crowe is that memorable character—flawed but vulnerable—who fails in fits and starts but engages the reader with her desire to rediscover life. Johnson writes with her pulse on the heart of the people who fly off the page. When she introduces Daniel, aching and shamed, she does not fall into sentimentality. Opting for truth, she creates depth, even when reaching back into Gaelic mythology to prove her point. Johnson writes music on the page with words. She is a lush writer who does not turn away from the heart."
— Julie Maloney, poet, author, director of Women Reading Aloud

"In this important novel, Julie Christine Johnson brings together a remote peninsula in the west of Ireland with environmental issues that threaten a local community and its attachment to the landscape...Written in a lyrical voice with honesty and authority on the environment, addiction and recovery, and the magic of the Irish landscape, *The Crows of Beara* is a passionate story of one woman's recovery of her soul." — Christine Breen, author of *Her Name Is Rose*

"Stirring and poignant, *The Crows of Beara* is storytelling at its finest—a heady mix of the familiar and new discovery. In her newest book, Julie Christine Johnson carries you on an emotional journey that you won't want to end as you travel alongside her beautifully drawn characters from both the natural and the mystical realm. I loved this book."
— Amy Impellizzeri, award-winning author of *Lemongrass Hope* and *Secrets of Worry Dolls*

"A beautiful, powerful novel about the mystical songs of ancient Ireland, two damaged souls fighting for the hope of a second chance, the healing power of place, and the importance of listening to your heart. My heart ached for Annie and Daniel and cheered for their resilience. This is not a novel I will forget." — Barbara Claypole White, bestselling author of *The Perfect Son* and *Echoes of Family*

THE CROWS OF BEARA

A Novel

JULIE CHRISTINE JOHNSON

Ashland
Creek
Press

The Crows of Beara: A Novel
By Julie Christine Johnson

Published by Ashland Creek Press
Ashland, Oregon
www.ashlandcreekpress.com

ISBN 978-1-61822-047-9
Library of Congress Control Number: 2016951335

Cover design by Rolf Busch (www.rolfbusch.com).

For Jon

The Beara Peninsula, southwest Ireland

March 2012

It is that nervous time between seasons, when chill winds skirr across faces upturned to the sun. Light spills over the eastern hills and dives into the valley, sparkles on the western bays. Two small crows reach with red feet and alight on the Hag. They dance along her spine with measured, delicate steps to the music of instinct. As one creature, the birds lift their heads to the bay and slice the air with their scimitar beaks. They affirm an unspoken request with an echoing ker ker *before swooping up and careering off air currents that take them south and west to their fragile home in Ballycaróg Cove.*

The crows leave behind the Hag, her sightless stone eyes fixed on a point far across Coulagh Bay where the silver-blue water roils across rocks and slips into the Atlantic. Her chiseled profile shows a long, straight nose falling from the soft curve of her brow. Gray hair streams behind her, caught in the forever wind that scours this small promontory, beating the grass down to a nubby carpet. Of her seven lives, she has been captured here in her prime, a woman full and complete, defiant in her solitude as she waits endlessly, some say for her husband, others for mercy that will return her stone body to flesh and blood.

Many travel far to lay a hand on the blade of her back, leaving tokens of gratitude or supplication at her feet, tokens that fade or are torn apart by the rain and carried away on the wind. Still others are born with the soul of the Hag—she who is the essence of Ireland—and carry her spirit into the world, seeking out those in need of her wisdom and lifting them to grace.

1

Seattle, March

Annie turned off the engine and rested her forehead on the steering wheel, gathering strength. Stephen's SUV sat squarely in the center of the carport, forcing her to park the Jetta on the street. He'd always left the covered space for her. The house hunkered in silent rebuke, complicit in the denial of this small gallantry.

Burdened like a packhorse, her gym duffel strapped across her chest, a canvas grocery tote in one hand, laptop bag hanging from a crooked arm, she trudged past the Koshals' minivan. The daffodils lining the sidewalk had bloomed with such eagerness just last week. Now they lay flattened against the cement, defeated by the day's rain.

The back door was locked. Annie dropped the bag of groceries to the cushion of her toes and fumbled in her jacket pocket for house keys. Slamming into the house in a cursing, spilling bundle of exasperation, she tripped on the straps of the tote. The bag went airborne as she yanked her foot free, pinballing loose fruit, containers of Greek yogurt, and cartons of deli takeout into the baseboards. Taking two jump-steps forward, fighting for balance, she met the edge of the cooking island with her hipbone. Profanity did little to ease the pain, but it kept the tears at bay.

The lingering scent of onions sautéed in butter told her that Stephen had eaten already. His anger lurked, tight and dark, in the shadows beyond the kitchen.

She collected the scattered containers and bruised fruit, depositing them in the fridge. Peeling away the foil from a burst yogurt carton, she dipped a spoon in what remained and stirred the chunks of black cherry from the bottom. Dinner. After a few swallows, Annie kicked off her running shoes and tiptoed across the polished fir floors.

Their bedroom door was open, but no lights were on; only Annie occupied that room. Light glowed from underneath Stephen's office door, and she wondered for the first time if he had returned to their bed during her weeks in rehab, or if he'd stayed in his office—spending nights on the long leather sofa, wrapped in a down comforter, watching ESPN. She rapped lightly with one knuckle and turned the cool brass knob.

He sat slumped on the otter-brown sofa, his feet propped on the coffee table, a beer bottle in one hand, balanced on the flat plane of his stomach. Annie had insisted he not deny himself alcohol because of her, but he'd cleared the house, hauling their prized cellar to a wine storage place down in SoDo. She hadn't seen him drink since she'd returned home from Salish. Her heart thudded at the evident end of his solidarity with her.

"Hey," she said to his empty stare at the muted TV. A sudden breeze tossed rain at the house, and the soft pattering of drops against window glass broke the silence. He flicked his eyes to her, then back to the blur of moving images. Annie rested her bruised hip against the doorjamb and pressed hard to sear the pain into her skin.

"Stephen, are you all right? Did something happen at the store?"

He exhaled a long breath from deep in his throat. She thought of the yogic breathing she used to relax her mind and sink into a pose: lightly in through the nose, audibly out from the back of the throat. But Stephen was not relaxed. Despite his slouched position, his knuckles were white and his legs were taut. The air around him hummed with an electric storm of tension.

The sudden lift of an arm. The arc of a wrist. Glass exploded beside her head and a tepid wash of acrid hops and sweet malt splashed over her. Stunned, Annie let the liquid drip from her hair to the floor, where the beer bottle lay in shards.

"Okay." She breathed, wrapping her arms around her rigid frame. "What did I do?"

"Did you think I wouldn't find out?"

"Find out what?" But she knew.

"Spare me the innocent routine, Annie. No more lies. After everything we've been through with you, after all I've done to get you back on your feet, you go and fuck some guy from your AA meeting. What a fool I've been." His feet crashed to the floor, and he dropped his face into his hands.

"How did you find out?" She began to tremble. She'd seen her husband cry only when he won triathlons. This vulnerability frightened her more than his anger. But the worst was over. Admitting to her betrayal was the uprooting of an abscessed tooth: the relief of released pressure greater than the acute agony of opening the wound.

He rolled his forehead between his palms and laughed. When he looked up, his face was dry, but his eyes were rimmed in red. "That's all you have to say? 'How did you find out?' What does it matter? I found out. That's enough."

Her cheek was beginning to stiffen with dried beer. Annie could smell the sweet and sour essence of orange and pine, thought of sticking out her tongue to taste it. She had to pee. She wanted to wash the barroom smell of the beer out of her hair and the gritty sweat from hot yoga off her skin. Maybe after a shower she'd feel less like she wanted to die.

"I'm sorry," she said.

"I can't do this anymore. I thought after rehab we'd have a way to start over together, that you'd have something to build on."

"It's been only two months." A protest, lamely delivered through her sludge of shame and regret, as if she had a right to be indulged because she was trying.

"That's right. Two months supposedly into a new life"— *supposedly*; the bitter word pierced Annie, but her small gasp didn't slow him down—"and you're having an affair. With another alcoholic, as if you couldn't wait to punish yourself even more." His voice barely rose above the rush of wind and rain at the window. "It's time for you to go, Annie. Go wherever you need to make you happy, or at least to get your life off the rails. You're my wife, and I love you, but I won't turn my life over to you."

Too weary to counter the dismissal, Annie eased out of the room. The bottom of the closing door slid over broken glass, sweeping it into the hallway.

"Annie."

She stopped just before the door clicked shut. Into the small sliver of light she said, "I'll go. Give me a couple of days to sort something out."

2

The faint patter of rain grew louder, finding perfect syncopation as it dripped from a loose gutter. Then the rhythm stuttered, and Daniel realized someone was rapping on his studio door. He yanked down the surgical mask that covered his mouth and nose.

"*Entrez!*" he shouted in mock-French. He pulled the mask back into place with one gloved finger and continued to gently stir sodium thiosulfate, concentrated nitric acid, and distilled water in a heavy glass laboratory flask.

"I can't! My hands are full of tea tray," Liam called back.

"For Chrissake." Daniel plugged the top of the flask with a rubber stop and stripped off his mask and gloves.

"Why did you come out here in this mess?" He held open the door for his nephew, and Liam backed in with the tray, shivering in his soaked T-shirt. "And why aren't you wearing a jacket?" Not that he needed an answer. Thirteen-year-olds didn't wear jackets in the rain. He took the tray from Liam's trembling hands and nodded to the line of coat pegs just inside the door. "Put on a sweater. There's a towel on that hook there. Dry your hair, and I'll pour you some tea."

The tea tray went onto the counter next to the deep

industrial sink. Daniel's three-meter-long worktable was taken up by a thin, rectangular expanse of copper. Liam yanked on a stretched and torn wool sweater, wiped his nose on the sleeve, and ran the sleeve across his head in a feeble attempt to dry his dripping crop of red-gold hair. Daniel snorted as he handed the boy a mug of tea with a tiny spoon inside to stir the cream and sugar. Liam took it with mumbled thanks and grabbed a handful of shortbread and cream biscuits from the tray. "Mom said to remind you that Mort and Michael would be over for supper tonight, to talk about the mines and stuff," he said through a mouthful of chocolate cream. Crumbs sprayed from his lips, and Daniel's heart swelled with love for this sweet, awkward kid. "She says to be at the table by six and not a minute later."

"Or we'll both be in for it, eh?"

"That's Mom for you."

"Don't I know it." Daniel winked. Fiana could exasperate the hell out of him, but he was careful to show only respect or a teasing affection for her around his nephew and Liam's older sister, Catriona. All that was good about his life he owed to Fiana and her children.

"What's that for?" Liam nodded toward the copper sheet. He walked to the table's edge and rubbed the flat of his hand against the lustrous metal.

"I'm not certain yet. The light will tell me its story."

Liam peered at the windows. "What light?" Under overcast skies, the studio's interior had dulled to pewter.

"Wait a few minutes, and I'll show you." Daniel placed a hand beside his nephew's. His, mottled with light-brown freckles from hours spent outdoors as a hiking guide and marred by cuts from sharp tools and small chemical burns; the boy's, still pale from the waning winter, hairless and delicate—a child's hands, really, though his fingernails were chewed to the quick. Daniel prayed Liam had only girls and homework to worry him for years yet. "Any calls from Aoife?"

"Aine."

"Right. Aine." Daniel corrected himself, swallowing a smile. "So, she called you?"

"We text sometimes."

"Ah, modern love. No one talks on the phone. They just text. Do you ever speak in person?"

"Daniel," Liam whined. Liam and Catriona hadn't called him *uncle* since he'd returned from Cork Prison. Fiana had insisted on the honorific, but Daniel told her once to let it go and they wouldn't speak of it again. She'd set her mouth in a thin white line but held her protest.

"I never know what to say." Liam blushed crimson to the roots of his orange hair. "I can hardly stand to look at her. She's so fine."

"She'd probably appreciate it if you did look at her every once in a while. Girls are like that. Any more thought of asking her to the Spring Ceilidh in Bantry?"

Liam hunched his bony shoulders, and his chest collapsed into a shrug. He crammed one hand into his jeans pocket and raised the mug of tea to his mouth, blowing apart the rising steam.

The light spared them both. Through the clerestory windows that ran in rectangles under the roofline of his studio, Daniel had watched as the snapping wind scraped the skies clean and the windows flashed with the late-day sun.

"There. Now we have a story." He squatted down, bouncing lightly on his toes, until his eyes were level with the surface and motioned for Liam to do the same. "Careful—those edges are sharp," he warned when Liam wobbled on his haunches and reached out to steady himself. But Daniel wasn't speaking about the table's edge. He had his eye on the corners of the copper sheet he'd picked up in Cork earlier in the day.

O'Meara's Roofing rang him when they received a supply of scrap copper—the kind he most preferred—sheeting that had been cut, trampled on, or left in the rain until it was bent and scratched and oxidization had started. This sheet, though largely intact, had been salvaged from the site of a housing estate that had stalled in mid-build when the developers declared bankruptcy. Yet another victim of Ireland's corroded economy. But this copper was a survivor. Daniel had a way with survivors.

"See the way the color is starting to change here." He pointed to the trails of iridescent pinks seeping into streaks of brassy yellow. "This hasn't been treated with anti-stain oil." He scooted to his left, running his fingers over a bend in the thin metal. "You can just see a shimmer of blue-green. That's oxidization. This piece has been outside a few weeks, and with this rain … " He spoke to himself now, and to the copper, imagining the shape it would take under his torch, hammer, and shears; the landscapes the patina would reveal as it ate away at the surface.

A shaft of sunlight shot through and bounced off the riotous copper. Liam fell to his backside, dramatically covering his eyes with his hands. Daniel closed his in thanks. He knew what to do. The light had shot a filigree of black veins across his vision that became an image of the gorse hanging on with fierce determination to the rocks of Ballycaróg Cove. This sheet would become the backdrop of those cliffs; he would etch the gorse needles and spines, the pockmarked cliffs, and the massive plates of rock into the copper, and then patina the sheet until the blue-green of the Atlantic glowed through.

He rose, grimacing at the sharp pop from each knee. "Thanks for the tea, lad. Just leave the tray, and I'll bring it in later. Tell your mom I'll be on time."

Liam shuffled off, pulling on the cuffs of Daniel's ratty sweater.

He didn't mean to be short with the boy, but when it was time to create, the world ceased to exist. Except the world of his copper canvas.

The two or three hours before dark were Daniel's favorite time to work. Gold and coral saturated the western sky, and the east bled shadows of blues and green—colors that lived in the fire and water of the metal and glass that filled his studio.

He sketched and discarded several ideas but felt his hands approaching the lines and shades of the copper sheet. He lost himself in the light that swelled and pulsed in the shed he'd renovated into his studio and living quarters. The hum of Fiana's incoming texts and calls was lost in the Mendelssohn violin concerto that filled the studio.

"Daniel, dinner!" Liam pounded on the door.

The fine point of Daniel's pencil snapped, and he swore softly. "On my way," he called.

His nephew, stripped down to his T-shirt once again, shivered on the small space of poured concrete that served as the studio's front patio. In the bedimming dusk, they tromped across the yard to the house. The calendar had declared spring several days ago, but tonight the clocks would change and the light would linger, dipping later each evening into the Atlantic, where the southwest coast of Ireland felt like the end of the world.

3

Racing up First Avenue, her ankles wobbling in stiletto-heeled boots, Annie slipped sideways between clusters of tourists descending toward Pike Place Market. It was raining, a soft weeping of the gray-white sky that epitomized late March in the Puget Sound. Rainwater filled the lid of her to-go coffee, and her dark-blond hair, pulled into a high ponytail, shimmered with moisture.

She pivoted out of the revolving door into the lobby and took the stairs two at a time to the mezzanine office of Magnuson + Associates: Strategic Communications. As she blew past the open threshold of Serena's outer office, she caught Beth's pointed look at the clock on the opposite wall. "I know, I know," Annie said. "There was an accident on the Aurora Bridge." The office manager waved a hand, as if pushing her through the air into the CEO's inner chamber.

Serena, her lips drawn into a thin line, squinted over the top of her crescent-shaped reading glasses. "Annie. Come in and shut the door. We need to talk."

Annie hesitated, swallowing back her dread. She was twelve again, called into the principal's office for a reprimand at best, punishment likely. She pressed the door shut behind her.

"I know what this is about. I haven't been pulling my weight." Not giving Serena a chance to respond, Annie rushed on, spilling out the phrases she'd picked up in therapy. "It's taken time to establish healthy routines, to get used to the idea of my life as a different person." *To get used to the idea of being alone.* But no one other than her AA sponsor knew the current state of her marriage. "This isn't me forever, Serena."

Her boss held up a hand and removed her glasses, leaving them to dangle on a thin chain around her neck. Aware of and yet unable to stop the protective stance, Annie crossed her arms over her chest, elbows braced in her palms. A shield against what was to come.

"The problem is, it's been you for a long time," Serena said. "The relief around here while you were gone was palpable. I can't deny that morale has tanked in the weeks since you've been back. This is a small firm, and we're all bearing the burden of your crash. Your colleagues have covered for you, taken over your projects, managed your clients. They've done it out of love and respect, but everyone is tired. I'm tired. We can't continue on this way."

Sinking into the chair that faced Serena's desk, she asked, "Are you firing me?"

"No." Serena let the word hang, and it drifted into an unstated *but*. "I don't know how much longer I can protect you," she said at last. "The partners want to renew your performance warning."

Cold fingers of dread squeezed Annie's belly.

"We can't—we wouldn't—fire you for being an alcoholic. We can, and we will, fire you for not doing the work you've been given. And we already have enough incidents on file to do just that."

Annie directed her gaze beyond the office's glass wall to

13

the bustle of the graphics studio, flooded with natural light, then to the boardroom, where a meeting was underway. Two of her colleagues walked by, their glances shifting sideways into Serena's office, then quickly away.

She'd met Serena at twenty-three, not long after a slide down a mountain trail had shattered her left leg and her dreams of a running career. Before her injury, Annie had been a darling of the running-shoe company that had built the university stadium where she'd risen to collegiate championship levels. The Olympics were in her sights. Two months after the accident, Serena had approached her with a job offer. "I've seen how you work a running oval, a press box, a crowd," she'd said. "You soothe egos and bring people together."

Back then Serena was a junior partner at a public relations firm in Portland that managed the shoe company's marketing campaign. She was setting up her own firm in downtown Seattle and brought Annie on board. They'd been together since the beginning of Magnuson + Associates; Serena had given her a first chance at a new life.

Fifteen years later, Annie sat in the silence of her shame. But she wasn't being fired. Not immediately, anyway. She trembled as relief seeped in. This was the last thing of her old life she could hang on to—proof she'd been worthy of trust and respect and would be again.

Yet even as she sighed into the reprieve, a hollow of disappointment opened up. Rehab had meant finding new ways to cope with life without numbing the pain. But rehab wasn't the real world. It was a controlled environment, deep in the woods, safe and protected and free from everything she'd been trying to escape. Returning to the same life she'd left to get sober felt like defeat. Without her job, she would be something undefined. But she would be free. Still Annie probed further, admitting that nothing had yet filled the cavern left by alcohol. And that terrified her. Where could she go but this place, at once so familiar and yet uncomfortable, no longer in need of her, no longer safe?

A sharp throat clearing made Annie refocus her attention.

"Look." Serena's brown eyes lost their hard veneer, and her shoulders dropped as she softened from boss to longtime friend. "I have fought to keep you. I'll keep on fighting. I believe in the passionate, funny, razor-sharp woman who is determined to rebuild her life, the Annie who kept running despite the shattered leg, who pulled herself up after she lost her brother—"

"Stop," Annie whispered, fighting back tears. "Just stop." Serena had pushed her to the edge. "What do you want me to do?"

"I've handed you soft assignments until you got back on your feet." Serena smoothed a hand across the pristine surface of her desk, and the moment of tenderness was gone. "But now I need you to pick up the slack. This contract with Eire-Evergreen is the biggest thing we've taken on since the viaduct campaign, and I can't have a senior associate writing press releases and proofing copy."

Annie held her breath, her thoughts spinning through the recent e-mails she'd only skimmed before dropping them into a virtual folder she'd then ignored. It hurt too much to be excluded from a project that once would have been her exclusive purview: a tangle of environmental versus business interests in a place she knew better than anyone here: Ireland. Eire-Evergreen Metals, an Irish-American subsidiary of an Australian mining conglomerate with a plan to develop a copper mine in a remote corner of southwest Ireland, had contracted Magnuson + Associates to develop its public relations strategy.

But Annie had shredded her credibility in the months before she'd entered treatment, and she'd done little to regain her footing in the firm since returning to work. She'd swallowed her protests when word got out that Jeff Franklin had been tapped to manage the Eire-Evergreen campaign. Perhaps she'd misunderstood. Perhaps Serena recognized her potential.

"If you want me to take a larger role, send me to Ireland." The idea occurred to Annie at almost the same moment she spoke the words aloud. Working in a place she loved would take her mind off her failing marriage and the drudgery of recovery. Someplace far away from the disappointed scrutiny here. And not just anyplace.

Ireland. She'd felt whole there. A high school summer exchange in Cork, chosen by her dad from the available list of his Rotary club, had led to a love affair with the place that she'd tried to sate with repeat visits to hike its many national trail ways. She'd brought Stephen along once, a few years ago, and they'd hiked the Kerry Way, but Ireland had always felt like hers alone.

Serena curled her sleek, mink-brown bob behind her ears. "You know we've already assigned the project to Jeff?" she said, her voice even and low.

"I heard, yes." Annie bit back the critical comments of her colleague that her fortified-by-booze self would have let slip through. Then she flushed with the sudden, manic conviction that she must be the one to go. Her knees knocked against the desk front as she sat forward, heart racing.

"Serena. Listen. I've proven I can take sticky environmental issues and spin them into pluses for the community. The Seattle viaduct campaign. I owned that." She pressed her hands tightly between her thighs to keep control. "I'll sell Eire-Evergreen's dream so the community thinks they dreamed it first."

She received a thin smile and a slight shake of head in response. "You're two months out of rehab," Serena said. "You couldn't possibly take on a major PR campaign five thousand miles away from your support system."

"What if I relapse? Is that what you're thinking?"

Serena raised her eyebrows a fraction.

"I mark each and every sober day on my calendar. One hundred five and counting."

"What would your counselors and your doctor say?"

What would they say? Annie had no idea, but she'd find a way to sell this to them, too. "What if they give the all clear?"

Serena sat for a long moment, eyes cast down to her hands, spread flat on the blotter. Then she drew her palms to meet, interlacing her fingers, tapping the lacquered red nails of her thumbs together. "You couldn't know this, but I've got a dilemma on my hands."

That dilemma played itself out in her uncharacteristic fidgeting. Annie held her breath.

"Jeff's wife has just been diagnosed with preeclampsia, and she's confined to bed rest for the duration of her pregnancy. Months. Jeff has asked to be taken off the campaign, and I need to make a replacement, immediately. Eire-Evergreen wants someone there, ready to go, in two weeks."

Hope rippled through Annie. *Please*, she pleaded silently.

"Perhaps your instincts are right—perhaps this project could be a lifeline to you. But it may also be your last chance at this firm. Do you understand what I'm saying?" Serena paused, her gaze fixed and unwavering on Annie's face.

Her boss's scrutiny and doubt were almost visible in the air as Annie weighed all the arguments against her and tried to quickly build a defense. "It will be the last one I need. I promise. I won't let you down. I'll have a project proposal to you by Monday." The AA insider's joke came back to her: *How do you know an alcoholic is lying? Their lips are moving.* She'd promised herself she wouldn't fuck up again. Which is precisely what she'd done in her marriage. But if she could just get out of here, away, *back to Ireland*, she'd be all right.

"Talk with your doctor," Serena was saying. "Then talk to me."

~

His 4Runner was gone—Stephen had left that morning for the IRONMAN triathlon in California—but Annie parked on the street anyway. The night he'd thrown the bottle at her, she'd found a room in an extended-stay hotel just off I-5, north of downtown. She hadn't gotten around to thinking beyond that. Their Green Lake Arts and Crafts bungalow was no longer her home. But she still had her key.

The plastic archive bin she sought was on the top shelf of the guest room closet. Annie clicked on the closet light and tipped the bin toward her, catching it in her outstretched hands as it began to fall. Sitting on the carpeted floor, her back against the bed, she opened the bin.

Two maps were rolled tightly inside a cardboard poster tube—they hadn't been unfurled since she and Stephen bought them at a Waterville souvenir shop during their hike four years ago. The top map was of the Iveragh Peninsula, the one they'd traversed on their walk of the Kerry Way. So enamored of their hike in Kerry, they'd decided to return the next summer and tackle the peninsula just to the south, which promised wilder beauty and more challenging trails than the Iveragh. But then her mother died and the world began to close in, one drink at a time. They did not return to Ireland that next summer, nor any that followed. The map became a memory never shared. The Iveragh remained curled shut beside her.

Annie held open the second map with one hand and her folded legs. It was an aerial drawing of the Beara Peninsula, the rises of its barren hills colored light brown, its pastured land in scales of soft green, the few villages a collection of white dots. Most of the space was devoted to blue: the Atlantic Ocean, Bantry Bay, and the Celtic Sea defined the craggy, narrow spaces of land. She ran her finger up one end of the peninsula and down the other, searching for Ballycaróg.

"It's not even on the feckin' map," she declared in her approximate Irish accent. "Oh no, wait. Oh. You've got to be kidding me."

Beara stretched away from the southwest coast of Ireland into the North Atlantic like the long foot of a lizard. At the tip of the foot was a gnarled knuckle of land: the Slieve Miskish mountains. The knuckle slid south to end in three claws—the westernmost tips of the country. Ballycaróg wasn't at the very end of the earth—that distinction belonged to the edge of Dursey Island, ten miles south—but it was tucked into a cove that looked toward nothing but ocean, all the way to Canada's Maritime Provinces. Annie lifted her hand, and Beara rolled up to the edge of Bantry.

She'd been to Bantry once, during her high school exchange in Cork. Her host family had taken her out for a Sunday drive, and by the time they arrived in that village by the bay, she was green to the gills from sitting in the backseat while her host father careened along the winding, narrow roads. She remembered the brightly colored buildings all in a row, their reds, yellows, salmons, and blues defiant behind sheets of June rain. The jumble ended where the hills began, covered in bright green pastures marked by hedgerows. Pastoral. Peaceful. Parish churches. And pubs.

She pushed back the rolled-up edge and searched again for the little cove that sheltered Ballycaróg. "What do you have in store for me?"

She tipped her head back against the bed, her finger still perched on the edge of Ballycaróg Cove. Her thoughts drifted away, but her eyes lit on a small black nylon bag sitting on a lower shelf.

Not long after she'd arrived at Salish Treatment Center in Port Townsend, Stephen had made the trip from Seattle with her Nikon. He'd pushed the camera bag across the cafeteria table, saying she was in one of the most beautiful places in the Northwest and that it might do her some good to show an interest in photography again. She took the bag back to her room and stashed it in her suitcase. The deeper she'd fallen into her addiction, the more she'd let her love for photography slip away, along with everything else that had brought meaning to her life.

Now, she rose and took another camera bag from the shelf. She carefully lifted out the camera, turning its cool, compact black-and-silver body in her hands. It was a Leica M-P Rangefinder, a manual camera that cost as much as a used car. Her parents had presented her with this camera fifteen years ago, while she was still in the hospital recovering from the shattered femur. But the camera had been Ryan's idea. Only her kid brother knew her well enough, had listened to her chatter about photographer Sebastião Salgado during the rare times she could get free of school and training to come home. After her accident, Ryan had researched the Brazilian and the equipment he used, and set out to save his sister's soul. She hadn't touched the Leica since Ryan died.

Annie repacked the Leica, grabbed the larger Nikon bag with its lenses and accessories, and set the camera bags in a large duffel. Around them, she arranged all she thought she would need for Ireland: rain gear, suits, blouses, sweaters, a pair of running shoes. She left the house the way she came, through the kitchen door, into the rain.

4

They were six squeezed around the table, elbows bumping as they ate. The windows were fogged with steam, the air thick with the odor of damp wool and fried onions. Daniel drifted in the warmth, his thoughts on the blank sheet of copper waiting in his studio. The edge of a knife ringing against a water glass brought him back to his sister's kitchen.

"My thanks to you, Mort and Michael, for coming out on such a night," Fiana said, raising her glass in a toast. *Not to think of it*, their small nods said in silent reply.

"You know the rumors about the mine this Eire-Evergreen Metals are building in the village, but no one seems to know what the truth is or what's to be done. Mort and I have been digging around, and it's time to let you"—she glanced at Daniel, one eyebrow raised—"know what we've found. We've got to have a plan, so."

Daniel was aware of the rumors circulating in the pubs and back gardens of southwest Cork since late last summer, but he hadn't paid them much mind. The rumors had coalesced into few solid facts.

"It's going to be tough, them coming in and promising jobs," said Michael Leahy, stabbing at a ball of potato and dragging it through the butter that pooled on his plate. Michael ran sheep on fields that drifted up boggy, wind-cracked Slieve Miskish. "There's not a soul in the whole of Beara who would deny we need the shot in the arm this mine would give. Not just the mining jobs but construction work on housing for the miners and their families, teachers for the schools, more traffic in the shops and restaurants. We'd seem like fools getting in the way of the economy. But is this what we want for our children's future?" The farmer pointed his fork at Liam and Catriona before cramming the potato into his mouth.

Liam hunched over his plate, fork grasped like a shovel, and he seemed to hardly chew his food before swallowing and going for more. Catriona's eyes had slipped down to the mobile phone hidden in her lap.

"We know what we're up against, and we can prepare for that. We'll know their arguments in support of the mine better than they do." Mort MacGeoghegan pushed his plate away. At seventy-five, the retired University College Cork professor of geology knew every layer of history the stones and sediment of the Beara Peninsula could tell. He'd been born just down the road and had spent all his life in West Cork, except for his PhD years at Cambridge University and fieldwork in the Pacific Northwest. He'd made the drive from Clonakilty to Cork for forty years. When his wife, Birdie, died two years ago, he'd finally retired and returned to his birthplace at the tip of this forlorn peninsula that thrust like an accusing finger into the North Atlantic. He was the closest Daniel had to a father figure, a man whose quiet confidence Daniel had been surprised—after all these years of building walls—to admit he sought.

"We must counter those arguments with a solid case of our own," Mort continued. "We've got to get across that restarting the copper mine industry would mean an end to Beara. Our protected corner of the world as we know it would cease to exist."

"Is that enough?" Fiana said, her hands raised and spread as if to show the emptiness of their argument. "Is saving the fragile ecosystem of Beara enough for families who are behind on their mortgages or can't pay their kids' tuition? Is it enough for Conor MacCarthy's pub that is about to shutter its doors or Emily O'Sullivan's dress shop that's gone since October or Fern Drummond's gallery?"

Fiana glanced at her brother. "We picked up the last of Daniel's pieces from the Niedan Gallery in Castletownbere two weeks ago. So few sold. Even the tourists—especially the tourists—aren't buying these days." She squeezed her hands around her glass. "I'm in full agreement with you, of course, but we can't come off like a pack of squirrely environmentalists or—forgive me, Mort—egghead professors. We have to give people a cause to rally behind."

Those unsold pieces from the Niedan Gallery sat wrapped in his studio, income delayed, but Daniel had grown used to the slow pace of sales. He'd begun his prison sentence when the country was as high on easy money as he'd been on drink and coke. Five years later, he'd emerged, diminished but clean, into an Ireland stupefied by failure, depressed, her eyes glazed over with shock. The high times had vaporized.

But here, deep in southwest Cork, the prosperity had made only a superficial flush on the tidy villages; the economic tide still ebbed and flowed with the fishermen and farmers. It was one of the reasons he'd returned, despite his shame. It was the only part of Ireland he still recognized.

"Did you have something in mind then, Fiana?" Michael asked.

"I do indeed." This time she held Daniel's gaze, as if trying to impart some meaningful message. He had no idea where she was headed with this, but Daniel knew his sister: She had a plan, and it involved him.

She pushed back from the table and picked up the cream-colored platter that had held the season's first tender asparagus and a ceramic bowl with two chunks of roasted carrots huddled together at the bottom. Michael considered his nearly empty plate with eyebrows raised in alarm. Daniel elbowed the dish of boiled potatoes toward the farmer, and Michael added a few morsels to his plate, winking his thanks. He'd watched Michael poking around his bowl of lentil stew earlier, looking for morsels of lamb or beef, until Daniel took pity and mouthed, "Vegetarian." Michael hid his dismay with a mouthful of soda bread, and Daniel swallowed back a smile. At least there were the potatoes, swimming in butter and salt.

On her way back from the kitchen, Fiana plucked a manila folder from the breakfront cabinet that held a jumble of schoolbooks, catalogs, and seed packets. "Gentlemen, and lady." She laid a hand on Catriona's head, and her daughter glanced up with rounded eyes. "I present to you the savior of Beara: our own Red-billed Chough." She dropped the folder on the table and returned to her chair, drawing the edges of her cardigan around her. The buzz of a muted phone sounded before anyone could respond.

"Cat, what have I told you about a phone at the table?" Fiana narrowed her eyes at her daughter. "Get started on the dishes. You're dismissed. You, too, lad. Homework. Now." Liam huffed his irritation, but he obeyed, flicking his sister's hair as he slumped past. Her face pink with embarrassment, Catriona palmed her phone in one hand and picked up her dinner plate with the other, mumbling her apologies. She returned to collect the rest of the dishes in silence, and Daniel caught her eye and winked.

His sister had opened the thick folder and pushed it to the center of the table. On top sat a large photograph of a jet-black bird with a long, crimson-red bill and scaly red feet that ended in pointed black claws. It was difficult to tell the bird's size from the photograph, but Daniel knew. He knew the chough like he knew the shape and feel of his hands. He'd held several at the Durrell Wildlife Park on Jersey, that island of rolling plains and rugged cliffs in the Channel between England and France.

Beara's elusive population of Red-billed Choughs clung to coastal cliffs or flitted in pairs through wet fields, low to the clumps of black, turned earth where they scavenged for loose grains, worms, larvae. At Durrell, Daniel had been able to study the bird in captive rehabilitation. He'd seen how a creature could be brought back from extinction. He'd learned how to represent what coming back from nothingness might feel like, how quickly freedom could be lost and what it cost to be granted a second chance. He would have scoffed had anyone said he'd found a spirit animal in this slight, strange crow, and he'd never spoken of his affinity for the chough; he let his art express what would have made him cringe to say in words. Barely a pound, the bird was the span of his forearm. Up close, the blue-green sheen of the bird's plumage made him think of the way copper aged under the stress of rain and cold.

Michael picked up the photograph. "The little chough. Used to see these everywhere as a boy on Dingle. Not as many here, but endangered? That's news to me." He dropped the photo onto the table and looked up to Fiana, but she was riffling through the stack of papers.

Daniel spoke up. "The Red-billed Chough has held its own

in most places, but it's on the Amber List in Ireland. Means it's vulnerable, and if we don't maintain local habitats, we'll lose it, like they did in Jersey." He traced the bird's image with a forefinger, imagining its shape worked out of metal. "Beara's got just the right mix of grazed land and protected sea cliffs where the choughs thrive," he continued. "But it wouldn't take much to tip the balance. They're what's known as an indicator species. Their health can indicate the health of the ecosystem they inhabit—"

"What does the chough have to do with the mine?" Michael interrupted.

Fiana extracted a laminated sheet from the pile and held it out. Michael accepted it and dropped the reading glasses perched on his head to the bridge of his nose. A moment's glance, then he slapped his knee. "Damn. I'll be goddamned. Forgive me," he said to Fiana, who waved away his curse.

"The chough's breeding ground overlooks the shoreline where Eire-Evergreen Metals have proposed to begin drilling," she said. "One of Ireland's remaining healthy habitats of the Red-billed Chough would be destroyed if that mine is allowed to open. This little crow"—she tapped the photograph on which Daniel's fingertips still rested—"will be the symbol of our fight against Eire-Evergreen Metals. He stands for all that is pure and unprotected on the Beara Peninsula." Circles of pink bloomed high on her cheekbones.

"If the chough is in such danger, how is the mining company able to begin exploration?" Michael asked.

Fiana and Mort exchanged glances, and she nodded for him to go ahead. "This is just an educated guess, but here's our theory," Mort said. "The whole of the Beara Peninsula is designated a Special Protection Area, meaning that no one can disturb the natural habitats of any species on public or private land without permission from the government. Part of any commercial development must be the Environmental Impact Statement, filed before development can begin, but not necessarily in the exploration process. My guess is Eire-Evergreen are in the thick of it now, figuring out how to get through the gauntlet of Ireland and European Union environmental regulations. But with the promise of jobs for the community and tax revenue for the state ... " He trailed off, allowing them to form their own conclusions.

"On behalf of this bird and our community, Michael's question is one we have to ask and ask loudly," Fiana said. "We—"

"We should have started before now," said Mort, "but it won't take long to round up supporters and form some sort of coalition. I can name every anti-mine family from here to Bantry." He plucked the photograph from underneath Daniel's hand in his excitement. "If I take this to the environmental studies and Celtic studies departments at the University, we can enlist students to build us a website, maybe get the kids in the Environmental Society to organize protests. It'd be a great research project for some young gun—somebody can quickly get us up to speed with the SPA requirements and file for the public notice documents at the Ministry."

"I'm going to put on some tea. Coffee for you, Michael?" Fiana stepped toward the kitchen, then hesitated and turned back. "There's more, actually," she said. "I just heard from Paula at O'Sullivan's Estate Agents. The McGuire place was just purchased by James MacKenna."

Mort was nodding as though he understood, but Michael and Daniel shrugged in tandem. "I'd heard it sold, but who is James MacKenna?" Daniel asked.

"Director of operations of Eire-Evergreen Metals," Mort answered. "He's an Aussie, but his family claims deep ties to the region, so it looks like they've used their gold-lined pockets to become Irish again."

A to-do list began to spill down one sheet of paper and a list of names on another—local supporters and those deep-pocketed transplants from the UK, Germany, and the Netherlands who visited Beara on holiday and fell in love with its wild beauty, buying or building second homes on this jagged slice of mountain and bog.

Daniel drifted away. His love for the peninsula was profound and complicated, twisted into thoughts of family, shelter, commitment, and obligation. His stomach knotted at the thought of a copper mine ripping into the cliffs and tearing at the coastline, changing this remote and quiet place forever. But someone else would have to take up the fight. He had none left in him.

"I agree," said Mort. Three smiling faces turned to him. "He would be brilliant."

"What?" Daniel hadn't heard a word they'd spoken for several minutes. His inner gaze had turned again to the sheet of copper waiting for him, his fingers twitching to feel the smooth, cool metal. "He who?"

"You, Danny," Michael replied. "You'd be perfect."

"For what?"

"The spokesperson for the Beara Chough Coalition," Fiana said.

"The what? You're joking." He pushed away from the table. "I'm not about to be the spokesperson for anything."

"Danny, listen. You are an example of what this land can do—heal and strengthen." Fiana placed a hand on his arm, eyes shining with her impassioned plea. "You are Beara's prodigal son, returned to rebuild his life in the shelter of his community. Your art represents us. Your story is our story."

Daniel flung off her hand and stood so suddenly his chair toppled to the ground. Fiana gasped and Michael started back in surprise, but Mort's blue eyes, bright against his trim white beard and hair, held Daniel's glare with somber empathy.

"My story?" Daniel snorted in disgust. "Fiana, my story is that I killed a child and destroyed a family. You've lost your mind if you think I'd present *my story* to the public. Leave me out of this."

He caught the tiny shake of Mort's white head before he barreled out the back door.

5

The basement of Green Lake Methodist served as a nursery and preschool during the day, but in the early mornings and evenings, it was Annie's go-to AA meeting place. Straight out of church basement central casting: beige-and-white checkered linoleum floors, garish fluorescent lighting, and the mingled odors of finger paints, sour milk, and pee. On wet nights, the addicts' damp clothing and skin carried a corrosive fug of cigarette smoke.

Motivational posters were tacked alongside cartoons of Jesus with his disciples: a rock climber clinging like a gecko to the face of a mountain precipice, with the tagline PERSEVERE etched in a giant red font above his daredevil figure; a sheer cliff face pummeled by massive waves with STRENGTH sketched solidly in white underneath.

Annie stared at the STRENGTH poster as she waited for the meeting to begin, imagining herself at the top of that cliff, her future swirling unknown in the turbulent waters below. Would she still be descending rubber-lined steps into stale church basements fifteen years from now? Would this become the badge that defined her: failed runner, failed wife, recovering addict?

The meeting ended precisely at eight with a recitation of the Lord's Prayer. As the group gathered their bags and briefcases, she lingered. Her sponsor's loose, watery laugh broke across the room like a stream over a gravel bed. Annie's inner Rolodex catalogued her fellow AA attendees according to first name and years sober, adding in details as they were offered, and when she had the energy to hold on to them. She recalled the story of the man whom Bill stood chatting with at the kitchen bar: Peter, nine years, software developer at the Google offices in Fremont. There was something fragile about his round glasses and flyaway hair that made Annie want to protect him, yet it was he who often led the evening meetings, his soft, steady voice a balm to jarred emotions.

As she helped break down the circle of chairs, a few long-timers acknowledged her assistance with a nod and a smile, but no one forced a conversation. Headlights flashed through the ground-level windows as cars pulled out of the parking lot, illuminating the silver strings of rain that cascaded into the barren flowerbeds lining the foundation.

"Annie, I have a feeling you're waiting on me." Bill's voice, as rough and comforting as a wool sweater, came from behind her. She turned, holding the metal folding chair a few inches off the ground.

When Bill had offered to be her AA sponsor after her second meeting here, she'd given a noncommittal, "Sure, thanks," wondering what she could possibly have in common with a sixty-year-old who looked like a cross between Santa Claus and a Hells Angel. Now she couldn't imagine navigating this over-bright, loud, racing-heart world of sobriety without him. Clean twenty years, Bill had named every single demon that sat on her shoulder, and he was helping her look them straight in the eyes.

"What gives?" He took the chair from her hands and added it to the stack propped against the wall.

She scanned the room. A handful of conversations continued, but almost everyone had made his or her way up the stairwell and to the exit. "I'm leaving town for a while," she said.

"Because of Stephen?" Bill had been Annie's only call the night she'd left home with an overnight bag and all her fears.

"It's for work. I'm headed to Ireland." Nervous now, she yanked the rubber band from her ponytail. Her scalp ached where the tight cap of hair fell free.

"Ireland?" Bill whistled soft and low. "That's a hell of a business trip." Bracing one booted foot against a cement pillar, he leaned back and tucked his hands into the pockets of his leather vest. "For how long?"

"I'm not really sure. A few weeks, a couple of months. I don't know. As long as it takes."

Bill raised an eyebrow.

"My doctor and my therapist both think that getting out of Seattle and away from some of my triggers is a great idea. Almost like a reward for what I did at Salish. And I need to focus on my job and my health right now. They're about all I have left." The explanation spiraled out of her in fragments as she tried to anticipate Bill's doubts.

She didn't tell him everything, however. Annie withheld how, after she'd promised to work her magic on the Eire-Evergreen campaign, the impulse to make a clean sweep had taken hold of her in a sudden fever. She'd rushed into her therapist's office with the notion she could walk away from her marriage, her job, and the Northwest to start over. She'd gushed about picking up photography again, freelancing, trying for gallery shows. How she'd lose her demons in art. Dr. Lamott had embraced a temporary change of scenery, but cautioned her against plunging into a new life without a plan.

"See this through first, Annie," he'd said. "Do the best you can for your job. Decide if your marriage is worth fighting for. Then come back and clean up after yourself. You have a lot of work to do."

Bill surprised her now by saying, "Seems like sound advice to me. I can hook you up with some buddies in Dublin. Just say the word."

"It's just that ... " Annie began, and then faltered. The knowledge that she'd be on her own if things went wrong loomed before her, a murky pool with no discernible bottom. "I'm hoping I can call you. Just in case, I mean. If I need to talk to someone."

Bill's myopic eyes were blurred by his fingerprint-smeared glasses, but his bearded cheeks rose in a smile. "'Course you can call. Being a sponsor doesn't stop when the time zone changes. And you'll bring me back some of those Cadbury chocolates, right?" He crossed his arms over his oil-drum chest. "You know you got this, Annie. You can fly from the nest and you won't crash."

The lights dimmed. "Hey, folks, we need to close up shop. Is everything okay?" Peter had his hands on the panel of switches, ready to flip the rest of the lights.

"No, we're done here." Bill pushed away from the pillar. "Right, Annie? Time to fly?"

"Yes." Her eyes welled with tears. "Just look at me go."

6

He'd been awake for some time, watching clouds slip over the stars and hurry out to sea. Finally, Daniel pushed back the wool blankets strewn across the bed. Sleep was gone for the night. He grabbed his watch from the straight-backed chair that served as a nightstand and squinted in the moonlight at the black numerals mounted on a white back. Three-thirty. Hours yet until dawn.

"Not so fast," he said to the old timepiece. The return to daylight savings time had occurred during the night. He pulled out the tiny knob on the side and rolled it between his first two fingers. "Four-thirty. Rise and shine." He snapped on the small lamp beside his bed, and its low light glinted off the copper figure at rest on the chair seat: a hand-beaten and brazed sculpture of a Red-billed Chough, one of his early pieces, worked from a two-millimeter-thick scrap. The bird appeared to be walking, one twiggy claw set before the other, its slender head thrust forward, long beak slightly agape, as if in mid-call. Daniel picked up the half-sized metal specimen and turned it in his hands. The bird's gaze was steady, the open beak an unspoken thought. He cursed softly and returned the chough to its bedside roost.

He wasn't ready to work. His cluttered mind raced with anger at his sister, guilt over the anger, and concern for the battle the peninsula had ahead if it really intended to fight this damn mine. He couldn't get Mort's clear blue gaze out of his head. In it, he'd read a mixture of disappointment and love. Mort's eyes mirrored his heart.

Daniel prepared a press pot of gut-burning coffee and dressed while it steeped. A ceramic heater kept his small sleeping space warm, but he could see his breath when he stepped beyond the screen into the large expanse of his studio. Coffee into a thermos, feet into battered leather boots, hands into fingerless gloves. He buttoned a flannel-lined Carhartt jacket over his wool sweater.

Fiana's house sat a heart-stopping distance from the edge of the bluff, where it seemed a rogue wave might sweep it out to sea. When she wrote to tell him she'd purchased Turlough Meaney's old homestead, Daniel was surprised that his practical sister would take a chance on so precarious a house. At last, her inner romantic had expressed itself—it was the Fiana she'd squelched decades ago, trying to create a stable life for herself and her reckless younger brother.

A steep, boulder-strewn trail led down to Ballycaróg Bay. Daniel held the thermos in one hand, extended the other for balance, and let momentum carry him to the shore.

There was no beach to speak of—none at all at high tide. The peninsula plunged into the sea in cracked, twisted clumps of black and brown sandstone and silt rock that was covered in patches of gray and white bird shit. The air tasted of raw oysters—briny and ripe with the tang of kelp and saltwater. Waves hissed and roared. There was never a moment's silence at this end of the bay. The ocean continued its incessant consumption of coastline, pecking away at Ireland millimeter by millimeter.

He walked to the edge of a narrow escarpment. The rock trembled beneath his feet with the force of the water. He could slip on the wet stone and tumble into the ocean, where the waves would slam him into the rock, drag him under, and carry him out in the time it took to heat water in a kettle. Not long ago he'd stood on this very spot, or dozens like them up and down this stretch of the Beara coast, considering such a tumble. It wouldn't have been an accidental slip. It would have been a dive into oblivion.

Above the sizzle of the retreating waves he could hear squawking and shrieking. Terns, herring gulls, and fulmars congregated at this prime fishing spot. It was as noisy as a pub during a World Cup match. Daniel continued north, until the land curved. A cove, bound by pockmarked cliffs, drew him into its shelter. The clamor in his head stilled as a certain listening quiet surrounded him again.

At first he heard only his own breath and the muffled sound of distant surf. A halo of light in the east cast shadows of silver and blue into the rock and earth that rose above him, and he tilted back his head, peering into the nesting area of the Red-billed Chough.

What Daniel waited for rushed over his head, swooping in from beyond the cove, a jet-black fleet of four in loose formation. A bright *chiach* sounded, descended, and was answered. One bird trailed with a bit of white fluff clutched in a tapered red beak—sheep's wool or dryer lint to line her nest. If someone could explain to these birds their possible fate, would they leave? Or would the choughs cling as stubbornly to their piece of this rock as he had learned to do?

He realized then he hadn't come out at dawn to relive his darkest hours. He'd come to be with a piece of the future he might have some hand in preserving. For this knuckle of Irish rock was the only thing that kept him grounded. The only way he knew he was home.

7

The cemetery sat atop Queen Anne Hill, surrounded by some of the oldest trees in Seattle. Annie loved to run on the hill—the views of Seattle to the south, the Olympic Mountains to the west, and the Cascades to the east were the best in the city. If she ran from home, across the Aurora Bridge to the top of Queen Anne—where the city slowed to the speed of a bustling village—she could get in ten to twelve miles packed with hills and stairways. The best therapy, and the cheapest. On the weekends, she'd meander through the farmers' markets in Fremont or Ballard before running the final miles to their Green Lake neighborhood.

Today she drove, the sun-warmed interior of the car relaxing her to the point of drowsiness. Opening the sunroof to allow in the cool air, she reveled in early spring's delicate beauty. The dogwood, cherry, and pear trees gushed in wedding-cake blossoms of white and pink, and lambs'-wool clouds drifted through a pastel-blue sky. She parked a few blocks away from the cemetery and walked through the old neighborhoods that ringed its south end.

Ryan's memorial was a niche set into a tall square wall, his name and the dates of his short life etched into ebony stone:

FEBRUARY 4, 1984–APRIL 14, 2002. Next to his marker, running six across and four down, were other memorial niches. Some had been left blank; the others stated simply the beginning and ending of lives. Ryan shared his space with strangers, but the blank squares below him waited for Annie and her father, John. They never imagined the youngest of them would be the first to take a place on the cold, hard stone. Her mother was buried elsewhere. It was a grave Annie had never visited.

"So, buddy, I won't be able to come by for a spell." She placed a clutch of tulips on the cement border at the base of the memorial, their pink innocence incongruous against the black slate. "I leave for Ireland in two days. Can you believe it? I promised to take you when you graduated, so this is a few years late, but how about you tag along? I'll need an angel on my shoulder."

She'd visited Ryan's memorial infrequently in those early years, but in the slide that began with their mother's death, she'd come more often, first monthly, then every couple of weeks, to talk through her hurts, to muster up the courage to change. She'd make him promises, only to break them in the days that followed. Few memories in Annie's hazy recollection of the recent past brought her more shame than those of leaning into this polished columbarium and smelling the fog of her own breath, rancid with booze.

She'd be in Ireland for the tenth anniversary of that terrible night; who would bring flowers to his grave? Dad would never make the drive from Walla Walla, and she couldn't ask Stephen.

An April evening, at the end of a day much like this, Annie had watched from the stands at Husky Stadium as her little brother kicked it, winning the 400-meter, the 1600-meter relay, and the long jump in the Evergreen Invitational. He'd just turned eighteen, high school graduation was two months away, and he would follow his sister's footsteps right into a track scholarship to the University of Oregon.

Annie found his voice mail the next morning. So many messages on her phone, consuming all available storage. But there was only one message from Ryan, and his was the only one that mattered.

He'd stayed in the city after the meet to celebrate, losing his ride home to Kirkland when his track friends hooked up with some girls from Spokane. Straight-laced Ryan, who never drank, never smoked, who turned his back on casual dating because it interfered with his training time, had just wanted to go home alone. He'd waited for over an hour before finally calling his mom.

How many ways had Annie replayed that night? She'd imagine the feel of the vibrating phone in her back pocket— she'd been only blocks away from Ryan, watching Beth Orton perform at the Triple Door—and she'd see herself answering the call. They'd meet up at their favorite Thai place on Pike, and she'd harass him about interrupting her evening, when in reality nothing could make her happier than to hang out with her little brother, whose lanky six-foot-five frame towered over her. She'd take him home, where Stephen would make late-night buckwheat pancakes and they'd all fall asleep on the sofa, watching *The Godfather*.

But it was too late. Her mother, senses dulled by vodka, had slammed into a cement median on the freeway hours before. An ambulance had transported her to Harborview with a broken pelvis, a broken collarbone, and a concussion from the force of the airbag. Ryan, asleep in the backseat, had been crushed by an SUV following too closely behind.

"I know Stephen would send his love," Annie said to her brother's stone memorial. "We're calling it quits, buddy. It's been a long time coming. Don't blame Stephen. He stuck it out with me a lot longer than most men would have. So, let's just forgive and move on, okay?"

An older couple came into view around the other side of the memorial. Annie fell silent, though she felt their questioning eyes on her. She wasn't the only one who talked to the dead. She'd overheard plenty of conversations in the past ten years and had placed a comforting hand on many shoulders. Some regulars she recognized by sight; a few she knew by name. The couple, their eyes dark with sorrow, passed without a word. Annie turned and set her hands on either side of Ryan's name.

"Well, Mr. Greenpeace, you wouldn't approve of the work I've got to do in Ireland. I'm off to convince a bunch of fishermen and sheepherders in the back of beyond that they want a mining company to set up operations in their village." She traced the etched letters and numbers on Ryan's stone.

"Don't think less of me because it's something you'd probably protest. It's not as black-and-white as you think." She paused, nodding her head once as if to acknowledge his objections. "It's my job, Ryan, and I need a challenge to wrap my head around right now. The development will be good for the local economy," she added, and her words rang hollow, even though she had the figures to make a credible claim. Figures she'd be citing to the community that had no idea she was on her way.

She waited, knowing the silence would reflect her conscience back to her, this place of rest making her disquiet a thing she could almost see. Her self-respect was like a broken plate badly glued and in use again. She'd voiced to Ryan what she wouldn't admit to herself: it wasn't just a job. What she'd been assigned to do in Ireland, what she'd *volunteered* to do, was akin to pebbles being piled on that vulnerable china. What would make the plate break and send her spiraling down again: losing her career, or compromising what few beliefs she held that still pointed her compass true north?

Annie kissed the stone, then wiped away the shimmer of her lip balm from the polished granite. "We leave Saturday," she whispered. "Pack light. I'm not carrying any of your shit. I have enough baggage of my own."

8

Fiana's whistling pierced into Daniel's studio, and he sat up with a start. One finger was trapped between the pages of John O'Donohue's *Eternal Echoes*, his other hand still clutching the pen he'd used to underline his favorite passages. He'd planned to set off for a hike in the Slieve Miskish the moment she left for Mass, but he'd fallen asleep just before sunrise. Sunlight now pushed past the half-drawn shutters on the west-facing windows. A stable door once occupied that space, but Daniel had removed it and installed a deep window seat where he could sketch, read, or simply watch the sky converse with the ocean.

He smiled. Fi whistled when she was angry, and this morning she was making a show of her defiant cheerfulness as she shoved the wheelbarrow across the gravel paths between her garden beds. She shouted now and again at Bannon, the blue heeler stray who'd arrived unannounced two years ago, establishing herself with immovable certainty at Daniel's side. A jangled crash signaled that a collection of garden tools had been dropped just on the other side of the plaster wall from Daniel's bed.

After storming from the dining room the night before, he'd spun out his anger in muttered, solitary arguments. The early morning walk had cleared the last of his self-pity. Whatever Fiana intended, it was with her bull-headed but loving heart. He shoved his stocking feet into mud-spattered Wellingtons just inside the door. "Right. Well. Let's get this over with." Daniel left the studio to join his sister in her garden.

"It's high time I get these onion sets and shallots into the ground. If I can chase down Liam, he's needed to mow this lawn." Her face shielded by a large sunhat, Fiana stabbed at the earth with a garden trowel.

"Can we talk a bit, Fi?" Not waiting for a response, Daniel brushed dirt from the brick edge of a wall that enclosed the newly seeded vegetable beds and sat facing his sister, his forearms on his knees. "I don't agree with what you have in mind, but it wasn't reason enough to lose my temper. I'm sorry."

Fiana sat back on her heels and pushed up the brim of her hat. "You've got nothing to apologize for. I should have talked to you first, before Mort and Michael arrived."

"It's not that. I have nothing to hide from either of them. It's the idea that I could represent this community. That they would allow me to, after what I've done."

"Daniel. I just—"

"You just want me to be more than I am. I'm not the right one to be a public face for anything, not even this, whatsit, this Beara Chough Council."

"Coalition," Fiana corrected. "It's the Beara Chough Coalition."

"That's a damn silly name." He lifted a corner of his mouth in a half-smile.

"Well, if you've got another, you're welcome to put it forward." She swatted at his knee with the trowel and then grew serious again. "But you'd better do it fast. We don't know how long this fight is going to last and what financing we'll need to seek, so we're doing this right. We're registering ourselves tomorrow with the Charities Regulatory Authority as a not-for-profit." Fiana attacked the flowerbed again, yanking out volunteer strands of ivy.

"Who is 'we'?"

"Mort, Michael, and me. And Denis O'Sullivan from the Beara Action Group."

"What about Alice?"

"She's pro-mine."

Daniel tipped up his chin in response. Alice Regan served with Denis as co-representatives from the Ballycaróg parish in the organization that acted as the voice of the greater Beara Peninsula. Already he could imagine the rift in this small community as families and businesses chose sides—save the economy or save a small crow—both claiming moral superiority, both with valid arguments that their cause was the just cause.

"This fight is going to tear Beara apart," he said at last.

"No, Daniel. This *mine* is going to tear us apart. And right when the economy is starting to turn around. Tourism is picking up, no small thanks to your guided hikes," she added gently. "The Germans and Dutch are building holiday homes again, the Americans are putting offices in Cork because it's so much cheaper than Dublin. And the weather's better."

He smiled weakly at her joke.

"We don't need this mine," she continued. "And what about when the mine leaves? And it surely will. Maybe not in our lifetime, but when it does, what will Liam and Catriona be left with? Unemployment and a torn-up peninsula." She waved the garden trowel, scattering damp black earth in her sweep, and stabbed again at the upturned bed.

Daniel watched her dig furiously in the rich soil as if in search of something. After a moment, he put a hand on her back, and she stopped, listening without turning.

"If I were to join this campaign, you know what would happen. It's one thing for an ex-con to sell his art—that makes me a story to tell around the pub. But if I supported your fight in any public fashion, what I did would become the focal point, not what I said or what I stood for."

Her back rose and fell in a silent sigh. Fiana set her trowel aside and joined him at the low wall. "Daniel, it was a terrible thing that happened. But you served your time, and there's not a soul in all of Ireland that would condemn you without turning away from his own conscience."

She'd all but said, "It was an accident." But he let it go. They'd had this argument too many times, Fiana insisting he drop the hair shirt of guilt, Daniel pleading to be left alone to deal with the remnants of his life as he saw fit. They needed one another—this family of two who had clung together through years in communes and New Age travelers' camps, linked to the shadow of a mother but no known father. Or fathers.

His sister had never wavered in her support. Not after the many times she'd collected him from the sidewalk in front of a bar after he'd been tossed out, or—more than once—from a drunk tank. Not after he'd wandered away from Cork, contacted her from Dublin, from Belfast, and finally from Manchester, asking for money each time. Not after he'd disappeared, only to call her from Cork jail six years later. That time, however, he'd needed more than money—he'd needed a criminal defense lawyer. Fiana, by then a single mother of two young children, breathed in deeply, cursed him once, and extended a hand to her brother.

She was the one waiting for him when he emerged from Cork Prison four years ago, the only father she could offer Liam and Cat after so many grim years with a man who ground them down with silent reprobation. Daniel felt her watching him with caution, one eye on her children, as he learned new ways of living with the world, with his addictions and his past. Fiana had allowed him to heal in his own way, through his art and the forces of nature that surrounded them on this peninsula, where the world seemed to spin more slowly, ancient legends knitting themselves into the present. Now he was a found thing, remade by regret and grief, and she a safe haven. They were, brother and sister, survivors.

"Would you at least be willing to lead some prospective supporters on the Beara Way? We want people to see what's at risk, to fall in love with this place. You know Beara like no one else, and something comes over you when you talk about it. We need that poetry, Daniel. We need everyone to feel it like you do."

He slapped his palms on his thighs and stood. "I can be a guide, not a spokesman. I can share with you all I know of the chough and their nesting ground in the cove. You keep me out of whatever limelight you've got planned, and I'll take punters through the mud and make them love it." He squeezed his older sister's shoulder. "Don't wait on dinner for me. I'm off on a hike."

Moments later, while gathering his gear, Daniel paused by the window overlooking the garden. Fiana sat motionless on the ledge of the brick wall, and her face in profile crumpled as if she might cry. Instead, she yanked down the brim of her sunhat, pushed herself up, and attacked the weeds with renewed vigor. The only whistling came from the chaffinches, which trilled with laughter as they darted in the fuchsia.

9

Annie's abrupt stop just past the doors leading from baggage claim into the arrivals hall at Cork Airport forced the other travelers to swerve around her. She had just enough time to shove a stick of peppermint gum into her stale mouth and wrap her hair in a chignon before James MacKenna, phone at his ear, noticed her in the crowd and waved her over. She pulled on the handle of her wheeled luggage and forced her stiff legs forward.

She recognized Eire-Evergreen's director of operations from the company's prospectus, running quickly through the few details she'd absorbed. The son of Redmond MacKenna, owner of Eire-Evergreen's parent company, MacKenna Mining, Ltd, James MacKenna been appointed to this role only recently, though he'd worked for his father's company since completing an MBA at the University of Melbourne a dozen years before. No one had warned her he'd be at the airport. She'd planned on an evening alone to prepare for the barrage of faces and voices that would surely hit her tomorrow.

"Annie! I was just calling you."

His familiar use of her first name took her by surprise, but she let it pass as she extended a hand to greet him. "Mr.

MacKenna. You drove all the way from Dublin to meet my flight?"

A bespoke black suit, light-blue shirt, and dove-gray tie complemented his gray eyes and black hair woven with silver. Annie caught a whiff of cedar-and-ambergris aftershave.

"James, please. I thought it would be a good idea if I took you to Beara to make introductions and give you the lay of the land and the politics, as it were. Here, let me." James took the handle of her suitcase and groaned at the weight. Her carry-on, with its laptop and camera gear, was strapped on top, but he flashed a smile to show he was joking. His accent, a blend of Irish warmth, round Aussie vowels, and clipped British consonants, reminded her of something from her recent past, a thread picked up by the streaming wind of her shaky memory. It was a puzzle to be reconciled, but Annie was too weary to sort through it now.

"This is so kind of you. I'd booked a rental, but honestly I wasn't eager to navigate the roads and drive on the opposite side quite yet." She tried to sound sincere, but having to make conversation and impress her client this soon, before she'd had time to rest? Dread piled upon weariness. Annie felt thin and dry, like a hollow reed. She excused herself to the restroom, where she scrubbed at her teeth with the travel toothbrush and paste she'd stashed in her purse, washed her face, and pinched some color into her wan cheeks.

James drove a late-model Mercedes, and despite the long hours sitting in a cramped metal tube, Annie sank into the smooth seat with a grateful sigh. Exhausted—she'd never managed the art of sleeping on planes—she watched the scenery unfold as the industrial end of Cork faded into pasture and rolling hills. They drove deeper into the country, where the land was boisterously green. They continued southwest along smaller byways, the powerful vehicle quietly dominating the road.

What do people do here? she wondered.

"Many of them make the drive to Cork, believe it or not," answered James, startling her; Annie hadn't realized she'd spoken aloud. "They buy a patch of paradise in some village, send their kids to day school, and drive more than a hundred kilometers round-trip to a city job to pay for it all."

"How about you? Country mouse or city mouse?"

"I rent a flat in Dublin and walk to the office. I've been in Ireland only since the new year, but I've just purchased a house outside Ballycaróg. I researched my family's records and found property the MacKennas had lived on as tenant farmers in the nineteenth century. Nothing felt quite as good as the day I reclaimed that property and put the MacKenna name on the title."

"Does that make you a local?"

James laughed. "Depends who you ask. I'm Australian, educated in the UK; most of my career has been in Southeast Asia and the Middle East. I spent a few school holidays in Ireland, but I've never considered it *home*. Those for the mine consider me the prodigal son, returned home to share his good fortune. For those against the mine, I'm an interloper."

"The fact that your history is linked to Beara is important," she said. "We'll emphasize your deep connections, your homecoming." One of his hands hung loosely from the bottom of the steering wheel; the other rested lightly on the gearshift. No wedding band. "Do you have any family here? Children?"

His glance was quick, but she caught the twitch of a smile at the corners of his mouth, the slight narrowing of his eyes. "On-again, off-again girlfriend in Riyadh, where I've spent the past two years working on the buyout of a Saudi mining company. She's French. Not remotely interested in living in wet, wild, southwest Ireland. So I suppose we're more off than on at the moment."

Annie held her face still. The implied closeness in a moment of personal disclosure. But her chest grew tight. Client flirtations were nothing new; a warm, open mien came naturally to her, but she'd learned to keep a careful distance. Never have drinks alone, never hold a gaze, return a smile with her mouth but never with her eyes if she felt the client had hazy boundaries. Then her own boundaries had grown hazy. The out-of-town meetings and conferences that led to dinners and drinks in dimly lit restaurants, stumbling tipsy and laughing back to the same hotel. Waking up in unfamiliar beds, head thick and pounding, stomach on fire, heart throbbing in shame.

James braked to a smooth stop. A moment later, two sheep stepped into the road, followed by a handful more. Then there were dozens—bleating, shoving, and bundling across the road, each sheep with a large splash of blue dye across its hindquarters.

A streak of black and white vaulted from the hillside. The sheepdog inserted himself between the car and the flock and crouched low, head tucked between his forelegs, rear end high in the air, tail wagging. He stood his ground before the car and barked in short blasts, jerking his head from the sheep passing by to the ones yet to come. A whistle sounded, sharp and shrill, and Annie heard the man's shout before she saw him. The dog bounded on, his head low, his taut body whipping with energy and joy. The flock curved as one, the wave of white and blue wool breaking on the other side of the road. The ewes crested the steep hillside with ease, but their lambs scrambled on spindly legs to keep up. A short, deep-chested man dressed in a ragged wool sweater, muddy jeans, and knee-high rubber boots crossed the road in front of the car. He waved his thanks and trudged on, over the hill, bringing up the end like a caboose.

James accelerated slowly and picked up the conversation. "My father financed the exploration off the Ballycaróg coast for years, certain there were copper veins waiting for the right mix of technology and tenacity. When his bet paid off last year, he plunged ahead and secured the prospecting rights. But he forgot about the locals. Or maybe he just assumed that since he was of Irish descent, they'd take him in as one of their own and be grateful for the jobs the mine will provide. You and I are here to show the community we've got their best interests in mind. And we start tonight."

He went on to explain he'd organized a dinner with the director of economic development and tourism from the Cork County Council, two councillors from the Bantry Electoral Area, and someone from some government planning commission—their names were a blur of rolled letters with too many r's and d's and g's to make sense of. "It's a gathering of decision makers, people who can really effect change in this community."

Annie swallowed back a groan. Once upon a time, she would have relished the opportunity to sort the jigsaw puzzle of issues, arguments, and opponents into strategy. Now the thought of spending her first evening in the spotlight, listening to and volleying back a lexicon of professional clichés, filled her with a soul-weariness that went far deeper than jet lag. Her first client dinner since rehab. Her first in too many years to count without cocktails or wine to ease the—

"Too much?" James's eyes lit on her, a furrow of doubt between his eyes. Had she said something? Had the groan escaped her?

"Not at all," she said, her mind whirring with the betrayal of her body. "It's a good opportunity to establish our talking points."

The Mercedes sliced sharply into a curve. Annie's legs stiffened, and she pressed her feet against the floor in a reflexive attempt to brake. Her shoulder brushed James's, and she shifted abruptly away. If he noticed her discomfort at his speed, he didn't let on. Nor did he slow. The gearshift glided underneath his loose grip, and his foot pulsed the clutch.

"My great-great-grandfather, Orin MacKenna, was twenty years old when the last of the copper mines still in operation on Beara closed outside Ballycaróg in 1882. Orin left Ireland the following year, like so many Irish during and after the Great Famine. He became a copper miner in Australia, as did my great-grandfather and grandfather. The MacKenna family didn't return to Ireland until my father purchased Leinster Metals in 1985. He'd already founded MacKenna Mining in Perth in '74. Mining is not just a part of my family's heritage; it's part of Ireland's economic future."

He slowed at a crossroads and looked at her, his expression unreadable. "How's that for talking points?"

Another Annie, a more affable version, perhaps loosened by gin, would have responded with approval that verged on flirtation, a stroke of the client's ego. This Annie was desperate to get out of the car, which seemed to shrink as their conversation intensified.

She'd tracked the signs directing them toward Ardgroom and Eyeries. They were close. Her legs ached and her head pounded. At last, James slowed and turned into a narrow gravel drive that descended toward the sea. The drive stopped just shy of the front door of a stone bungalow.

"Is this your house?" she asked.

"No, mine is on the other side of Ballycaróg. This is yours." James turned off the engine. "I'll bring in your bags and make certain everything's in working order. And then I'll leave you to get some rest."

The sensation of being watched whispered over Annie just as she reached into the trunk for her carry-on. Turning, she saw a man dressed in the same browns and greens of the hills behind him; the noonday light brought his features out of camouflage. The air suddenly seemed heavy and palpable, and the whisper that had made Annie look in his direction became a low moan. The man broke his stillness with one step toward her. Then abruptly he pulled back and strode away.

10

Daniel descended from Knockoura, skirting the backside of the village, and continued along trails and dirt roads until he arrived at the small clutch of houses that dotted the headland. Each was distant enough from its neighbor to allow for privacy but not so far you couldn't dash over for a needed cup of sugar or a dram of whiskey. Fi's house was at the end of the headland, splendid in its isolation for most of the year. The two nearest houses were vacation rentals that hosted a rotating collection of northern European families, the few tourists who thought Beara's summers—gleaming with rain, pushed on by the incessant wind—were an improvement on their own.

A late-model Mercedes crunched down the driveway and pulled up in front of the Moyle place. The house had recently been smartened up with an expensive renovation and let out as a holiday home after the Moyles retired to Wicklow. Daniel whistled low at the car's finely sculpted bones and iridium silver skin. It must have cost close to what Fi had paid for her house.

The driver rose from his seat, as sleek and polished as the Mercedes, and stepped to the car's boot. Joining him was a slender woman with dark wheaten hair twisted at the nape of her neck. Her legs climbed high in her tight-fitting jeans and disappeared under the loose folds of her sweater. She lifted a smaller bag from the back and turned in his direction.

A sighing seemed to rise from the earth, a sound that made no sense on this unusually still afternoon. No wind swept up and over the bluff or came rushing down from the mountains behind. The aural stirring echoed like a woman's voice, low and soft, in the space between the woman and himself. She paused, her head tilted as though listening. Daniel moved a step closer, but the air's weight lightened, then vanished.

Abashed to have been caught staring, he walked on but kept the house in his periphery. A husband and wife, or lovers, here for a week's getaway. The trunk slammed shut with a heavy thud of solid steel. The couple crossed the paving stones and entered the house.

Daniel drew nearer and saw Dublin plates on the car, confirming the two were a city couple in search of a quiet idyll. He was sure to see them hand in hand on Ballycaróg's one high street or perhaps at the Beara Artists' Cooperative in Castletownbere, where he put in a few hours each week—a local artist hoping to connect with well-heeled tourists and collectors.

A few minutes later he heard the low rumble of the Mercedes engine. The driver executed a tight three-point turn in the small parking area and ascended the drive. Alone in the car, he lifted a hand from the steering wheel in a casual wave as he passed.

Daniel glanced over his shoulder at the house as the road fell away behind him. A large patio extended over a short cliff, anchored to the rocky ground by long stanchions. There she stood, her hair now loose and swirling around her shoulders in long waves that shone almost white in the sudden, bright light. She pulled a tangle of hair back from her face, secured it behind her ear, and turned. Again they locked eyes, and she froze, her fingers still clutching locks of her hair. Then she hugged herself and turned away.

A chorus of barking forced his attention from the Moyle house. Bannon hurtled down the road, and Fiana's Glen of Imaal terrier, Kennedy, scurried behind on squat legs; the dogs' underbellies were caked with mud. Bannon leaped and twirled in midair, knowing better than to smear her soaked body on Daniel but unable to contain her joy. An irresistible scent distracted Kennedy, and he halted his trajectory halfway down the path.

Daniel removed his muddy hiking boots on his small patio, clapping the soles together to knock off the earth caught in the deep tread. He could just see the tile roof of the Moyle house from where his studio was perched.

Fiana's sensible Ford wagon wasn't parked beside the house—he'd ask her about the house's occupants later. As a social worker in Castletownbere, she'd know all the comings and goings of the tightly knit neighborhood. He took a quick shower in the stall he'd rigged up in the studio and dressed in haste. The AA meeting in Bantry started at six o'clock, and it was pushing five.

11

The bungalow was spotless, though the air was chilled and smelled of sea and wet stone, as if the windows had been open only minutes before. James had been true to his word; he showed her how to work the thermostat, made certain the refrigerator was plugged in, handed her the keys, and closed the door behind him. The sound of his voice, the smart click of his shoes on the tile floor, and the scent of his cologne lingered. It seemed to Annie she didn't breathe until she heard the heavy purr of the Mercedes recede up the drive.

Keeping in motion would help set her body to Irish time, but Annie longed to curl up on that sofa in the sunny extension of the kitchen, where floor-to-ceiling windows overlooked the cove. There was a soft, down-filled duvet folded neatly at one end of the sofa, tea and biscuits in the cupboard, and she'd started a Kate Atkinson novel on the plane. Work could wait, couldn't it? James would be back at six-thirty to pick her up for dinner in Castletownbere. She had hours to unpack and sift through her notes.

She stepped onto the patio that wrapped around the back end of the house, forming a balcony where the cliff dropped toward the cove. The aspect of the narrow peninsula was such that sunrises would pour in from the continent and sunsets would bleed away to North America; the house would remain suffused with light as long as the sun hung in the sky. Accustomed though she was to Seattle's breathtaking views, her heart still soared at the vast expanse of water smashing into the broad toes of rock. With no mountain ranges to break the horizon, the sky was massive and in constant flux. The sharp, briny air revived her. Annie shook out her hair and let the wind snap it around her face.

The same wind that snarled her hair delivered the voice in a tendril of sound. It was a rush of tide swirling in eddies of sand and stone. It was the whoosh of birds' wings banking just over her head. It was a woman's voice, emanating from deep in her throat and cascading to Annie's ears.

Mór mo phian, it whispered—a surge of round vowels and soft consonants, one hardly distinct from the other. Annie pulled her hair back from her ear, and the voice rushed again, closer:

Mór mo phian.

She turned to see the same man who had watched her arrival just a short while ago. He was tall, not as tall as James, but easily over six feet, and stockier. His head was covered by a blue knit hat, his age indeterminable from this distance. Thirty? Fifty? He wore an outfit not unlike the shepherd they'd passed on the road to Ballycaróg, but his boots were serious hiking gear. He stopped, she stared, the voice disappeared. Spooked, she reentered the house and watched from the shadows.

A mismatched pair of dogs tore down the path that led over a slight rise, and their joyful presence reassured her. The blue heeler clearly knew her master; she spun in paroxysms of delight as he approached. The man walked on, out of view.

After she scrubbed the travel grime from her skin in a hot

shower, Annie curled on the sofa under the down blanket in the glassed-in room beyond the kitchen and unpacked her camera equipment. With a map of the Beara Peninsula spread in front of her and a collection of camera lenses nestled in the blanket's folds, her chin fell and her breath slowed. She slept, and the wind whispered.

~

The voice stayed with her through dinner that evening, holding her hands in check when they longed to grasp one of the dewy pint glasses filled with molasses-rich ale posed like satellites on the table, or the burnished bronze whiskies emitting a rich, sweet-grass decay that concluded the meal. As she spoke of interest groups and community meetings, of job fairs and corporate sponsorships, she imagined that rich and steady voice was her own. Voices around the table rose and fell with stories and local politics as the assembled group expressed their combined hopes and expectations for the economic development the mine would bring to their constituents and businesses.

Just when she felt the evening might get away from her, when holding up her end would be made all the more tolerable if she could just soothe her raw nerves with a whiskey balm, the man sitting to her left, Des Pattwell—one of the local regional council members—spoke softly in her ear. "You look like you're wanting your pillow, so."

"I've never been able to sleep on planes," she said. "It feels like the hours I lost over the Atlantic were drained out of me."

"I live just out of Ballycaróg. I'd be happy to give you a ride back when you're ready." He hadn't had anything stronger than a Club Orange soda with dinner, she noticed. Relieved by the offer, she let him announce their leave-taking, gathering the last of her energy for handshakes and promises to meet again soon.

James waited with her outside the restaurant while Des brought the car around. A soft rain fell, and they stood under the vinyl awning, the glow from the windows reflecting off the shallow puddles forming in the street.

"I've booked us a guided hike of Beara tomorrow. I should have thought to wait a day, until you've had a chance to rest. I can cancel and reschedule—"

Annie was shaking her head before James finished his thought. "No, that sounds perfect. Fresh air and exercise are the best antidote to jet lag. Just—" She stubbed a mental toe. How to get away, alone, to make it to the AA meeting by six o'clock? "I'd like tomorrow evening to myself. I need to sort through what was said tonight as I consider how best to present this to the community." *Safe enough.*

"No worries. I'll have you in Ballycaróg by teatime. Really, I could take you to the Beara Way on my own, but this guide is supposedly an expert on the peninsula. It'll be a good local history and geography lesson for us both."

A trim white subcompact pulled up to the curb, and James opened the passenger door. He bid a good night to Des, then stood aside for Annie. "Hope you get a good night's rest."

"I will, thanks. What time tomorrow?"

"Ten-thirty."

Annie nodded and shifted toward the space of the open door. A hand pressed lightly against her shoulder, a familiar touch that lingered a moment too long. "I'm glad you're here, Annie. It's good to see you again."

A brief nod of her head, an invisible brush that just lifted the corners of her mouth. "I'll see you in the morning." She folded herself into the waiting seat. James brought the door to the frame, and it shut with a firm but muted thump. It wasn't until the car pulled away that she thought to wonder what he meant by *again*.

12

Daniel parked in Castletownbere's central square lot and checked his watch—it was just past eleven. His hiking clients would arrive at any moment. He grabbed the folder from the front seat and checked the details again: *Monday, 2 April, 11:00 a.m. CTB central car park/Family (3), Danish: Kai (M, 40), Britta (F, 38), Lisbet (F, 14) Andreassen.* Malcolm had scribbled next to the computer-printed data: *Experienced, even the daughter, they don't want a stroll.*

His phone chimed with an incoming text: *This is James MacKenna. We're in the car park, silver Mercedes.*

"MacKenna? The hell?" Daniel muttered. The Mercedes sat at the far end, and the man who'd appeared at the Moyle house the day before was reeling out his long limbs from the driver's seat. He couldn't be anyone other than the corporate arm of Eire-Evergreen Metals.

Daniel scrolled through his contact lists and pressed *call*. Malcolm answered immediately. "Hey, mate! Where are you?"

"Castletownbere. Where I'm waiting for the Andreassen family. Mal, why is James MacKenna here, and how did he get my number?"

"MacKenna? Of course, you're taking him and—wait, I've

got it right here—a Miss Annie Crowe on a short stretch of the Beara Way this afternoon."

Daniel watched as the man walked through the lot in search of the guide he'd arranged to meet. He appeared to be alone. Daniel waved, pointed to the phone and held out his palm. MacKenna waved in return and remained where he was.

"My pick-up sheet says Andreassen, family of three."

"Oh, shit." Daniel heard a clacking of computer keys. "Danny, I sent you the wrong sheet. Which means Niamh's got yours, and she's in Glengarriff looking for MacKenna. What a cock-up! Are they with you now?"

"Your man MacKenna is here, Mal, but I don't see her. Look, I'll figure it out. You call Niamh and get things sorted. I've got this."

~

"James MacKenna?" Daniel approached, pretending to glance at the paper on his clipboard. "Daniel Savage from West Ireland Excursions."

MacKenna extended a manicured hand, and Daniel clasped it, aware of his own palm and fingers roughened by weather, chemicals, and cuts from metal-working tools. "I was expecting two of you," Daniel said.

"Yes, my colleague. She's just fetching a coffee."

My colleague. Not a spouse or lover. Not obviously, anyway.

Then he heard her speak as clearly as if she stood at his side. *Mór mo bhrón.*

Daniel had picked up a bit of Gaelic— a handful of poems and songs, bits of conversation—from a few old timers who would eventually leave Cork Prison in hearses. The English translation of the words now in the air came to him in a rush of understanding: *Great my sorrow.*

Mór mo bhrón.

The voice was low, emanating from deep inside and exhaling from her throat in a warm, calming breath.

Just then, she crossed into the street and stopped. The voice resounded, soothing and rich, at the same moment as a low-slung Renault picked up speed through a turn and flew down the street. It seemed to be aiming for her slight frame, almost a shadow in the narrow lane, her hair bound in braids that fell over her shoulder, a tall disposable cup clutched in one hand. He held his breath, waiting for her to quicken her pace and cross to safety, but she was frozen in place.

13

The alarm emitted a series of slow beeps that accelerated to a rhythm just shy of frantic. Annie buried her head beneath the pillow and groped the nightstand for the offending clock, knocking it to the floor. The insistent noise stopped. Moaning, she drew her knees to her chest, her eyes squeezed shut. Five minutes later the alarm sounded again, fainter, but driving into the edge of her consciousness.

Kicking off the covers, she cast blurred eyes to the floor. The digital face stared back at her, blinking as it passed seven-thirty. Still so early—she had three hours before James arrived—but she wanted get into some sort of recognizable routine. A recovering addict was at her most vulnerable when her routine was thrown off-kilter. She stretched until her elbows and spine popped.

There was a tin of instant coffee on a tray in the kitchen, along with tiny packets of creamer and sugar. Annie's head pounded as her bloodstream realized it hadn't been injected with espresso in nearly two days, but this would have to do until she could get some ground coffee for the French press in the cupboard. She stirred, sipped coffee that tasted like cardboard, and grimaced.

Colm Fahey, the mine's project manager, was due in Ballycaróg that afternoon with a company car for her. Then she'd explore on her own, stock the refrigerator, suss out some running routes, and get to the AA meeting in Bantry. There was a Monday night meeting in Castletownbere, but that was too close. Someone might recognize her, or hear her American accent and put things together.

Annie smacked her mug on the counter. The addiction was like parenting a toddler: You couldn't take your eyes off it for a minute. In hindsight, being a drunk seemed almost simple. She felt miserable, she drank, she felt better for a few breaths. The guilt and shame followed soon after. The cycle was just shy of unbearable, but it rarely held any surprises.

But recovery. God. It was so complicated. Your entire day directed by the care and feeding of The Addict, the name Annie had given to this unwanted extension of herself. She didn't want it hanging around, didn't want to be associated with a disorder that felt like a failure of character, but it was a dependent child and she couldn't turn her back. She dragged it along to meetings, checked in with her sponsor, made certain it ate right and got enough sleep, and, above all, she kept a constant vigil so The Addict didn't get into the wrong things. Alcohol, prescription medication, a line, a pipe—pick your poison—the forbidden toys were so easy to find.

"Enough!" she shouted, and the sparsely furnished house echoed her condemnation. How amazing to shout. In her densely packed Seattle neighborhood, noise carried from open windows into backyards and side gardens and onto the sidewalk; she never dared to release her voice there. Here, she couldn't even see the next house over.

"Welcome to Ireland," she said and dumped the muddy brown coffee down the sink.

~

"Are you certain you're up for this? These hills may not look very high, but the ground can be rocky and full of bogs." James steered with one hand along the blind curve. The Mercedes took up the whole of the narrow road, and again Annie's foot pressed down on an imaginary brake pedal. They were on their way to meet the hiking guide in Castletownbere.

"More than ready for fresh air and a leg stretcher, trust me. I'm aching to get out."

"You were a champion runner in college, right? Do you still run?"

"I'm not the runner I once was, but I get out there." A slight chill rippled through her as James touched this part of her past, but of course it wasn't a secret. Anywhere her bio was listed—Magnuson's website, her LinkedIn profile—the bright star of her running career glittered.

"And you were an Olympic Trials finalist at university?"

Annie flinched, and her hands gripped her thighs reflexively. "Yes, I was. My ambitions were big. But they ended during a trail run in the Oregon Cascades. I tripped over a rock and tore my right thigh to shreds when I slid down scree. My left tibia snapped like a cracker and burst through my skin."

James responded with a sharp intake of breath.

"Sorry. Didn't mean to be so graphic. I was able to run again, after surgery and years of physical therapy."

They continued in silence. Annie waited for the questions that inevitably followed when people learned her dreams had been dashed by a slip and a stumble, but none came.

James deftly wove into a roundabout before an approaching car and spun through, exiting like a needle pulling closed a stitch. He took the straightaway and entered Castletownbere, where the street became a small canyon bordered on either side of the road with buildings colored like a child's finger painting: dashes of primary reds, blues, and greens squeezed between buildings of delicate pastels. Annie watched the village take shape. The vibrant rainbow defied the dreary Irish weather and drearier economy. It declared hope and life in this land whose history was written by disaster and conflict.

He parked in the town's central square. "I'm sorry I pressed you about your injury," he said, closing a hand over the keys and releasing his seatbelt. "It was a clumsy attempt to get to know you better."

Annie offered him a half-smile, wanting to steer the conversation away from her past. James unnerved her. His familiarity, the way his cologne lingered in the air. *Dammit.* She had to put things back on safe footing.

"Annie?"

"Sorry. Lost in thought." Lost in the repulsive thought that James would learn the facts of her addiction and the infancy of her recovery. At least here she could hide among people who were ignorant about the worst of her past; for a few weeks she could be someone else, in this place that was beautiful enough to be make-believe. She'd become particularly adept at pretending.

"That's one of Beara's iconic pubs." James pointed to a three-story building across the way, its top two floors built of white plaster with black trim. The ground floor was painted fire-engine red, with the words GROCERY and BAR spelled out in blocks of cursive gold letters on either side of the door, and MacCarthy's proclaimed in white block letters in between. Baskets of flowers hung from a lintel across the front façade.

Patrons were already seated at the outside tables, sipping pints and poking through fish and chips, even though it was just past eleven. Annie prayed James wouldn't suggest they stop in for a pint later. Last night's sweet-sharp tang of beer and whiskey had been nearly too much. "I'm desperate for some decent coffee," she said. "Do we have a moment to stop?"

While James sent a text to the guide to let him know they'd arrived at the rendezvous point, Annie jogged across the street to a café and ordered the largest coffee they had on the menu. Back outside, she popped off the lid, blew over the hot surface, and took a tentative sip. Freshly ground, hot and black.

She started back across the road, remembering to look to her left before stepping into the street. Leaning against his car, his arms crossed over his chest, James was in easy conversation with ... well, damn.

It was the man who had watched her from the road yesterday. He wore the same outfit—canvas hiking shorts, a ratty wool sweater, and sunglasses pushed back on his head. Annie snorted a private laugh. "Our guide," James had said. *Of course.*

Mór mo bhrón. The wind whispered past her face.

Except there was no wind. She could hear the clink of china plates and the hum of voices from the open windows of the restaurant behind her, the clatter as a recycling truck dumped bottles into its hopper, the echoing clang of a buoy bell in Castletownbere Harbor.

Mór mo bhrón. A woman's voice, murmuring words that sounded like lullabies, in syllables distinct but unintelligible.

And then, the man rushing toward her, his face open in alarm.

The rasping whoosh and grate of car tires coming to a sudden stop and the angry blare of a car horn jolted Annie out of her reverie, and she found herself standing in the middle of the road. She mouthed an apology to the enraged driver and silently ordered her feet forward, embarrassed and bewildered. Where was that voice? *Who* was it? It was the same voice, if not the same words, she'd heard the night before, standing on the deck, buffeted by the ocean wind. The thought that she was hallucinating, after all the months of sobriety, made her whimper even as the normal sounds of ships' bells and passing conversation flowed and ebbed around her.

"You all right then?" He met her at the street's edge, reaching out as if to draw her into the shelter of his embrace. "Daniel. I'm your guide for the day."

She met his hand with her own, wondering what cloud he'd been dropped from. Her guide. "I'm Annie."

"*Céad mile fáilte*, Annie. Welcome to Ireland."

His voice was warm, but Annie felt absurdly self-conscious under his gaze. "I saw you last night, from the house where I'm staying," she said. "Are we neighbors?"

He blinked, tilted his head, and gave it a slight shake, as if wiping away a thought. "We are. I live just up the hill."

She took refuge in her coffee, grateful for something to do with her hands, covering her silence with a sip. Yet she longed to continue on with him, past this street, beyond the village, just walking and talking, as soon as she could figure out what to say. A longing that seemed to be a lingering echo of the voice that had stopped her in the street, the voice that had stopped her heart the evening before.

"So, I've done a little exploring of the Beara Way." James appeared, inserting himself into their stalled conversation. "Where are we headed?"

None of the place names or the directions Daniel explained made any sense to Annie, so she drifted, observing the two men. Other than their height, they couldn't be more different.

James was polished, not a black hair out of place except for a finger of curl that spilled over his forehead. His build—just like a runner's, with lean limbs and an arrow-straight carriage—brought Stephen to mind, a visual she'd rather not carry around. His clothes were REI-approved: Arc'teryx jacket, convertible nylon pants, boots tastefully scuffed. She wondered if the boots could be ordered that way and had to stifle a laugh.

Daniel, well, he didn't look as though he'd *just* rolled out of bed, though his clothes probably hadn't seen the inside of a washer in a few wears. Several days' growth on his jaw and around his mouth caught the sunlight and glowed red-gold, but his hair—curling just above his ears and collar—was soft amber. Legs like tree trunks covered in fine red-gold hair. Blue eyes like the inside of a glacier. The very vision of an Irish Celt.

They left the Mercedes in the lot and climbed into Daniel's battered Range Rover. Annie sat in front, a pack, her camera inside, at her feet. She turned to see James settling in the backseat. From his pursed lips and narrowed eyes, she read his disgust at the dog hair clinging to every surface. Daniel introduced Bannon, who stood with her wiry tail whacking the car door, directing her steamy breath at James's face. Annie turned back before he could see her grin.

Daniel leaned across her to shove the clipboard into the deep glove box. He slammed it shut and uttered a simple "Oh." She followed his gaze down to her feet.

"What? What's wrong?" Annie bent over just as he sat up, his head colliding with her nose. She yelped in surprise. Hot coffee sloshed over one hand, and the other flew to her face. She watched Daniel's face twist in horror as she cupped her palm over her throbbing nose and waited for the warm trickle of blood.

"Jesus, Mary, and Joseph. Are you all right? Here, let me

take a look." She allowed him to lift her hand away from her face, watching his eyes for signs that it was as bad as it felt.

"No blood. You've got a hell of a solid *gaosán* there." He rubbed the back of his head. Her stomach flipped.

"A what? A geesun?" It hurt to talk, hurt worse to smile, but she couldn't help it.

"*Gaosán*. It's Gaelic for nose."

"You're soaked. Annie, you can't hike in those." James's voice collapsed the moment. With him over her shoulder, leaning between the gap in the seats, Annie considered the mess in her lap. A dark-brown stain down one thigh had bled into the crotch of her pants.

"Damn it to hell," Daniel muttered. He hopped from the Rover, and there was an opening and slamming shut of the back hatch door. Moments later he returned with a towel. Annie was surprised to see it was clean and neatly folded. "I keep a stash in the back," he explained, reading her expression. "Hikers get more soaked on Beara than they imagine possible." He began to dab at her pants, but, realizing where his hands were, he stopped abruptly, giving her a stricken look. That's when she began to giggle. She took the towel from him, shaking with laughter, and he mercifully pulled the coffee cup from her hand to save her from upending the rest.

"It's fine. I'll be fine," she choked out. "This is quick-dry material, right? There. See? Good as new." She displayed the stain, now lighter brown, before strapping on the seatbelt. She retrieved her coffee from Daniel's grasp. Their fingers brushed and in the touch, the woman's voice: *Mór mo bhrón*. Mournful. Resigned. The same emotions she saw reflected in his eyes. *I'm your guide,* he'd said. And their hands pulled away.

"Let's go. Day's a-wastin'," she said, trying to return them to the earlier lightness of mood. A small rumble of laughter spilled over, and the release was a revelation: It was the cleanest she'd felt in months. The hollowness had been replaced by something. What was it? What was this sensation that was so foreign, yet reminded her of what she used to feel? *Hope.*

For the first time in recent memory, she felt hope.

14

From Castletownbere, Daniel drove west before turning onto a lane only wide enough for one vehicle. But they encountered no one. Then the road narrowed even more, the tarmac ebbed away, and they bounced along tracks of dirt and rock.

He came to a stop in front of a fenced pasture. Several cows watched them in solemn contemplation, their jaws shifting sideways as they chewed at the grasses that hung in tendrils from their lips.

They descended from the Rover, and Daniel pulled a large pack from the back of the SUV, releasing Bannon at the same time. She sailed between fence rails, scattering a trio of calves. Their lithe little bodies bounded and bucked in the air. It was hard to believe they'd become great, lumbering creatures in a couple of years. The cows appeared unconcerned with the commotion, though one called out in a low, irritated bellow.

"Here's where we start," he explained. "Cross through this field and head into those hills." He pointed into the distance. "We'll have excellent views of the Skelligs once we're up. Maybe we'll see as far as America," he joked. "Is this your first time to Ireland?" he asked Annie.

"No." A shake of the head and a half-smile in silent memory.

"I've been a handful of times, hiking ... once with my husband. But I've never been to this part of Beara."

Husband. There it was. Absurd how the word flattened him. *Mór mo bhrón*.

The voice that had coursed the road, seeming to pull them together. Had she heard it, too? Daniel wanted to ask, wanted to hear Annie speak, to elicit another smile, another heedless laugh, but this was ridiculous. Whoever this woman was, she was married. And she was James MacKenna's colleague, which meant she worked for Eire-Evergreen, which meant she stood for everything he abhorred: development for profit's sake, tearing apart this land that belonged to no one but the creatures who were dependent on its integrity. Those who loved Beara as he did were merely its stewards.

"You wouldn't have a sturdier pair of shoes?" He lifted his chin to indicate her trail running shoes.

"Oh." She chuckled. "Is this why you nearly broke my nose? Because of my shoes?"

"They do present a bit of a challenge," Daniel said. "We'll be crossing some boggy terrain. A bit of boulder hopping as well."

"You lead the way," she said. "I'll be fine."

"If it gets too slick, we'll turn back. I won't sacrifice your safety for a view." Daniel hoisted his pack and pointed to the tall, laddered stile that straddled the fence. "All set? Up and over."

Annie hitched her small pack over her shoulders and shook out her pants. The coffee stain had spread across the thin fabric in the shape of stretched-out South America, but it was almost dry. James was closest and climbed over with ease, jumping from the tallest step into the field.

"I wouldn't advise that," said Daniel. "Surest way to snap an ankle if there's boggy ground or rocks at the bottom."

James's pale skin flushed. "It's solid dirt."

Annie caught Daniel's eye and winked, but he held his tongue and motioned for her to go next. James walked ahead along the trail, until a cow with a sleek black coat and a giant white heart on her forehead heaved to her spindly legs and began to amble toward him. He halted and backed up a few steps, and then looked over his shoulder, lips pressed tight as he tried to cover his alarm. Annie almost tripped down the ladder with the effort of holding back her laughter.

"She's just curious," Daniel said.

James scowled. "I prefer my beef on a platter."

"These ladies would make for poor eating. They're milkers. Aren't you, girls?" He hailed the herd, which watched them with soulful eyes. "Friesians have the black-and-white spots, and those russet beauties are Guernseys." Daniel moved past Annie and James, following the well-worn path. Even though few tramped the Beara Way this time of year, generations of farmers and sheep, and eventually hikers, had carved the most logical way up the hillside until the grass no longer grew in between the stones and patches of bog.

Annie caught up to him. "Where is your office?" she asked.

"You're in it."

"Ha. Of course. Have you always lived on the Beara Peninsula?"

"Long enough so it's home. I was born in England, but my mother's Irish. She brought me and my sister to the west of Ireland when I was a toddler."

"Is she here still?"

"Ah, no. She married and moved to New Zealand a long time ago. I've got a whole passel of half-siblings I've never met."

Not waiting for—or wanting—a reply, Daniel set the sunglasses hanging from a strap around his neck into place on the bridge of his nose and stepped up his pace. James and Annie proceeded in single file behind him along the steep hill track.

What was he doing out here, with this pair? With his thoughts of this woman who drew him in like a selkie? And if they knew who he was—that a few nights ago he sat at his sister's kitchen table, plotting opposition? Well, they'd find out soon enough, and whatever connection that might run between him and Annie would be lost.

15

After a climb that had Annie grabbing for balance at huge stones sunk into the hillside and wishing for sturdy boots to steady her ankles, they emerged onto a flat spine of land. The sun had passed its zenith, and she shielded her eyes with the flat of her hand.

The Atlantic Ocean stretched in a sparkling sheet of blue-gray with great black pools where clouds reflected from miles above. Narrow brown fingers of headlands stretched away from the green mass of Ireland and dipped into the sea. Low mounds like the humps of whales and jagged peaks like shark fins rose from the water. Annie stared in wonder, overcome by an emotion she couldn't name, some mixture of transcendent joy and raw sorrow. Her heart felt as if it sat outside her chest, drawn from her body by the sheer beauty of Beara.

Her eyes smarted with tears. At the top of this steep hill, the wind was fierce, and she could hide her brimming lower lids and the sniffled inhale behind the harsh turn of the weather. She wiped the back of her hand across her eyes and swiped at her cheeks. "I could live inside this view," she said when Daniel joined her. It made no sense, but that's what she felt—wanting to lift off the earth and into the dream of the panorama before her.

"There is no place quite like this place," Daniel agreed. "The near islands are Scariff and Deenish." He pointed out the gray-green islands just offshore, then shifted his finger a fraction to the left. "That jagged tooth in the distance is Skellig Michael."

"It's extraordinary," she whispered. She could say no more.

Daniel excused himself. "Got to see a man about a dog," he announced and walked over a rise and out of sight. James joined her, their shoulders nearly touching.

"How are those shoes holding up?"

"I wish I had my boots. These are fine for the moment, but I want to come back here. I want to go there." She pointed to a bluff where suicidal cliffs dove into the water. The scene reminded her of the poster in the Green Lake Methodist basement. "And there." Below them stretched a green valley with a clutch of gem-colored cottages nestled in the center.

"And there." James guided her hand farther to the left, where the coast curved in, as if a primordial sea creature had taken a massive bite of earth and stone. "That's Ballycaróg Bay. Underneath that water is a treasure of copper that will change this peninsula forever."

Annie's hand dropped to her side. "Yes. There," she echoed in a hollow voice. Bannon nosed her leg, and she bent to scratch the heeler on the dog's chunky shoulders.

"This isn't just about what's best for Beara or even for Ireland." James squatted on his heels and gathered a handful of small stones. "Copper is one of the most important mineral resources known to man. Your mobile phone and computer couldn't function without it, nor could the transmission of data. Electric motors. Semiconductors." He hurled a rock sideways, as though skipping a stone on the surface of a lake. "I bet you had an MRI after your leg injury. Do you know what protected you from excessive radiation? Copper. There is copper in car brakes. In that tractor." He pointed down the hill, to a farmer churning up black sod. "It's also one of the most widely recycled metals. Most of the copper that has been mined since the fifth century BC is still in use. I think that's amazing, don't you? Beautiful, really."

Not as beautiful as this. She held her thought in check, her words in safe silence.

"Our campaign must convey the message that Eire-Evergreen Metals will respect Beara and work to preserve her beauty," James said. "I want people to see us as the key to preserving the peninsula for generations to come, so that their children's children can enjoy this view."

"A coastline degraded, a fishing industry destroyed, mammals and birds made extinct, and piles of seabed and pits of earth dug up and dumped, all in the name of exploration and profit." They started and turned to see Daniel just steps behind them, his eyes opaque sea glass, his voice cold ocean. A vein in his neck pulsed.

Annie straightened suddenly and had to close her eyes against a wave of dizziness. She opened them as a massive cloud eclipsed the sun, turning the day's fulgor to a slate-gray lassitude.

James's fine features dissolved into a mocking smile, but Daniel hadn't finished. "You do realize if the Eire-Evergreen mine opens, this cove will be destroyed, and the choughs that live there won't survive," he said.

"The birds won't relocate?" Annie asked.

"It's not as simple as that. The birds are dependent on a particular habitat, one that offers them a consistent supply of the invertebrates they eat. And those invertebrates thrive in specific conditions—sea cliffs on the edge of sheep and cow pastures. The exact conditions found in Ballycaróg Cove, oddly enough." A shake of his head and a huff of air that might have been a laugh, but Annie knew it conveyed sour irony.

"You might think the west of Ireland would be rife with coastline that offers these cliffs, but you'd be wrong. Our cove is the only place on the Beara or Kerry peninsulas with the right conditions. If this mine goes in, our children and their children will face an environmental disaster." Daniel spoke to her, looked only at her. His words were matter-of-fact, and his tone barely concealed outrage, but his eyes implored her to think twice. *Reconsider.*

Mór mo phian. The strange words carried on the shadow of a cloud for only an instant, before dissipating with the sound of James's voice.

"That is precisely the misconception we are here to destroy." He stayed by Annie's side, speaking to her the words he really meant for Daniel. She felt like a cue ball between the two men, taking the hits. "You might have your work cut out for you, but once we show the good people of the peninsula the jobs and the euros behind this project, false Cassandras won't have much to complain about, and there won't be many who'll listen."

The cloud that passed over Daniel's face was darker than the one blocking the sun. Annie stepped out from between the two men. "Well, now, what do you say we get out of this wind? I'm starting to take a chill."

The day seemed soiled, and suddenly she truly was chilled and deeply tired. Daniel dropped his sunglasses over his eyes, and as he turned, he paused briefly before her. Annie saw herself reflected in the mirrored lenses; her face was drawn tight with tension.

They returned to the trailhead and descended the hillside. The rain began as they crossed the cow pasture, and the beasts regarded them dispassionately, unaffected by the intrusion of humans or weather. Annie realized, as her pack thunked into her back, that she hadn't taken a single photograph.

~

No one spoke on the way back to Castletownbere. The wipers slashed through the sheets of rain in a metronome of cracked rubber while the radio delivered a low murmur of incomprehensible Gaelic. It wasn't quiet. But it was silent.

Annie had soaked her shoes trudging through the middle of a boggy patch in the pasture, and the damp had seeped to her skin. She flexed her toes, squishing her socks in time to the wipers. Bone weary, she closed her eyes, and the views of southwest Ireland breaking, tumbling, sweeping into the Atlantic Ocean played across her inner vision.

Back in the parking lot where they'd met up that morning, James leaned over the seat and offered Daniel a precise rectangle of folded euros. Daniel held up the palm of his hand. "Can't take your money."

"Can't? Or won't?"

Daniel chuckled, but his hands gripped the steering wheel and twisted the faux-leather cover as he stared through the windshield. "No need. West Ireland Excursions takes good care of me."

"Right. I'll make certain you're paid for the day. Cutting short the hike wasn't your fault. I should have arranged decent boots for Annie."

Daniel responded by addressing Annie directly. "What size do you wear?"

"Me? You mean my shoe size? Nine?" Flustered, she did that thing she hated when she heard other women doing it:

ending every statement as if it were a question. "I don't know what that would be here."

"About a seven, I would think. Your feet look the same size as my sister's. I'll bring down a pair if you want to go hill walking again. Save those"—he nodded to her soaked feet—"for walking on the roads."

She nodded her acknowledgment before opening the car door. It wasn't likely to be a genuine offer, knowing now who she was, that they were on opposing sides. Still, she wanted to say something … an apology, an explanation. But with James still in the car, meaningful conversation was impossible.

"Thank you," she said, one foot already out the door. "I'll let you know."

16

He set off across the lot to the Spar as the Mercedes drove away. Annie turned his way … did he imagine a hand raised, bidding him farewell?

After purchasing several gallons of distilled water and loading them into the back of his Range Rover, he allowed Bannon to leap free. She accompanied him into Dunne's Farm Supply Store, where her best friend, Hilary, a black lab with a grizzled muzzle, greeted her with subdued wags and gentle sniffs. After a moment, Hilary settled back on her squashed square cushion.

"Not feeling well today, girl?" Daniel bent to rub Hilary's warm, bony head. She responded with a few licks, then rested her long snout between her paws. Bannon nosed around Hilary's ears before she trotted off to the paint section, where the clerks kept a supply of dog biscuits.

"She's not long for this world, our Hilary." Maeve Brady clucked with regret from her perch on a step stool, where she was arranging hoes upside down on a display mount. "But she made it through another winter, the old girl. Maybe the sun will see her through the spring and summer." She climbed down. "What can I do you for, Danny?"

"Another special order." He unfolded a list and placed it

on the counter. Maeve retrieved a pair of reading glasses from the side pocket of her cardigan.

"Let's see. Five hundred mil bottle of ammonium hydroxide, a case of five hundred gram ammonium chloride. I've got a case of this ferrous sulfate in stock. I'll let you take that now and just order more with this lot."

Maeve called in the order to the chemical supplier in Cork, while Daniel grabbed bags of dog food and birdseed. "That's in, then," she said when he returned to the front. "Should have a delivery by the end of the week. What are you working on?"

"O'Meara's landed me several sheets of roofing copper," Daniel said. "This"—he waved at his list—"is for experimenting with different patinas. Just making sure I've got the right chemicals on hand when inspiration strikes."

"Well, as long as you don't blow up half of Beara with your science experiments." Maeve winked. She leaned over the counter and in a stage whisper asked, "You'll know who was in town last night, right there at MacCarthy's?" Not expecting a response, she hurried on. "Your man James MacKenna, with his mine and his Mercedes. I was enjoying my Sunday pint with Mr. Brady, and he breezed in with a pretty blonde on his arm. They joined a group in suits. Even Des Pattwell was there. On a Sunday!" she crowed, delighting in her outrage. "I heard her talking. American. What do you suppose an American is doing here?"

"She's with the mining company, doing PR work for them." Daniel tried for offhand, but Maeve wasn't having any of it. She raised her eyebrows in surprise.

"Listen to you, Daniel Savage. A man in the know."

"It's not me—it's Fiana. I've gotten the full rundown of who's who. Fi's organized an anti-mine movement with Michael Leahy and Mort MacGeoghegan."

"The Beara Chough Coalition."

Daniel snorted. "So, you know."

"Know? I'm an official member." She nodded to the window. Daniel had missed the display, focused as he was on getting through his errands as quickly as possible. Distracted by thoughts of Annie.

Plastered on a front window were several A3 flyers with a crudely drawn and colored Red-billed Chough set against a green-and-blue backdrop of what Daniel supposed was land and sky. BEARA CHOUGH COALITION! UNITE AGAINST THE MINE! PRESERVE PRISTINE BEARA! was etched in thick black marker underneath the bird. MEETING: THURSDAY, 5 APRIL, 7:00 P.M. BALLYCARÓG COMMUNITY CENTRE. Fiana's mobile phone number was listed. He groaned and accepted the copy that Maeve thrust into his hand.

Daniel left Dunne's with his supplies and returned to the mud-spattered Range Rover. Bannon jumped into the back, and he slammed shut the door behind her. "Lie down," he called. The heeler circled three times, gazed beseechingly at Daniel, and then sank onto her bed. Daniel looked again at the poster before sailing it over his shoulder onto the backseat.

17

"That went well, don't you think?" She didn't try to keep the sarcasm from her voice.

"Are you on his side, then?" A punch to the gas and a swift downshift of gears as they turned out of the village.

Annie braced herself against the sudden uptick in speed. "Of course not. But there's no point in being deliberately antagonistic."

With a bend in the road uncomfortably near, James passed a slower car. She closed her eyes. "It's so easy for us to talk about changing this place when we don't live here," she said when she could breathe again. "We don't know what it's like for those who've spent their whole lives trying to make a home and a living at the end of the earth."

"This isn't Borneo or Mongolia, Annie. Don't treat them like poor savages."

"Isn't that exactly what we're doing by telling them that Eire-Evergreen is here to save the day and the mine will be the answer to all Beara's woes? What if things are fine just as they are?"

Exhaustion had dissolved her professional boundaries and perhaps her common sense; she kept going, even as a small voice pleaded for her to stop. "How much of a minefield am I walking into, really?" she asked. "I'm beginning to wonder why I'm here. Why don't you just use your in-house PR people?"

James took his time responding. So long, in fact, she wondered if she'd offended him. "You came all this way as our strategic communications specialist, and you don't know why you're here?"

Annie turned her face to the window, hoping the pink flush that crept up to her hairline wasn't as obvious as it felt. What would he say if he knew she was riding the edge of a ruined career, that this was the first project she'd been put in charge of since her slide turned to a plummet last year?

"Yes, I know why I'm here. Eire-Evergreen bungled it from the start. The community has seen only the corporation, the logo, the suits, the government badges. I'm here to smooth things over, bring a face to the industry, show them it's a family affair."

"The family affair is why *I'm* here," James said.

Moments passed, and Annie felt an entire conversation happening around her, unspoken, heavy with misunderstanding.

"You don't remember?" he asked. "Last year at the SME conference in Chicago?"

She hesitated, her mind racing past bewilderment into the recesses of recollection. The Society for Mining, Metallurgy & Exploration annual conference had taken place last September. She'd been part of a panel of public relations experts with experience in environmental issues, a presentation she'd eased into after a lunch of Bloody Marys. But later, the evening functions ... what had she done, and with whom?

The blackouts had become more common around that time. Not a blanking out of body—she remained able to function. No, the blackouts robbed her recall. She'd lose hours. Whole nights.

The weekend of the SME conference had been a blur of mixers and happy hours. The final morning, she'd woken up alone in the hotel, but the room wasn't hers. Shame had driven that image from her mind. Until now.

And then there was James's distinctive voice, that puzzling blend of accents she'd recognized at the airport, which still hadn't reconciled itself into concrete memory.

Her belly clenched. It couldn't be. *No. Please not that. No.*

Not long after Annie had returned to Seattle, Serena and the director of HR had called her to a closed-door meeting. There they'd presented her with the performance warning that still hung over her head. Although they hadn't mentioned her conduct at the conference, she'd had to wonder what they'd heard. Vodka that smoothed the rough edges had also fallen over her memory like a heavy curtain across the sad stage of her life.

"Yes, I remember." The lie was delivered. Too late to take back.

"I wasn't even considering your firm," said James. "Then you approached me and made a hard pitch. You were so confident, made such a compelling case. I realized if you could sell me, you just might be able to sell a few thousand Irish."

He had to be bullshitting her. The first she recalled hearing of MacKenna Mining and Eire-Evergreen Metals was a month, maybe six weeks ago, after she'd returned to work. How could she have pitched last year? What else was missing? *Who* else was missing? *Think, Annie.*

"And I believe I will," she said.

"Do you? Because the Annie sitting next to me is nothing like the Annie I met on the thirty-fifth floor of the Chicago Hyatt. You know how to win people's hearts. That's what we're after here. You're terrific at your job. Or at least you were."

Annie pressed herself against the seat, her body braking

against innuendo. She breathed in through her nose, practicing her yogic breath to steady her mind and body.

James silenced an incoming call with the push of a button on the steering wheel. "When I contacted Magnuson, I asked for you personally. But I was told you were occupied with other projects. When I pressed, Serena told me you weren't right for this project. She said you'd been out of the office on extended leave and weren't up to the demands of an intense campaign."

Serena had known all along, had withheld this from Annie. But why? Why flirt with violating her privacy and set her up for certain failure?

"Extended leave."

"That's what Serena said."

"I suppose you'd like to know what that means."

"It's none of my business."

"That's a true statement." Annie waited a beat, but James left her response hanging in the thick air. "Maybe I had chemotherapy. Or I was on bereavement leave. Maybe I had a facelift or a nervous breakdown."

"I'm not asking you to tell me." His lip lifted at one corner, but if it was a smile, Annie couldn't tell. She didn't think so. Their awkward exchange rang in her ears, his pointed remarks digging into her most tender parts. She folded her ice-cold fingers in her lap to keep them still.

James pulled into the drive that led down to the bungalow on the cliff. Parked in the paved lot just outside the front walk was a late-model Opel. "Good," he said. "I meant to tell you earlier. Colm texted that he delivered the car. Keys are under the front seat. He'll meet us for dinner at the Ballycaróg pub at seven. Would you like me to pick you up, or do you want to meet us there?"

Annie's hand on the door latch froze, but her mind

scrambled. The AA meeting in Bantry was at six. She had to go. She *wanted* to go.

"Jet lag kept me up most of the night," she said quietly. "Let me get one good night's sleep, and I'll be on fire tomorrow." What about tomorrow night? Could she find a morning meeting? Maybe she could Skype with Bill—she'd already set up a weekly Skype call with her therapist.

James considered her a moment, and she felt a flash of anxiety, sensing he measured her against his expectations and that she fell far short. From a deep side pocket of his hiking pants he retrieved a large, folded sheet of paper and handed it to Annie.

"You'll want to make time for this."

Her eyebrows knitted in a question as she opened it. It was a large flyer with a child's rendering of a black crow. Except this crow had a red beak and red feet. Urgent messages were printed in heavy ink:

BEARA CHOUGH COALITION!
UNITE AGAINST THE MINE!
PRESERVE PRISTINE BEARA!
MEETING: THURSDAY, 5 APRIL, 7:00 P.M.
BALLYCARÓG COMMUNITY CENTRE

"What's the Beara Chough Coalition?" she asked.

"Our greatest challenge," James replied. "Do your research. Get your rest. I'll call you in the morning."

18

Terry Mullen kicked up the doorstop and guided the door shut. Daniel refilled his coffee and walked toward his preferred seat on the far left side of the room. Rows of chairs were arranged classroom-style in two sections, separated by a center aisle, and nearly every chair was filled.

In a lull of conversation as the gathering found their seats, he heard a familiar voice call, "Wait, please!" Terry pulled back the door, and Annie Crowe entered, her face flushed, her smile strained. She mouthed her thanks and nodded as Terry pointed to empty seats in the back row.

"Good to see you, lad." Bea Moriarty slipped her arm through his. "How's the art coming along?"

He allowed himself to be escorted by the hummingbird of a woman who, proudly sober for forty years, had devoted her career to counseling addicts across Cork, dispensing her warmth when needed and tough love when that was called for, too.

"It's coming along. Good days and bad days, like most everything else."

"What was today, Danny? A good one or a bad one?"

He ushered Bea into the chair next to his and took one

last look at the back of the room before sitting down. Annie wriggled out of her raincoat, steam wafting from her as the chilled air she'd carried in met the heat of the room, stuffed with bodies in waterproofs and wool.

Annie, an alcoholic. Fifteen years around addicts of all flavors and he'd developed a good sense about these things, but this one he'd missed.

"Today?" he whispered against Bea's rouged and wrinkled cheek. "Today was interesting."

The room fell silent, and with one voice, punctuated by nicotine-laced coughs, the group recited the Serenity Prayer. Daniel heard voices speaking in English, Gaelic, German; the two brothers seated one row ahead and few seats down recited the prayer in their native Polish. They were construction workers who'd brought their families to Ireland three years ago, settling in a Polish enclave outside Bantry. There was Mawusi across the aisle, wearing a long wool sweater draped over a brightly patterned skirt of kente cloth. Originally from Ghana, Mawusi had earned a master's in social work in Dublin and now worked as a drug and alcohol counselor out of Skibbereen.

Daniel considered these changing sounds and faces of Ireland—the ancient and the new—brought together by addiction, joined in fellowship and need. A hush descended again as voices trailed off, ending the prayer.

Mór mo náir.

The voice rang low, vibrating in the air like a gong. He lifted his head. Denis from Bantry rose, the Twelve Steps pamphlet shaking slightly in his hands, and began to read in a halting voice.

Mór mo náir.

Great my shame, she said, a mother's croon to her child, Leda's murmur to her swan. It was the same voice he'd heard in the car park that morning in Castletownbere. And, like those words—*mór mo bhrón*, great my sorrow—he understood the Gaelic but could not place the meaning.

Many recovery stories were shared that evening, but Annie's was not among them. In the meeting's final minutes, someone in the back stood to introduce herself as Margaret and declared she'd been sober for eleven months and fourteen days. As the gathering greeted her, Daniel shifted in his seat to see past the speaker's body to the row behind, where Annie sat. Where Annie had been sitting. The chair one row behind and to Margaret's right was empty.

~

"Bea, you're a Gaelic speaker, aren't you?" The hour had come to an end, and the room rumbled once more with conversation, chairs scraping across the linoleum, cell phones beeping, feet pounding overhead as the group filtered up the stairs and through the hallway above.

"Of course, Danny. I'm from Letterkenny; we spoke only Gaelic at home. But in secret, you know. Wasn't allowed in school. You're needing a translation?" In a pink hand-knit cardigan stretched over the round ball of her torso, with hair like white floss, Bea resembled a wrinkled but still-fresh rosebud.

"Not exactly. I understand the words, but I don't know where they're from."

"Let's have them."

"*Mór mo náir*, which I'd translate as 'great my shame.' *Mór mo bhrón* means 'great my sorrow,' I think. I feel as though I've heard them before—maybe a song? I just can't place when or where."

Bea's round, pink face crinkled like crêpe paper with her smile.

"Daniel Savage. For shame. Don't you know your Irish history?"

He held up his palms in surrender. "I skipped that day?" he offered. "Matter of fact, I skipped most of high school. Though I thought I'd made up for it prison."

Bea placed one hand on his shoulder, one on her heart, and closed her eyes. The Gaelic poured from her throat in syllables that had all their rough edges rounded off as they passed over her tongue.

Mise Éire: Sine mé ná an Chailleach Bhéarra.

Mór mo ghlóir: Mé a rug Cú Chulainn cróga.

Mór mo náir: Mo chlann féin a dhíol a máthair.

Mór mo phian: Bithnaimhde do mo shíorchiapadh.

Mór mo bhrón: D'éag an dream inar chuireas dóchas.

Mise Éire: Uaigní mé ná an Chailleach Bhéarra.

The room hushed as Bea recited, though several voices joined her in the familiar phrases. She finished and opened her eyes to applause and "We love ya, Bea." At a half-shouted *"Erin Go Bragh,"* laughter rippled around the room.

She winked a shining eye at Daniel. "Ring any bells?"

"You had me at *Mise Éire.*" Of course he knew the poem. It had been written by Patrick Henry Pearse, a leader of the 1916 Easter Rising, the greatest battle of the Republican Irish against British Home Rule. *Mise Éire* translated to *I am Ireland.*

"Good boy. Now, are you going to make me ask why you're wondering about *Mise Éire?*"

"I won't make you ask, but I don't have much of an answer. I've heard those phrases in recent days, but I couldn't put them in context. Now at least I know where they come from, though I still don't know how they found their way into my head."

"Well, if you're hearing things now, at least you're hearing the right things, so. God bless you, lad."

He stood and bent to kiss her powdered cheek. "Thanks for the chat, Bea."

"That kiss'll keep me alive at least another week." She patted his cheek in return. "You're a good man. Now go off and do good things."

19

Hidden in the back of the room, Annie felt comforted by the familiar give and take of sharing, acknowledgment, readings, confessions, and reassurance. The accents were different, but the stories were the same. Even the basement, with its smells of stale coffee and nicotine, wet wool and cologne, could have been copied and pasted from one of a half dozen church and community center meeting rooms she'd sat in since January. She was safe here. If this meeting was at the end of each day, she could get through whatever the hours before it held. She might even start to invest in the task before her. Might care what would happen if she succeeded in selling the mine to Ballycaróg. Or if she didn't.

But then the sight of a head of reddish-brown hair and solid shoulders jolted her, and she shrank back in her chair. She was certain he hadn't seen her. Fairly certain. But beyond shocking her into embarrassment, Daniel's presence filled Annie with sadness. She had to sit for a few minutes to pick apart why. He'd seemed so solid, connected, and certain up on the mountain, and his anger at James, at the mine (*at me?*) righteous. Yet here he was. As fallible and flawed as she. She'd wanted him to be as magical and mysterious as this place, and now, suddenly, in this church basement that was like any church basement, he had a past like any alcoholic's, full of mistakes and regrets. When attention was turned to a speaker at the front of the room, she slid out of her seat, tiptoed to the door, and slipped out.

Dusk was just easing down as she sat in the car with her phone to her ear, listening to it ring in late-morning Seattle.

"Annie! How's the Emerald Isle? The old country." Bill affected a lousy Irish accent, and his familiar, gravelly voice suffused Annie with warm relief.

"Hey there, Bill. Is this a good time?"

"It's always a good time, kiddo. How about you? Are you having a good time?"

"A laugh a minute."

"Better than crying, right? But you didn't call me just to tell me about the weather, or how green it is, did you? What's up? Are you in a safe place?"

"In a church parking lot. I'm good. Just a little lonely." She squeezed shut her eyes. *Don't cry. Don't cry. Don't cry.* "A lot lonely."

"Tell me."

And so she did. She told Bill about feeling that a shadow of herself had come to Ireland, while the rest of her sat at the bottom of a bottle somewhere. Of her uncertainty about this project, now that she was here, seeing this place and the beauty that would be so compromised if she succeeded, and still she was terrified to lose the last piece of her shredded identity—her job—if she didn't. Yet what a relief it would be to start over. She told him how good it had felt to laugh in Daniel's car and how feeling good left her vulnerable. She tried to tell him what she'd felt as she stood on top of that hill overlooking Ballycaróg Bay a few hours before.

"It was so profound. I wanted to cry and shout with joy all at the same time. That much beauty just shatters my soul. I can't comprehend how something so perfect could exist in a world with so much pain." Her voice caught, and she swallowed back a sob. "I don't want to be an alcoholic. I don't want to be around other alcoholics. I want to know normal people. People who aren't in pain."

"Ain't nobody I know who isn't in pain. Non-addicts all around us, and they're in a different world of hurt. Most of them don't even know why. You and me, we know why. We think we know how to make it stop. A drink. Maybe a couple. It would feel so good, smooth everything out so you just can't feel, right?"

Annie's throat clenched with tears, but her silly gesture—nodding as though Bill could see her—made her smile. "Right," she whispered.

"But you know that's the road to hell. We're the lucky ones, Annie. We're the ones who know just what to do to keep the worst pain at bay. We don't drink. Ever. You know what you felt today?"

She shook her head, her shoulders starting to hitch. "No."

"You felt the exquisite pain of being alive. There you were, full of endorphins from physical exercise—that shit makes you feel great, I know, even though it would kill my fat ass—but you're still jet-lagged, running on borrowed energy, maybe feeling vulnerable around the one guy you have to impress, the other you're attracted to."

Annie snorted and blew her nose into a tissue she'd scrounged from her purse, the phone clenched between her shoulder and her ear.

"Oh, yeah, I noticed the way you described your guide. *Your neighbor.*" She pictured Bill making air quotes. "I'm jealous already. Of him, let's make that clear."

She laughed aloud, but her stomach rippled. *Attracted to Daniel?* Her gaze was drawn to the church entrance. Why hadn't she simply driven away?

"And then you see this vision that must look like heaven," Bill was saying.

"I wanted to slip inside it," she said, her voice raspy with tears. "I thought if I could stay on that hilltop forever, I'd be healed. I'd find out who I am and what I should be doing with my life."

"Ain't no leaving yourself behind, Annie. There's only facing who you are. But where you are doesn't sound like such a bad place to be at all. Who says you have to come home?"

"Ha. Wouldn't that be nice? Just run away. Doesn't seem like very sound advice coming from the guy who's supposed to keep me grounded."

"Me? Nope. That ain't my job. I don't do the groundwork. You do. You had a moment of feeling alive, a moment you probably felt just like the old Annie, the pre-drunk Annie—strong, hopeful, powerful—and it scared the shit out of you. But I will give you one piece of advice."

"What's that?" She pulled at a loose thread on the seam of her jeans.

"Go hike that mountain again."

20

"Lad, start another row at that end, eight across."

Liam grabbed more folding chairs than he could carry, and Daniel closed his eyes against the ensuing crash. Fiana spun around as several chairs slid across the cement floor and landed near her feet. "Liam!" she shouted. "Use the good sense God gave you."

"He's been a great help, Fi." Daniel came to the rescue of Liam, who'd blushed to the roots of his red hair. He saw his own adolescent self reflected in the boy's thin face and pale blue eyes. "He's just excited. Kind of like his mom."

Fiana unfolded one chair and bent to pick up another. "I know. I'm sorry, son. My nerves are on edge. I just want everything to be perfect. We both need to slow down." Her phone rang, and she pressed one hand over her free ear, moving into the hallway as she spoke to the caller.

"Women," Liam muttered, and Daniel laughed.

"It only gets worse, lad." He ruffled the boy's hair so that it stood on end. "You think mothers are bad," he whispered conspiratorially. "Just wait until girlfriends."

"Not happening," replied Liam. "I'm through with women."

He shoved open a chair, and with the coast clear, planted it with a bang.

"Things with Aoife not working out?" Daniel followed his nephew, straightening out the rows.

"Aine. I told you, her name's Aine. We're not together anymore."

"Last week you still hadn't actually spoken with her. How can you now not be together?"

"We weren't getting along."

Daniel stilled the flicker of a smile. Nearly thirty years had passed since his own entangled adolescent love life, and the memory of those awkward days—the parade of teenage girls in their school uniforms, all two heads taller than the lads, their limbs growing into their blossoming bodies with grace, while the boys chafed at their own squeaking voices and scrawny chests—belonged to another life. *Another century.*

Between January of his third year of junior cycle and the end of the following summer, he turned sixteen, grew fifteen centimeters, and gained eighteen kilos. He'd put on most of that weight over the summer after joining a construction crew. The money and freedom were better than school and a rotating roster of foster families, so he didn't go back to either.

But in his early years, he'd attended a community school like Liam and Catriona, and he figured that formative time, in the peace of Skibbereen, under the close watch of foster parents and the grip of Fiana's love, had kept him from his troubled fate long enough to build a foundation of common sense. The waters of petty crime and addiction had eaten away that foundation, but it never collapsed completely. It became his sole means of rebuilding his life. He would finally earn his leaving certificate in prison, eighteen years later. And in the end, he'd returned to Fi and her family.

"Hey, Daniel, watch this!" Liam lifted a crumpled sheet of paper with his instep, flicked it into the air, and kicked it in a fine arc across the room, where it circled the rim of a rubbish bin and tipped in. "Goal!" he shouted, and offered a bow to his imaginary fans. Daniel prayed Liam would not lose his artless approach to love for years yet. There was time enough for a truly broken heart.

Liam retrieved the paper from the can and tossed it to Daniel, who caught it on the front of his foot. He let it sail high into the air before delivering a wallop that sent the wadded paper straight back to his nephew, just as Fiana returned with Mort MacGeoghegan. She flung her hands up in a gesture of hopelessness. Daniel stared at her hard, hoping to beam a strong signal. If a man had paid this kind of attention to him when he'd been thirteen, had listened, joked, kicked around a football made of paper … *Let it go, Fi*, he pleaded silently. *See what's happening here.*

It worked. She rolled her eyes and set her mouth but flashed Daniel a look that said *thank you*. He shook his head at Liam, and the two resumed their setup of the meeting room, the football match left until the coast was clear.

"How many are we expecting?" Mort stepped in to give Daniel and Liam a hand setting the final chairs into place while Fiana did a quick count.

"We've got forty chairs. The room holds seventy-five people, but who knows? It's just the first meeting. We probably won't need so many." Arms akimbo, she scanned the room and sighed.

"I tell myself there's time to build support, but then I realize how quickly this could spin out of our hands. We have no money, no power, nothing to offer except our belief that sacrificing Beara is wrong. It's just wrong."

Liam placed an arm around his mother's shoulders and

gave her a quick squeeze. Daniel realized with a shock how quickly his nephew was growing—when had he surpassed Fiana's height? It seemed just last week he'd barely reached her shoulders.

"You worry too much, Mom. It's going to be fine. You always get your way. You'll see." Fiana returned the laughter that followed Liam's declaration with a scowl but patted her son on the cheek and gave him a kiss. "You're a good son, Liam. You two"—she frowned at the men, but her eyes shone—"mind yourselves. You could stand to learn a thing or two still."

The front door to the community center opened, and the first familiar faces appeared. Fiana left them to greet their neighbors from across the peninsula who may be willing to join the fight to defeat the mine.

~

An hour later, the hall was in violation of multiple fire codes. Standing room only in the back, with several of the youngest and most limber sitting on the floor. Bottoms perched on windowsills, and bodies blocked the door and spilled into the hallway. Moira Kearney's oatmeal biscuits were mere memories, and one lone candied cherry was all that remained of Tess Flanagan's whiskey-soaked fruitcake.

Fiana's face was no longer flushed and sweating. She sat beaming in between Michael and Mort at the head table, wholly in her element. The first community meeting of the Beara Chough Coalition was ready to be called to order, and her fears that no one would come, no one would care, had been laid to rest.

A sudden, shrill blast sent gasps through the din of voices and hands flying up to ears. Michael Leahy dropped the dog whistle that hung on a chain around his neck and sat back with his arms crossed over his chest, the picture of satisfaction.

"Michael Christopher Leahy, for all that is holy!" scolded his wife from the front row. Titters of laughter rippled through the room. Fiana mouthed "thank you" to Michael.

"I'm so pleased to see you all here." She stood with her hands folded in front of her waist, about to address a group of people she'd lived near for most of her adult life. "Of course, you know that I'm Fiana O'Connell, and you all know Michael Leahy." The farmer raised his whistle, and the crowd laughed. "Many of you know Dr. Mortimer MacGeoghegan, professor emeritus of geology at University College Cork. Dr. MacGeoghegan has lived all his life in West Cork and moved to Beara two years ago. " Fiana turned and motioned to Mort, who half-raised from his seat and waved.

"Mort, please," he said. "Only my students are allowed to call me Dr. MacGeoghegan." Gentle laughter followed, and he settled back into his chair.

Fiana continued. "You all know the rumors floating around that copper has been found in the waters off Ballycaróg Cove and possibly new stores of it well inland." The assembled group nodded their heads as one.

"While we understand the excitement about new jobs and new industries possibly coming to Beara, this all seemed hush-hush and too good to be true. Some of us started asking questions. We learned that Eire-Evergreen Metals are owned by the Australian conglomerate MacKenna Mining. And this MacKenna Mining own mines all over the world." There was some shuffling of feet and shifting of bodies in the overheated room.

"Turns out all the land, including the coastline, that

MacKenna Mining want is owned by the Irish government—none of it is in the hands of any private citizen. The government has worked closely with Eire-Evergreen Metals, and the proper exploration permits have been sought and issued by the Department of Communications, Energy and Natural Resources. The DCENR has also allowed exploratory drilling offshore. All of this is happening right here, right now, on Beara land, and no one has said a word to us." She let that statement echo. A low murmuring and shaking of heads followed.

"We learned that before any work can be done on land or any actual mining can take place in the ocean, there must be a series of community meetings. Eire-Evergreen Metals are required to file an Environmental Impact Statement and obtain an Integrated Pollution Prevention and Control license. What's most important is that the whole of the Beara Peninsula is designated as a Special Protection Area. No one can just come in here, wave around a bunch of euros, and start drilling."

"Oh, yes, they can, Fiana. This is big business! Who are you kidding?" Nicotine and whiskey had grated Niall O'Carroll's booming voice to a rasp. The room erupted in conversation, and more voices rang out: "I'll take some of those euros!" "They're welcome to drill in my backyard—nothing but rocks and sheep dung!" The good-natured shouting went on.

Fiana held up her hand. "Listen, all of you. The three of us"—she motioned to Mort and Michael—"we've been researching copper mining in other countries, and we're concerned. This mine would have some very serious effects on Beara. If it stays out to sea, it might not seem so bad, but our fishing economy will suffer, and not one of us will see a job from the mine—offshore mining is all done by experts and machines on one of those giant rigs. If the mining comes onshore, sure, yes, there will be jobs, but at what cost? Do you know what seabed mining does to the environment? To commercial fishing? I've got a Greenpeace report right here. And another from the European Environment Agency." She waved around a thick clutch of papers. "Are we going to destroy one industry for another?"

More muttering followed, but no one interrupted Fiana. "This peninsula will be turned into a giant pit of tailings. Our waterways and coastline and forests will be polluted. Our villages, small schools, and the isolation we love—our very way of life—will be changed forever. We've survived the lousy economy better than most because we never soared to crazy heights in the first place."

Fiana squared her shoulders, her confidence growing as the crowd leaned forward, taking in her every word. "Things are turning around in Ireland. Little by little, it's true, but it will happen on Beara if we're just patient. Are you sure you want to sacrifice our way of life for empty promises and a destroyed environment? We—Mort, Mike, Daniel, me, and all of you who've signed our petition—we've all decided that we're not. So we've formed the Beara Chough Coalition."

She grabbed a meeting flyer from the table and held it up for all the room to see. "You know this bird, of course. It's the Red-billed Chough. Beara has got one of Ireland's last populations, and they are one of the reasons the peninsula has the Special Protection Area designation. You all know where they live—in the cove, just past Glass Beach. If this mine goes through, the nesting grounds of the Red-billed Chough will be destroyed, and we'll likely lose this bird forever. So we chose the chough as our symbol. We hope we can count on your support in fighting this mine. Any questions?"

What questions there may have been were drowned out in the applause. Fiana stood tall, her mouth turned in a faint smile and her eyes shining. From the back of the room, Daniel lifted a hand and flashed his sister a "V" sign. She nodded once in return. He scanned the crowd. Not everyone applauded, and several heads were bent together in intense conversation or turned around to catch the eyes of their neighbors. A few were scribbling notes on the back of the flyer, and as the applause began to die away, a number of hands shot up. A man stood and waited until he could take the floor without having to shout.

"Fiana, that's a fine speech," he began. "I've lived on this peninsula all my life. For the two of you who don't know me, I'm Noah Scott, born in Eyeries, and I've been running sheep in these hills since I could walk. I'll die here, probably next week unless Burns there repairs that railing on the Knockoura Creek bridge he took out last week with his tractor." Good-natured laughter followed.

"But, Fiana, my sons have no interest in tending sheep. They're not much made for university, and they're talking about moving on to Britain or even Australia to find work. I read in the *Times* last month that nine out of ten of our youth in the rural areas are leaving Ireland because they can't find work. Not just good-paying jobs but any jobs. How can we turn away this mine? How can I let my sons leave Ireland?"

"How indeed?" Annie's voice rang from the back of the room. She strode down the center aisle, stepping lightly over outstretched feet, her eyes making contact with the faces that turned nearly in unison at the sound of her clear voice. This confident woman was the opposite of the one Daniel had seen that night in Bantry, whose unsmiling face had revealed her vulnerability.

21

She'd walked into Ballycaróg from the bungalow and waited in the half light of a bus shelter until the doors of the community center closed, signaling the meeting was underway. The last to arrive were stuffed in the doorway of the meeting room and turned as she slipped inside, but they forgot her when Fiana began speaking. Annie surveyed the room from a sheltered angle just beyond the threshold.

Entering the room, she shifted into her public relations persona. The room was a stage, and she played her role with a confidence she knew how to exude, whether on a running track or in a boardroom, even if she didn't feel it.

Yesterday she'd stood on a cliff above Ballycaróg Cove with James and Colm, surveying the proposed mining site. Already there were stakes with orange strips marking out construction areas. Colm had spread waterproof maps on a flat patch of ground to show her where the operations would take place, both on land and offshore. The sea had been too rocky to pay a visit to the spot—a half mile out—where the platforms would be built over the massive underwater mining operation, but she'd seen the blueprints, read the estimates of mineral extraction tonnage, and noted the millions of euros

Eire-Evergreen Metals were prepared to invest in anticipation of harvesting billions in the years to come.

Her public relations challenge depended not on understanding the intricacies of extracting copper from the earth or beneath its oceans, or in explaining the growing world demand for a precious metal that played such a significant role in green energy, electronics, and the transfer and security of data. Her mission had everything to do with making a connection between the health and stability of this community and Eire-Evergreen's interests in what lay beneath its surface. Statistics embedded in arguments and counter-arguments gleaned from white papers and studies filled her head. Her fingers had flown across her laptop's keyboard these past days, transforming the reams of technical data into talking points and outlines.

Now she faced the opposition. This gathering would be her first chance to gauge how Eire-Evergreen was perceived by the community and whether there were any pro-mine feelings to be cultivated.

"Mr. Scott, how can you let your sons leave Ireland, when there will be good-paying jobs—with salaries your families can live on and save to buy homes, pay school fees, send your kids and grandkids to university—right here?" She strode to the center of the room as she spoke, turning here and there to catch and hold gazes. Her voice was warm and calm, as if she were simply having a conversation with a group of friends. "If your sons want to stay on the Beara Peninsula, if they want to raise your grandchildren here, Eire-Evergreen can help to make that happen. We can be a part of ensuring Beara remains beautiful, pristine, and healthy for generations to come."

She turned to take in the entire room. And there was Daniel in the back, standing next to a gangly teenage boy. They had matching blue eyes and prominent noses, the boy's hair bright red, Daniel's a softer auburn. The boy mimicked Daniel's posture, one foot set against the wall, arms crossed over his chest. The connection was unmistakable.

His son. She hadn't noticed a ring during their hike, but that meant so little anymore. She wondered, with a twinge—envy or curiosity?—if any of the women in this room could claim Daniel Savage. The thought was fleeting and foolish, and she let it go.

"I apologize." Now she addressed the head table, showing careful deference to the opposition. "I didn't mean to crash your meeting. My name is Annie Crowe." She paused to let her solid Irish name sink in, hinting at an ancestral connection. In fact, her grandfather had changed Chrzanowski to Crowe when he landed at Halifax, Nova Scotia, from Lódz, Poland, in 1921. But today, let them wonder. Let them assume. Let them think she was one of the vast Irish diaspora come home.

"I work for Eire-Evergreen Metals in America," she explained, wringing a mostly true statement out of a business relationship. "My job is to make certain your voices are heard. I'm here to listen to your concerns and to provide you with the information from our company that will help you make the best decisions for your community and your families."

The woman who had spoken so compellingly a few minutes before—what had Noah Scott called her? Fiana—seemed nonplussed by Annie's interruption. She stared at her with a hurt expression, as if Annie had betrayed some solidarity between them.

Fiana opened her mouth but then turned to the two men seated at the table behind her. The smaller man, with a snow-white shock of hair and a neatly trimmed white beard, rose and placed his palms flat on the table.

"Ms. Crowe, Ballycaróg is pleased to meet you. I'm Mort

MacGeoghegan, and on behalf of our village, I say *Céad mile fáilte* to you: one hundred thousand welcomes. Thank you for coming all the way from America with our best interests at heart."

Some tittered at Mort's irony, but Annie knew she'd made the connection. People listened when jobs were on the line. James and Colm assured her they'd listen even more closely if American dollars were behind Irish euros. No matter how bad the downturn, American investment still meant something in Ireland.

The skill that allowed her to size up her opponents and zero in on their strengths and weaknesses told Annie that Mort MacGeoghegan was not to be underestimated. The lines around his sparkling blue eyes and the dimple on his left cheek told her that he smiled often and deeply. Something ancient and sad in those blue eyes held her gaze. He could see through her, see past her smooth confidence into the well of ambivalence that was filling even as she remembered to keep her shoulders back, her chin up, to push the easy smile on her lips into her eyes. To convince them she was worthy of their time, their trust.

Annie pulled her eyes away from Mort's. "I lived in Cork as a student." She turned again to the crowd. "I brought my husband back to the west of Ireland a few years ago." This she said to reassure the women that her blond hair and American accent posed no threat—she was one of them, a married woman with a husband to manage. "But it wasn't until Daniel Savage took me into the Slieve Miskish mountains two days ago that I really understood how precious this land is."

All heads swiveled to the back of the room to Daniel. He pushed himself away from the wall, his face registering surprise. Annie turned back to Mort, Michael, and Fiana, whose mouth was dropped in shock, her face flushed. Annie followed Fiana's gaze to Daniel and the boy standing next to him. The boy had his mother's mouth, the shape of her eyes.

Fiana and Daniel?

"Daniel took James MacKenna, the director of operations of Eire-Evergreen and son of the founder of MacKenna Mining, and me on a hike into the hills above Ballycaróg Cove. It is one of the most beautiful places I have ever been. At that moment, I knew we—Eire-Evergreen Metals—had been given an opportunity to help the Beara Peninsula protect its unique beauty."

"Aren't you just in it for the money, lass?" shouted a voice from the crowd. Laughter and murmurs of assent and indignation followed.

"Of course we're in it for the money. MacKenna Mining employs four thousand people worldwide; Eire-Evergreen is just one small subsidiary. It's about creating jobs, sustaining a business, growing opportunities, and yes, answering to our shareholders."

She addressed the room once more. "Mr. MacKenna recently purchased a home in Ballycaróg on the very same land his great-great grandfather, Orin MacKenna, helped homestead in the 1880s."

Bodies leaned in again, eyes followed her, heads nodded. Time to make the connection, to bring it home and close the deal, at least for tonight. "Orin MacKenna mined at Minach Mòr until it closed in 1882. He left Ireland the following year to seek his fortune in Australia. It took four generations for the MacKennas to return. But here they are, hoping to create an industry on Beara so your sons and grandsons will never have reason to leave." As she spoke, she looked right at Daniel.

Mise Éire, the voice whispered, and the room seemed to

fall away. So low, the voice could be a woman's or a man's, or simply the wind moaning through the door that opened and shut in the hallway beyond.

Mise Éire, and she stared at Daniel, waiting for him to acknowledge the sounds that echoed between them. His eyes widened, as if he, too, heard the call. Then a shadow seemed to cross his face, leaving something like sadness trailing behind.

That's it. Her convincing argument had alienated the one person here whose approval she yearned for. *He's gone.*

22

Annie was good. More than good. Daniel actually believed her. Or believed that *she* believed what she claimed. She spoke with confidence, making eye contact, yet with her pale, clean face, her simple blue jeans and sweater, her blond hair swept back in a band so that it cascaded over her shoulders, she seemed so vulnerable, like an Alice in Wonderland in denim. How could you think that the company she represented would ever bring harm to Beara? How could you not want to wrap this woman in your arms and find out what was behind those haunted eyes?

The questions began in earnest after her poised and friendly speech, but Annie deftly deflected them, promising that Eire-Evergreen Metals would hold a community meeting in the coming weeks, where she and her colleagues would be on hand to present the mining project to the community and answer questions about the available jobs, the sustainability of the mine, and their plans to protect the peninsula from environmental degradation.

The Beara Chough Coalition had their work cut out if they hoped to defeat this mine. They'd have to make it through the gauntlet of multinational corporation money, expertise, and sophistication. And Annie Crowe already had them eating out of her hand.

But she couldn't have surprised Daniel any more than the moment she'd said his name. No, that wasn't it. He couldn't have been more surprised by how he *felt* when she said his name. He was filled with that same mix of wonder and bewilderment as when he'd heard the voice. The one that had been whispering lines from *Mise Éire*.

Annie left shortly after her speech, having the good sense not to steal any more of Fiana's thunder. But the meeting broke up soon after. It was a school night, and many had left their dinner dishes in the sink in their rush to make it to the meeting from their distant farmhouses or seaside cottages. Daniel remained to fold the chairs and waited for Fiana to corner him. She was uncharacteristically subdued, but it didn't take long.

"Why didn't you tell me you'd met her?" she hissed in his ear while waving farewell to Simon and Paula Coogan.

"Fi, they were clients. We went on a short hike. There isn't much to tell."

"She seemed to think it was a life-altering experience."

"Would you rather the opposition crashed through here in suits, throwing money around? Looks like we'll have someone reasonable to work with. Maybe we can find a compromise."

"Compromise? Daniel, you don't negotiate with these people. What, oh, you want only a small mine?" She snorted. "You'll destroy only half the cove? Right. Have at it. It takes one beautiful American, and suddenly everyone's all for the mine."

She shoved her hand into the arm of her coat, where it stuck. The more she wrestled, the more tangled her coat became. Daniel set a chair aside and tried to help his sister, but she jerked away. "Leave it be," she snapped. Then her shoulders sagged. "Danny. Damn. I'm sorry. Tonight didn't go as I'd planned. I never thought someone from Eire-Evergreen would show up. I thought we'd have a chance to rally this community, get them fired up, before … "

Fiana looked as though she might cry. Daniel turned his sister around, pulled up the half of her coat that dangled on the floor, and eased one arm and then the other through the sleeves. He turned her back again to face him and kissed the top of her head.

"You're doing the right thing, Fi. You were brilliant tonight. Everyone was with you, even those who still want those mining jobs—they know you're right. This isn't a setback, it's the very start. You've been given a gift—you know what you're up against. Keep going, sis. Beara needs you to fight for it."

23

She sat on the sofa in the dark, her hands pressed between her knees, rocking slightly. What she offered up at the meeting had taken all her reserves. Being inside that room, seeing a community that might be at odds yet still shared a bond of place, of history, brought home how outside the world she'd grown, how very alone she was. The way Daniel had looked at her: regret and disappointment mingled with confused desire—emotions that have been mirrored in her own expression, for it was what she felt in her soul.

Intense thirst grabbed her throat, set her fingers trembling and her skin crawling. The Addict who huddled inside her was in fact a deep, abiding loneliness. An ache for companionship. A fear of the quiet. Shame.

At Salish, there were meetings from dawn until bedtime. When she returned to her room each night, she could scarcely think to brush her teeth and wash her face before collapsing onto the hard twin mattress.

Now she longed for that structure. To wake up morning after morning and know that your day was planned to the minute, that you had little time to think or little room to wander on your own. After rehab, she'd filled her days with

AA meetings and work. Getting through the day wore her out, which was exactly what she'd wanted—to be exhausted to the point of numbness; it seemed easier than facing the shadow of her marriage.

The loneliness washed over her in waves, and she let it come. Was this the part her therapist thought would be good for her? To listen to the blood beating in her ears, to feel the tightening of her chest as the panic pulled with icy fingers at her sanity? To feel the pull of alcohol so strongly that she pictured herself rising from the sofa and climbing into the car to follow the winding road into Ballycaróg, to the pub with the football pennants in the window and a mural on the outside wall depicting a pint glass filled with dark, rich beer, its creamy head dripping down the side? Once inside that pub, she'd opt for a Jameson's with a splash, the mellow whiskey draining down her throat, coating her mouth with the taste of malt and toffee.

During the six weeks in rehab, as she moved from desperate detoxification into resistance, depression, and, finally, toward a slow, stuttered healing, Annie had encountered suffering she hadn't known possible. She'd met alcoholics who drank rubbing alcohol, hand sanitizer, and cough syrup. The shower stall offered rare moments of privacy, and she compared her body—still a finely honed instrument of muscle and ligament, not yet destroyed by her addiction—to those whose very insides seemed rotted from years of heroin or meth, their teeth destroyed, skin ravaged. *There but for the grace of God go I* became her mantra during those exhausting weeks in the woods west of Port Townsend.

She rose from the sofa and stood with her hands clenched at her sides. Tilting her head back, she let forth a holler that began somewhere near her toes and smashed into her ribcage.

It exited her throat as a bellow and ended as a screech. She nearly tipped over with the effort, her knees locked, her body rigid. She laughed, coughed, swallowed from the glass of water on the side table, and tried it again. She shouted because she could, because it was fighting back. Because it was better than drinking.

A face flashed past the window, a shock of white skin and pale eyes descending along the side of the house. She screamed again, this time in surprise. The sound of feet stomping up the outside stairs that led to the patio shook her into action. She ran for the kitchen and grabbed a knife from the wood block on the counter. Peering around the threshold into the sunroom, she saw Daniel tugging at the handle of the patio door.

"Annie!" He pounded on the frame support. "Are you in there? Annie?"

She stepped forward, the knife held out in front. Daniel bent and dropped his hands to his knees to catch his breath. He kept his eyes on her and shouted through the window. "Are you all right?"

"You scared me half to death!" she yelled back. "What are you doing?"

"I heard you screaming. I thought you were being attacked. Jaysus. You scared *me* half to death."

"You could hear me at your place?"

"I wasn't home. There's a path that leads to the beach over there." He waved his hand to some vague distance. "It cuts through the Moyles' property. I passed the house on my way back, and that's when I heard you."

Annie pulled up the handle of the door to release the lock and opened it, still brandishing the knife in her other hand. She stepped aside to let him in. Daniel braced himself on the doorframe but didn't cross the threshold.

"You heard it all then," she said.

"I heard everything."

"Ah." She started to close her arms over her chest but realized she still gripped the chef's knife. "Why don't you come in? I need to put this away before I hurt someone. Myself, namely."

She turned away and heard the door click shut. When she returned to the room, Daniel stood just inside.

"Do you want to talk about it?" he asked.

"I was just letting off a little steam. Really, I'm fine."

"I saw you in Bantry on Monday. The AA meeting."

"Oh." In one moment, the façade torn down. It was like being outed as a spy by another agent. A relief. At last she could drop the pretense and slip into a familiar language. "How long have you been sober?"

"Nine years, eight months, sixteen days." He glanced at his watch. "Nearly seventeen."

"Congratulations." Annie wondered where she would be in ten years. If her sobriety would hold. It seemed an impossible distance from now to the end of a decade. But standing before her was proof—healthy, empathic proof—that it could be done.

"How about you?"

"Three months, thirteen days."

"Were you close to not making three months, fourteen days?"

She sank onto the sofa and let her hands dangle between her knees. She was spent. Her throat hurt. "So, this is the part where you tell me it gets easier, right? Even if you don't mean it."

"Have you got a sponsor?" Daniel sat across from her in a rattan Papasan chair, and the alarm on his face as the giant moon swayed slightly under his large frame sent a ripple of giggles through Annie.

"Sorry. I'm tired. Yes. Bill. My sponsor. He says hi, by the way. I told him about you."

Daniel shook his head but smiled. Annie curled her legs under her, tucking her hands between her knees, settling in. "You forgot to tell me that it gets easier."

"Can't tell you what you want to hear, Annie." His words sounded like a shrug, but he didn't brush her off. In that moment, he reminded her of Bill. No apologies. Just reality. "Do I feel like drinking? No, not really. I miss the idea of it, more than the actual memory of what alcohol tastes like. How it makes me feel. Maybe it's like being an amputee. That pain of a ghost limb haunts me sometimes, but I understand what it is, and I get through it. For me, being an addict is wrapped up in all sorts of other pain. Pain I can't imagine getting over. So, no. I can't say it gets any easier."

"Well, shit. That's depressing. It sort of makes you want a drink, doesn't it?" She meant this as a joke, but from the look on his face, her caustic humor sank.

"You'll look back ten years from now and be so relieved that you're out from under the burden of booze. Now, that much I can say is better. Time really does heal some things."

"But not all of them?"

"Of course not all of them. Who's Stephen?"

"What?"

"You sent up a string of curses directed to Stephen."

"Did I? Yes, I suppose I would have. He's my husband."

"I see."

"Things are a little complicated on that front."

"So I gathered."

"Your son is a dead ringer for you."

"My *what*?"

"The boy standing next to you in the meeting. He's even

got your gestures, or at least he's mimicking them. Though there's no mistaking his mother, either. Fiana, right?"

Daniel dropped his head back in laughter.

"What? Sorry, I think it's wonderful. You don't see many kids so connected to their parents, certainly not at that age. He's what, thirteen? Fourteen?"

"Thirteen. He's not my son. Liam's my nephew. But you're right about one thing—Fiana's his mother. My older sister."

"Your sister." Relief prickled her face, and she allowed a soft chuckle. "Right. Now I feel like an ass."

"Liam *is* like a son to me. His dad is mostly out of the picture—lives in London—so I'm the best male figure he's got, for what that's worth."

"Considering how closely he watches you, how much he tries to act like you, I'd say it's worth a lot to him."

Daniel's silence told her she'd struck a chord. "That's quite a lot to put together about people you don't know."

"My job is to see what connects people and what separates them. Obviously, I'm a little off my game for not catching that you and Fiana are siblings. I'll blame it on jet lag. And your funny accents." At last, she crossed the space between them and was rewarded with a smile. "But mostly, I'm good at what I do."

"I see that. You put on quite a show tonight."

"Hey. That wasn't just a performance. I meant what I said. That moment on the hill, something inside me clicked. I can't explain what happened, but it was powerful. I'd like to go back there again."

"The offer of my sister's boots still stands."

"Are you sure about that? After tonight, I can't imagine your sister would let me in the house."

"Fiana's a good soul. She's just fighting for her piece of earth."

"I don't blame her. What about you? Is this your fight, too?"

"These questions." He exaggerated an exhale. "Why does it feel like I'm consorting with the enemy?"

"We're not the enemy, Daniel. At least I'm not. Don't you want to see this region grow, these families stay together because they can earn a living right here in Ballycaróg? I think you want to do right by the town."

"See, there you go again. Being good at your job."

She raised her hands in a gesture of supplication and laughed. "Okay, I'll lay off." A moment of silence shifted the energy between them. "So, you live with your sister and nephew then. Fiana and Liam, right?"

"And my niece, Catriona."

"Was she there tonight?"

"Catriona? Nah. The last place a sixteen-year-old girl wants to be is at a community meeting with her mom and uncle. She's a good girl, but—"

"But she's sixteen. I know. I was once, too. A long time ago."

This made him smile. "With Liam, it's easy," he said. "He's so hungry for approval, and he's still just a kid. He'll listen. But Cat. I've been with them for four years, and it seems she changed overnight from a sweet child into a whining brat. She fits her nickname—contented purrs one moment and all claws the next."

"I'll bet she's just as hungry as Liam for approval. Despite what her body might show and what her mouth might say, she's still just a kid."

"Perceptive."

"That's why they pay me the big bucks."

"They probably do, too."

"If I mess this up, they won't," she said, and then pressed a palm over her mouth and winced. "Did I say that out loud?" she asked.

"You did."

"I seem to have lost my filter in this place. I swear my thoughts are only in my head, but my mouth has other ideas. I'm hearing things, too. Maybe I'm possessed by a leprechaun."

"There haven't been leprechauns here since the nineties. The Celtic Tiger ate them all."

"And that Celtic Tiger died when the economy tanked, didn't he?"

"You could say that."

"So, maybe I brought a little Irish magic with me. What was it that man, Noah, said? Nine of out ten Irish youth in rural areas are leaving the country to find work abroad? Seems you could use a leprechaun or two around here."

Daniel sat forward, bracing his hands on his thighs. "We could use a little truth around here. The promises of a mining company will mean as much as little men in green suits if those jobs destroy this peninsula."

That look of disappointment she'd seen in the community center made her long to come clean. Admit to her ambivalence. Confess it was more act than conviction. The same need for acceptance by someone who understood the struggle was what put her into the arms of someone other than her husband. The need that had led to so many mistakes.

Perhaps mistaking her silence for exasperation, Daniel slapped his palms on his knees and rose awkwardly from the curved valley of the chair cushion. "I should go. Will you be all right?"

"I think that tonight, I'll be fine." She walked him to the front door. "Thank you for making certain I was okay. It was very chivalrous of you," she said, trying to toss her embarrassment into the safety of a joke.

"If you feel like screaming, or drinking, or doing anything

else you might regret, I'm just on the other side of the hill, not even a five-minute walk."

"I rather liked the screaming, though. It's very cathartic."

"Well, I've got some good yelling spots near the water, if you don't want to terrify the neighbors."

They said good night, Annie not daring to meet his eyes. She closed the door and rested her cheek against it, waiting to hear his boots crunch on the gravel. But nothing stirred on the other side. The shadow of his head was visible through the window mounted high in the door frame. Perhaps he was waiting for her to flip the dead bolt and extinguish the hall light. She thought she could feel his steady breath, his rough, warm hand resting on the wood, just where her cheek lay. She could open the door, lace her fingers around his neck, curl her shoulders into his chest and be lifted up, cradled, held. That was all she wanted. Simply to be held.

Her hand slipped down to the door handle, and she pressed gently until she felt it catch.

Then she heard the scrape of footsteps across the gravel. She released the handle, flipped the dead bolt, and pushed off the light switch. The hallway went dark, and the sound of footsteps faded.

24

Amy, Mort MacGeoghegan's beagle, bounded past the window where Daniel sat on the long, cushioned bench, a sketchpad propped against his knees. He stilled his charcoal pencil and watched as Mort appeared in the driveway, proceeding at his dignified pace with a tall walking stick in his right hand, pulling the earth toward him in stretches his elderly legs could manage.

Daniel rapped on the window, and Amy dashed back, her tail slicing the air like a wiper blade. Barking, she ran to meet the incoming bullet that was Bannon. By the looks of the heeler's mud-caked fur, she'd been rolling in just-turned fields, nosing around for moles, or chasing seagulls. Daniel closed his sketchpad, knocked on the window again. Mort opened the studio door as Daniel clicked on the kettle.

"Danny. Just the man I was in search of." He propped his walking stick against the wall and sat on a bench to unlace his boots.

"Beautiful morning for a walk. I was planning a run up Hungry Hill after lunch."

"That it is. Wish I could join you. I might make it up in time, but I'm afraid this arthritis would make coming down damn near impossible, unless you carried me." He massaged his swollen knee joint. "But I'll manage my five kilometers today."

Mort, despite the pain and the deterioration of his joints, maintained a rigorous daily walking habit—more exercise than most people a third his age managed. Love and frustration for this vital man, who refused to quietly accept the degeneration of age, surged through Daniel.

"I'm on my way to see your sis, but if you've got a spare moment or two?"

"For you, Mort, always." The kettle clicked off. "You're just in time for tea." Daniel pulled a carton of milk from the small fridge and put a mug together the way Mort preferred: black tea, a healthy splash of whole milk, no sugar. "But you know Fi's in Skibbereen this morning?"

"Yes, but she rang to say she'd be home by lunch." He checked his watch. "I've timed it just right. Half an hour, at the most." Mort took the tea with a sigh of gratitude and stretched out his legs, wiggling his stockinged toes. Daniel pulled around a chair and sat across from him.

"Great turnout at the meeting last night," Mort began. "I was mighty proud of Fiana. But the American woman was a surprise."

"Yes, I got an earful from Fiana as soon as the meeting broke up. You'd've thought we were conspiring against her."

Mort's blue eyes, so like Daniel's own, sparkled with laughter over the rim of his mug.

"Yeah. Don't you start." Daniel grew serious. "Sure, she's lovely, but if that interested me, there's no end to the punters hanging out in the pub if I wanted a fling. Why are we talking about this?"

"Because I sense that it matters to you. That she matters." Mort, in his gentle way, held on like a dog with a stick, daring

Daniel to wrest it from him and toss it far.

"Matters? Matters how?" Daniel set his mug on the worktable with a smack. "She's an alcoholic." The older man raised his trim, white eyebrows. "Not that I plan to invite her into my life, but that one I didn't see coming."

"How'd you find this out?"

"I saw her at an AA meeting in Bantry." Daniel wasn't ready to admit he'd been inside her house, nor could he begin to explain the shouting episode. He was getting too close.

"I'll leave you be, lad. But don't be afraid to listen. I think you know what I'm talking about."

Daniel's thoughts flashed to the soft, throaty voice that delivered lines from a famous poem into the air, reaching for him with some purpose he couldn't yet understand. "'Fraid I don't. But if it makes you feel any better, I spend most of my days in silence. If there's something to be heard, I'm sure I'll catch it. Did you really come here to talk about Annie?"

"Not exclusively. I wanted to catch you before I talked to Fiana. Just the two of us. I've been doing a little advance legwork, so to speak." He grimaced as he flexed his aching knee. "A great group of kids from UCC have been scrambling to rally the troops. I didn't want to bring this up last night in case it was premature, but I received the word just this morning."

He took a swallow of tea before continuing. "The Beara Chough Coalition have enlisted the support of BirdWatch Ireland and the Irish Wildlife Trust, and together we've prepared an injunction against Eire-Evergreen Metals. We'll be filing by the end of the day, using a pro bono attorney in Dublin. We're invoking the strictures of the Special Protection Area Act to halt further development of the mine."

"Will it work?"

Mort raised his shoulders and pressed his lips together.

"Likely it'll at least stop Eire-Evergreen until they sort things out. The more time we have to mount our campaign, the better prepared we'll be."

"Fi'll be thrilled when she finds out."

"Oh, she knows most of the story already. I just need to bring her up to speed on this morning's events. I really came to ask you to reconsider."

"Reconsider?"

"A video production class at the university has offered to film a promotional spot. The kids think they can get it to go viral on the Internet." Daniel held back a smile at this elegant man's colloquial phrasing. "They want you to be the face and voice."

"Isn't this about the chough? Why is there even a need for a spokesperson?"

"You're handsome and well-spoken. You're the antithesis of the bleeding heart environmentalist. You look like you should be in that mine, but instead you're fighting for a little black bird."

Daniel snorted his contempt. "I'm not an actor."

Mort held his gaze. "Exactly. I think you should do it for the very reason you don't want to. Because of what you represent."

"What the hell do I represent?"

"A man who has rebuilt his life after failure, whose story is the story of Ireland. A man whose life's work is devoted to sharing the beauty of his country."

"I am a man who took the life of a five-year-old boy. Let that story get out, and your campaign will be in the viral bunghole. Ireland is a survivor; that is true. I'm an ex-con with a drink-driving manslaughter conviction on his résumé."

"We would never try to hide your past, Danny. But I wonder if you will ever accept the Burkes' forgiveness and do as they asked: Turn what you've done into something good."

Daniel whistled low. "You've been taking lessons from my sister, haven't you?"

"I can't tell you what to do, of course. But you're like a son to me, lad, so I'll tell you what I think. I think you should let go of this self-flagellation. What is served by hiding away, denying yourself a future, a family, any measure of happiness?"

"Happiness is temporary. It's shite. I gave up the right to happiness when I killed that child. All I want now is to be at peace. The art, the guiding, it's enough. Why doesn't anyone believe me? I have enough."

Mort swallowed the rest of his tea, set the cup on the floor, and retied his boots. "You're what, forty? Barely half your life behind you. I'm looking at it from the other side. And what I'm proudest of are the fifty-five years I spent with Birdie. I had the good sense to marry her when we were eighteen, and I never regretted a day. It's hell now, being alone. Maybe it's time you let someone else in your life."

Daniel choked back angry retorts that burned like bile in his throat. Slapping his hands on his thighs, he said, "I've got some work to do here. The house is open if you want to wait inside for Fiana."

Mort ran a hand over his jaw, rubbing the white patches of beard. Daniel waited for an admonishment. Instead he said, "Understood, son. Thank you for hearing me out."

Daniel watched as the old man leaned into his walking stick and hoisted his thin body to standing. He turned before the door closed behind him.

25

Annie entered the Ballycaróg Bayview Hotel lobby just before lunch to find James and Colm sitting on adjacent sofas in front of a low coffee table, papers spread out before them, matching laptops open.

Colm stood and greeted her with a peck on the cheek. Much preferable to the bone-crushing handshake he'd offered when they were introduced at dinner four nights before. "You look like the cat that ate the canary," he said. In his corduroy suit jacket and shirt in shades of mustard and olive green, with a brown oilskin coat draped over the back of the sofa, Colm looked more suited to a barnyard than an office tower. His wispy blond hair held memories of red. Red bloomed in his nose and cheeks as well, and in the tiny veins of his pale green eyes—signs of the heavy drinker Annie recognized him to be the moment they'd met.

"I think I was the canary," Annie replied. "The one who went down into the copper mine." Before offering an explanation to the puzzled men, she looked around for listening ears. The front desk was unstaffed, and she could hear the hum of a vacuum cleaner down one long hallway.

"I went to the Beara Chough Coalition meeting last night."

She perched on the edge of the sofa across from Colm and James. "The village has organized, and they have valid concerns. They're aware that if the mining remains an offshore operation only, they won't see much benefit in the way of jobs or a bounce to the local economy. So, that's got to be addressed."

James nodded and waved her on.

"They're serious about this bird, the Red-billed Chough," she said. "Have you been down to see its nesting grounds?" The men shook their heads. "Well, we should go."

"It makes me think of the controversy in your part of the world several years ago," Colm said. "Something about logging and an owl?"

"The spotted owl. It was more than a controversy. It was a federal lawsuit. The spotted owl became the symbol of all that is wrong with development and industry. If we aren't careful, that little crow could become the spotted owl of the Beara Peninsula."

James dismissed her with a huff. "Ireland isn't the United States."

"I wouldn't say that with such confidence. Ireland *is* part of the European Union, and I'll bet the EU environmental regulations are tighter than they are in the States." The men exchanged looks, and the certainty they were withholding something rippled through Annie like a cold current.

"The upshot is this," she continued. "There are some pretty strong pro-mine sentiments in town. I don't think people felt completely free to speak their minds last night, seeing as it was a meeting of the anti-mine coalition, but when I spoke to them—"

"What do you mean, you spoke to them?" James interrupted.

"I introduced myself. I introduced us. I told them we were as committed to keeping this peninsula beautiful and protected as they were."

He flexed and released his fingers, then pressed his palms together. "Annie."

"Why does this surprise you? I thought winning them over was exactly why you brought me on board. You can't just come in here waving euros around and start drilling." She repeated Fiana's words, shocking herself that she'd absorbed them, believed them.

"No one said we were." James's tone was conciliatory. *Condescending*, Annie thought fleetingly. "But the stronger message would be that this is a business the Irish government supports, rather than worrying ourselves with cozying up to the locals."

"What is it exactly you'd like me to do?" Annie asked, keeping her voice low and measured. "Look pretty and keep my mouth shut?"

James exhaled through his nose, a soft hiss of annoyance.

"So, there is good news that should make all our jobs easier." Colm inserted himself into their tension. "We secured the State Mining Lease." He made the announcement under his breath while scanning the otherwise empty lobby. "The paperwork is being processed, and the lease hasn't been announced officially, so let's keep it under wraps. But we spoke with the DM of Exploration and Mining yesterday, and it's green lights all the way."

The news shook her. Annie looked to James for confirmation, and he shrugged his shoulders in an offhand acknowledgment of their success. She sank back into the sofa. "You've had the prospecting license for only six months. I thought these things took years to put into place. The Environmental Impact Statement and the Pollution Prevention and Control license— what about those?"

Again, a meaningful look flashed between the men.

Colm—leaning forward with his forearms on his thighs, hands clasped—spoke first. "Of course those will need to be completed. This is why we must keep quiet about the lease. The deputy minister is on our side, ready to do what it takes to make this project succeed."

James coughed into his fist and punched a couple of keys on his laptop. "Colm, you make it sound like a conspiracy." He tried to make light of it, but Annie caught the flicker of narrowed eyes. "We've still got a long road ahead of us before mining operations can begin. The DM isn't taking sides or slicing through the red tape."

Her internal alarm pinged quietly. Why mention this if it wasn't precisely what was happening in Dublin? "Who's the DM?" she asked.

"Hugh Doyle," Colm replied, without hesitation. "A Cork man. He's got a particular interest in what happens here."

Annie filed the name away. "So, now that you've secured the lease, to hell with public opinion? Isn't this exactly how Eire-Evergreen bungled things in the first place—muscling into the community, throwing around promises without taking its pulse?"

James snapped shut the lid of his laptop and turned his full attention to her. "I think if we took a pulse, we'd see the patient is failing. There are, what, six thousand people on this peninsula? How many were at last night's meeting? Fifty? A hundred? I don't think we're going to see a tidal wave of resistance, Annie."

"I've been in the strategic communications business a long time, James," she volleyed back. "As you have noted, I'm very good at my job. I know that one of the biggest mistakes you can make is to underestimate public opinion. If this community gets wind that you are taking their support for granted, expect a tsunami of resistance. As your strategist, I advise you not to wait for the peons to fall at your feet, thanking you for the jobs. I advise you to show your faces as supporters of Beara and its environment. You should make plans to save this little bird before the rest of the world learns it's in danger."

"Bravo. Nice speech." James tapped his hands together in mock applause. "It sounds like you've got your work cut out for you."

"Indeed." She turned his sarcasm into a challenge. "Our next step is to initiate a community meeting of our own. Glossy brochures and a slick video might work in Dublin, but you'll only alienate the residents here. Of course I'll coordinate this meeting, and I assume I will have your full support, that you will provide me the resources I need, and you'll be there, ready to face the people who will be behind the increase in your company's share prices." She sat with her back ramrod straight, her words pouring forth in a low and even tone. It felt like achieving her perfect stride in a race, when her whole body clicked into one seamless, coordinated flow of breath and muscle.

Colm broke into the tension again. "Annie, you're right. I think Beara will respond best to the human touch. Fine work you did last night. James and I are returning to Dublin this afternoon, but you can count on us for whatever you need. Just ring."

James opened his laptop again, and as his fingers flew across the keyboard, a lift of his chin indicated his grudging consent. His cell phone rang, followed half a heartbeat later by Colm's. Just beyond the hotel doors, a large white van with tinted windows disgorged several men. The lobby filled with commotion as the men burst in with loud voices and American accents and golf bags. James and Colm turned away, palms pressed to their exposed ears.

Annie took the opportunity to leave. She'd said enough, and she had work to do. As she walked through the now-chaotic lobby, she angled her scowl and the hard green chips of her eyes toward the flirtatious hellos the golfers tossed in her direction. One face made her pause. Sunglasses hid his eyes, but she felt she was being watched behind dark lenses. The tilt of his head, the angle of his body, directed at her. Something familiar that sent a tremor of anxiety through her. The same she'd felt when she first heard James's voice.

The whisper of recognition was ephemeral. Then it was gone.

~

The car steered right instead of left, pulling Annie away from Ballycaróg. She turned at the Old Iron Forge, merging onto the R571 toward Eyeries and Ardgroom. She needed to breathe, to get some perspective.

As the green and blue scenery slipped past her, she wondered for the first time how she could continue to work on a campaign she was losing a grasp on, one she'd never held firmly except as a lifeline to sobriety, a purpose to get out of bed every morning. It wasn't enough. It hadn't been, not for a long time. She should quit now and go home.

"Home," Annie said aloud. The word fell flat, sucked away by the whump-slap of tires on tarmac. She scanned the passing scenery, looking for meaning in the simple, complicated word. Ireland's blue-green was so much like the Northwest's; if she squinted, she could be on the Olympic Peninsula, rounding Discovery Bay toward Sequim.

The adrenaline from her confrontation with James had

seeped away, taking her bravado with it. In its place was the black hole of uncertainty. She'd thought she could hang on to her sobriety as long as she had her marriage and her job. After Stephen asked her to move out, she figured she could limp along with the crutch of work holding her up. Now her job dangled on a thread. The full force of her life disintegrating and blowing away like flakes of soot discharged from a chimney hit her on that sweet stretch of country road.

She braked into a turnout and stepped out of the car, working to calm herself. *Breathe.* She was past Ardgroom, and the farms were sparse, hidden behind tall hedges of fuchsia, lilac, and gorse. Kenmare Bay winked in the distance; clouds drew shadows across the brown skin of the eastern hills. A sagging clump of palm trees on a distant knoll looked as lost as she felt. Annie leaned against the hood of the car, drawing the curiosity of a few sheep pulling up grass near the fence. They paused and watched her with wide-set eyes.

A flicker of black against the green grass beyond the sheep: two crows hopping in tandem toward a small mound of earth. Small, delicate things. No, they couldn't be crows. Swallows, swift, sparrows—Annie hardly knew the difference. It was their *pas de deux* that held her, bobbing as though attached to the same string, their bodies dipping toward each other and away in a waltz of instinct. Then one called a questioning *chi*, and the other echoed with a descending *ach*. They turned to show their profile, and Annie stopped breathing. The light broke against the birds, illuminating the flaming orange-red of their beaks and feet. She extended a hand as if to preen their glossy black feathers and then looked around, wanting to share her discovery. Red-billed Choughs, a pair stepping to a pattern of mating, or perhaps already bound and now seeking out fodder for their nest.

The tightness in her chest and the racing of her heart had eased, but the anxiety was replaced by an ache like homesickness, a longing to belong to someplace, to know her place, to whom she might belong. Yet, as she put herself back into the bungalow she and Stephen had so carefully renovated in that shining, lovely city, it wasn't the waters and mountains of the Pacific Northwest she craved, or the market full of flowers and fish, the cafés smoky-rich with coffee steam, the bookstores, or her running routes. All that seemed to belong to a life far more distant than the one week she'd been away. The dreams she and Stephen had built in that house in Green Lake were over.

She craved this. This blue-and-green peace, this sense of hovering above it all, never landing, never touching ground, never having to return to the Annie Who Was. She wanted to remain here, in the Annie Who Is. Without a past. *Clean.*

26

"Maybe I should invite her to dinner? What do you think? Too obvious? Would it mean I'd have to invite James MacKenna, too? I'd lose all credibility with the village if they thought I was cozying up to the mine's owner. No, I can't. I just can't be seen with her. None of us can. Who is she, anyway? Not that a woman can't be involved with mining, but she doesn't look like she's seen the inside of a car garage, much less a copper mine. She must be some muckety-muck in their corporate office. In Seattle, of all places. Do you suppose she's sleeping with James MacKenna?"

Fiana's nattering slipped over Daniel like tepid, bitter tea. Until her final sentence. He slammed shut the refrigerator door, where he'd been rummaging mindlessly, not hungry but seeking to fill an emptiness, the image of Annie brandishing a chef's knife teasing at his mind's shadowed corners. His sister's words caused that image to dissolve into one of Annie in the embrace of the dark-haired interloper who drove a Mercedes.

"If you had her over to dinner, you could just ask her outright. Clearly, it's relevant to your campaign."

"Don't tell me you wouldn't like to know the answer." Fiana swiped a damp sponge over the same spot on the counter she'd just wiped dry. She kept her hands in motion, her eyes away from Daniel's.

"What a ridiculous thing to say, Fi."

"Why would Daniel care who James MacKenna is sleeping with?" Catriona was standing at the threshold between the kitchen and the glassed-in back porch, one hip braced against the frame, watching her uncle and mother with narrowed eyes.

"What are you doing here? Why aren't you in school?" Fiana shooed her daughter away from the door and followed her onto the porch. "Off with your muddy shoes."

"Mom, it's Friday afternoon."

"Right. Well, why aren't you studying for end-of-term exams?"

"Mother! Polly is meeting me here in an hour, and you promised to take us to Kenmare. I want to know who is sleeping with who, Daniel!" She cupped her hand around her mouth and shouted through the glass.

"It's 'who is sleeping with whom,'" he shouted back.

Catriona returned to the kitchen in her stocking feet and headed for the refrigerator. Behind her, Fiana made a slicing motion across her neck. "And it's none of your business," finished Daniel, reading his sister's motion to end the conversation. But Catriona refused the hint.

"It's that American who showed up at Mom's meeting last night, isn't it? Now I wish I would have gone." With an exaggerated sigh, she pushed shut the refrigerator door. "There's nothing to eat." She sagged against the counter. "Liam's told me all about her. He's mad for her. Annie Crowe," she teased in a singsong voice. "He says she knows you, Daniel. You took her on the Beara Way."

"Step aside, kid." Daniel elbowed her away from the counter. "I'll make you a toasted cheese."

143

Catriona snorted. "Yeah, right. I know everyone lives like it's a monastery around here, but trust me, the rest of the world is making up for what you two deny yourselves."

Daniel turned from slicing cheese to see his sister's face bloom red to the roots of her dark-brown hair.

"Catriona Margaret O'Connell." Fiana stood on one side of the kitchen table, gripping the back of a chair. "I have half a mind to smack that smug grin clean off your face. What would possess you to say such a thing?"

"I'm sorry." Contrite but not ready to back down, Catriona pressed her back against the counter. "I didn't mean to be nasty. But it all just begs the question, doesn't it?"

She looked to her uncle for support, but Daniel was as bewildered as his sister. Not quite embarrassed to be almost talking about sex with his niece—in front of her mother—but getting close to it. Melted butter foamed in the waiting pan, and he set a sandwich onto the hot surface, pressing it gently with the back of a spatula. Still, he wanted to see where this conversation was going. Anything to distract from talking further about Annie. "What question, Cat?"

Behind his niece, Fiana shook her head in warning. But Catriona had something stewing inside. "You two live like hermits. I mean, it's not normal. Mom, when's the last time you had a date? Daniel, seriously, like, do you even want a girlfriend?"

Fiana's face remained pink, but the knuckles that gripped the chair were stretched white. If Cat had intended to push her mother's buttons, she'd succeeded. Daniel braced himself for the firestorm that would surely follow.

"You're being perfectly horrible, Catriona. Go to your room. I can't bear to talk to you right now."

"Mommy, come on. I'm not trying to be awful. I just want

to know. You are two of the loneliest people I know, and I don't understand it!" Her voice rose sharply in her frustration. "There's so much we're not supposed to talk about around here. Your past—" She flipped a hand to Daniel. "You pretending you don't ever want to be married again." Her palm turned up to her mother. Catriona's shoulders hitched with emotion. "I'm not talking about sex. We've had that talk. I get it. I'm talking about love. I just don't want to end up like either of you."

Fiana's mouth opened, closed, and she shook her head.

"Oh, just forget it. You totally don't understand. There's something wrong with both of you!" Catriona wailed and ran from the room.

Daniel and Fiana stood in place as Cat's stocking feet pounded up the stairs and her bedroom door slammed. Daniel felt a little weak, as though he'd just come inside from a tempest.

"Out of the mouths of babes, so." His sister broke the tense silence.

"She's not such a babe anymore, Fi. Those were some pretty astute observations. Do you want me to go up and talk to her?" He slid the crisped bread with its thick center of now-molten cheese onto a waiting plate, wondering who still had the appetite for lunch.

"No, this is definitely a mother's job. But I'll let her cool down first. I need to cool down first." She pulled out the chair she'd been gripping for support and sank into it. "You reckon something's really wrong with us?"

"Because we're two lonely adults with abandonment and commitment issues who resent our mother and have no idea who our fathers might be? One of us a recovering alcoholic with a manslaughter conviction under his belt and the other with a Mother Theresa complex? Where's the problem?"

Fiana laughed and dropped her face into her palms. "Know any nice men at your AA meetings you could set me up with?" Her voice was muffled, but Daniel was relieved that she didn't seem to be crying.

"I wouldn't do that to you. Taking care of one of me is enough."

"You know you don't need me. You can take care of yourself." She placed her palms flat on the table.

He pulled out a chair and sat across from his sister. "You're wrong there. I'm fairly certain you all need me, too. We do all right together, don't you think?"

She gave a quick nod, as if she really might cry.

"But Cat's got a point," he said. "You should get yourself out there. Meet someone. It doesn't have to be serious—just get out there and date. Have some fun."

Fiana dug into her pocket for a tissue. She laughed as she blew her nose. "Fine one you are for giving advice to the lovelorn."

"It's different for me."

"How so?"

The slam of a car door cut into the conversation. Fiana peered at the wall clock and shoved herself up from the table. "It must be Polly."

Feet thumped up the back steps, and a high ponytail swung into view. Polly clattered in with a heavy book bag, smacking her gum. "Hi, Mrs. O'C," she chirped. But her "Hey, Daniel" was delivered in a softer voice, and her cheeks blazed. Fiana lifted her eyebrows at Daniel and said, "Cat's upstairs, Polly. Take off your shoes in the house. Take this sandwich upstairs with you. Have you eaten? Do you need lunch?"

"I'm good, Mrs. O'Connell, thank you, no." The very portrait of a dignified woman, rather than the effervescent teen who'd blasted into the house, Polly glided past, trying to catch Daniel's eye as she took the plate from his outstretched hand. Moments later came Catriona's excited shriek to see the friend she'd left at school just an hour before. Apparently the storm had passed.

"See, little brother. No shortage of interested parties. Her mother's keen on you, as well."

"Perish the thought. Both of them." He pushed back his chair and grabbed an apple from the bowl in the center of the table. "I need to get back to the studio. I'm headed to Kenmare late this afternoon to sort through some pieces for the show with Margitte."

"Daniel, as if Catriona doesn't hate me enough. I'd promised to take the girls into Kenmare this afternoon to the cinema. They're desperate to see the new Gerard Butler film. But if you're headed that way, it'd save me."

"Fiana."

"I'll invite Annie Crowe to dinner. Just for you."

"That's supposed to convince me to do you a favor?" Daniel opened the door to the back porch, then paused, leaning slightly into the room until he could see Fiana. "I'll take the girls, no worries. But wait on the Annie thing. I don't know, Fiana. I just don't."

~

Stopped on Shelbourne for a passel of tourists ambling over the road, Daniel saw Annie crossing the lawn of the Adult Education Center. She stepped onto the sidewalk and walked in the opposite direction, her hands stuffed in the pockets of her jacket, her shoulders hunched. His throat moved, her name on his lips. He'd seen the look on her pale face before she'd turned away. Thirst and despair. Her slim figure jogged across the road and into the car park of a hotel.

The road was too narrow to do a three-point turn, and the center was aswarm with exiting cars and small groups lingering in the fine spring evening. Daniel drove toward the hotel, slowing as he passed. Two men stood to one side at the door of the adjacent pub, and one held the door open, letting Annie enter first. The beep of a car horn urged Daniel on. He swept the roundabout, gunning his engine as he exited, and jerked the wheel to the left, entering the hotel car park with a grating downshift of gears.

Inside the pub, a football match played silently on a large TV screen hanging at the far end of the bar, and young Van Morrison sang of foghorns and gypsy souls. Laughter and the click of billiards filtered out from a room beyond. The sweet-sharp aroma of deep-fried chips in vinegar. The scene was of a cheery, companionable Friday night.

Annie sat alone at the bar, with what looked like a glass of water before her. The men who'd ushered her into the pub were hunched over their pints, watching. Daniel leaned in between two barstools and placed both hands flat on the bar, softly clearing his throat. Annie turned her head slowly to look at him, resignation etching her lips into a hard line. There was a red tinge to the rims of her eyes, as if she'd been crying.

She began to laugh. Softly. Then a giggle that she tried to stop with a hand pressed over her mouth. Her irises, large and black in the dim light of the pub, shone, and the tears spilled over, collecting in the crevices between her fingers.

"What are you doing here, Annie?" he asked in as quiet a voice as he could and still be heard over the music. He took a seat beside her.

She squeezed shut her eyes, breathed in deeply, and the

giggles subsided. She ran a finger under each eye and patted her cheeks dry with the back of her hand. "I was planning to get something to eat. I haven't eaten since breakfast, and my blood sugar tanked." She took a long drink and set the glass down carefully on the paper coaster. "What are *you* doing here?"

Daniel turned his head toward the bar. No one paid them any attention. The men who'd been leering at Annie when he entered were gesticulating at the football match. "I saw you walk into this pub," he admitted at last. "And I followed a hunch."

"A hunch that I'd come in for something other than sparkling water."

"Yes. I'm sorry I doubted you."

"What if I said you were right? That I *did* come in here for a drink. Would you be disappointed in me?"

"Disappointed?" He pulled his stool in closer, and the temptation to take her hand nearly won out over his common sense. If she thought he was making a play for her when she was most vulnerable, he'd lose her completely. "Annie. Never. Come on. I live this addiction twenty-four seven, too. Maybe I saw myself walking into this bar instead of you."

"I really was just hungry."

"Then why were you crying?"

A young woman appeared in front of them and looked expectantly to Daniel. "Can I get you something, love?"

He glanced at Annie.

"You know what?" She pushed herself back from the bar and dropped her feet to the floor. "I'm not hungry anymore. I'd like to get out of here. I was planning to visit some galleries in town before heading back to Ballycaróg."

"Can I recommend one of my favorites?"

"Of course." Her face softened into the hint of a smile. "I'd appreciate that."

"The Vaughan Gallery on Henry Street. In fact, there's a photography exhibit you shouldn't miss. I know the gallery owner pretty well. Would you like to meet her?"

"Why on earth would she want to meet me?"

Daniel raised a shoulder. "Just a feeling you'd get on well. Parking can be a nightmare. Why don't we meet there?"

27

She took her time on Henry Street, pausing in front of galleries and craft shops, absorbing the landscapes painted in oils or sketched with pastels, the carved and polished woodworks, the pottery in shapes and colors of the hills, clouds, ocean, and rocks of the west of Ireland. She kept an eye out for Daniel, half in anticipation, half in dread. Their sudden intimacy in the pub, that cozy space as ripe for confession as any curtained booth in a church, had shaken her. As if conjured from her faulty conscience, he'd appeared to save her from herself. She'd gone into that pub to flirt with those bottles displayed in tiers behind the bar, to see how far she could take herself to the edge, an exquisite torture of willpower, like penitents whipping their bare backs, thinking their blood and pain would cleanse their sins. She hadn't wanted to be rescued. She'd wanted a drink.

Annie had made her decision to bolt from Kenmare when a window display stole all thought. Mesmerized, she drifted the few steps forward, brushing her hands against the glass. Framed photographs held aloft by wire floated on the other side: seascapes bursting with waves of power and profundity; forests deep with secrets and soft with moss, sunlight filtering through evergreens; panoramic landscapes that caught the coaxing blush of sunrise and bittersweet glow of sunset and every tempest and dance of the clouds that towered or drifted across the Irish sky. The work spoke of the magic and art of the creative process—that seamless communication between the eyes, the heart, and the hands. It pulled at Annie like the sight of a familiar face she couldn't place. It had been so long … would she recognize that feeling if it came her way again? She felt the cool weight of the Leica in her hands, the narrowing of her mind's focus down to thoughts of aperture and exposure, the meditative state of her brain as it entered the scene before her. Annie broke away and stepped back, not surprised to see that she was standing in front of the Vaughan Gallery. She floated inside, collecting a brochure from the young man seated on a stool at the counter.

The work belonged to Grainne Petitt, a landscape photographer who lived just outside the village. Each framed print mounted throughout the whitewashed space held Annie spellbound for long moments before releasing her to the next. She stepped back to study the compositions, seeing the landscapes as she would through her camera's lens, imagining the patience required to anticipate and wait for just the right play of light and shadow. She smelled the decomposing leaves on the forest floor, sensed the shifts in the light and the wind, the feathery touch of meadow wildflowers as they brushed their fingers across her bare calves. Seeing Grainne's work was like finishing an earlier, interrupted thought—her state of heart had traveled full circle, from the despair she'd felt at the bar back to the balance of acceptance and a measure of peace.

A doorway opened into another display area, and she passed through into the adjoining room, expecting to see more photographs. This space, too, was bright white, with poured concrete floors, but it was an exhibit in the making; only a few pieces of glinting, glowing metalwork were mounted.

Annie started to step away, but a sculpture on the far wall pulled her further into the room. At least three feet in diameter, the piece glowed with the light of setting suns and rising moons. Dozens of circles cut from copper, bronze, and chrome formed spheres within spheres, each shining in its own glorious universe.

She approached it as she had the photographs, and the present fell away until she could see only the vision in front of her, offering itself to her imagination. But unlike the photographs, which showed a familiar world at its most evocative, this piece was *of* the world, made from its elements, its meaning left to be divined by the beholder. Annie was drawn to its warmth, how it seemed to move as the light shifted, radiating heat, vibrating with secret music. Her hand raised of its own volition, but she pulled it back at the last moment, before her fingers connected with the living work of art before her.

28

It took him longer than he anticipated to find a space near the gallery's back loading door and to bring the last of his pieces inside, but when Daniel walked into the gallery, Annie was standing transfixed in front of the sculpture he'd titled *Grian/ Gealach—Sunrise/Sunset*—her hand reaching for the delicate spheres of metal. She withdrew her hand before touching the piece, though her body leaned in still.

"Go on. It's all right," he said over her shoulder, removing a pair of stained and torn leather work gloves.

She seemed not to register him. Then she turned and nodded at the gloves he clutched in one hand. "Do you work here?"

"I'm delivering pieces for the installation." He waved around the exhibit space. "We've set up just a few so far, but they give you an idea."

"Is the artist a friend of yours?"

"Some days, yes. Some days I really can't stand the sight of the bastard. But mostly we get along." He winked and motioned her toward the sculpture. "Really, it's meant for all the senses, not just visual. Go on."

She drew the tip of her finger down one large round of

metal. It blazed like firelight, catching the dipping sun, but the metal was cool. "It's beautiful."

"I like for people to handle these pieces—I want them to feel the texture and temperature of the materials." Annie turned in surprise, but Daniel pretended not to notice. "Fingerprints leave marks and oil—that's a good thing, at least for my work. People change my art as much as I hope it changes them."

"I didn't know you were an artist."

"I do the guiding to keep a steady income coming in, but this is meant to be my day job."

Giant parcels wrapped in quilted moving blankets leaned against the walls; only one other piece had been unwrapped, a protective cover draped over the corners. It was a tall, narrow triptych of patinated metal with a background of aquamarine. Gracing the foreground was a long hawthorn stem of leaves and berries that shimmered and waved in a silhouette of red and gold.

"This is copper," she said in wonder. "You work with copper."

"Copper mostly. Some bronze, chrome. I'm just starting in with glass—studying with an artist out of a cooperative here in Kenmare."

"But, Daniel. Copper."

"Recycled copper. I use discarded materials, from building sites mostly. Ironic, right? I don't want the mine in my backyard, but I'm willing to exploit it nonetheless—is that what you're thinking? I'm not so naive as to think we shouldn't have mining."

He pulled the cover away from the sculpture's sharp edges and let it drop to the floor. The hawthorn was in a cow pasture where he often sat, watching for the Red-billed Chough that foraged for seeds in the manure. "But in my own way, maybe I can show that the earth's resources aren't ours for the taking wherever, whenever we want. Art is a way to connect people with their environment without polarizing, without politicizing. It can be used to that purpose, but it belongs to everyone. I want my art to show nature as a cultural artifact. I made a very deliberate decision to use what's already been taken from the earth—what had been stripped from Beara's earth more than a century ago. Maybe that *is* my political statement."

At that moment, hearing the words in his own voice, speaking his heart out loud, Daniel made his decision. But it was something he needed to sit with, to form more fully on his own. And he couldn't forget, no matter how enchanting this woman was, *who* she was, why their paths had crossed.

29

Nature as a cultural artifact ... Daniel's words were ringing in her mind when a willowy woman wearing a long, clinging dress of gray jersey, her face framed by silver-gray hair, emerged from a hallway that extended to the back of the gallery.

"Danny, so sorry to have run off and left you like that—I'd been waiting for that phone call from New York for hours. Hello, I'm Margitte Vaughan." She posed an elegant hand in the air, and a row of thin silver bracelets ran up her arm in a symphony of delicate clinking. Annie took Margitte's hand, expecting a cold, bony clutch. She was surprised by the strength and warmth of its grasp.

"Margitte, this is Annie Crowe, visiting Beara from Seattle; Annie, Margitte owns this gallery. She's been a champion of mine for a long time, far longer than I deserve."

"Nonsense. Daniel is one of Ireland's most important metal artists; Ireland just doesn't know it yet. But they will, if I have anything to do about it. A pleasure to meet you, Annie. Are you in the arts? A friend of Danny's?" Words delivered with a sylvan accent of Scandinavia lined with London.

"I—well, no." Annie's face flamed. "I'm in the area on business. It's just a coincidence that I'm in Kenmare today."

Coincidence seemed too cheap of a word for all that had happened this week. It couldn't be coincidence that Daniel had found his way to the bar where she'd been plotting her destruction. This trip was beginning to feel like fate sticking out its foot as she ran toward it, heedless, blind.

"And you'll be here for Daniel's opening next week, of course?" Margitte swept her hands around the room, and her bracelets set off a shower of chimes like fairy bells. Annie imagined if this woman wriggled her nose, the art would fly free of its wrappings and settle itself on the walls and stands according to her whim.

"I didn't know ... " She wouldn't admit this was the first she'd heard of Daniel's show. She cringed in embarrassment for them both.

"Annie's a photographer." Daniel stepped in. A small flush of pleasure to hear him claim her as an artist. But how she wished not to be the center of attention.

"Then you must see Grainne's work. What sort of photography do you do?" Margitte slipped her arm into Annie's and steered her toward the photographer's collection.

"I just dabble. Landscapes, mostly. I was looking at Grainne's work when I came in. She uses a four-by-five large format, doesn't she? It's something I'd love to learn."

They stopped in front of a photograph of a storm brewing over the Skelligs. "Grainne's work is exquisite. It's what brought me inside."

Margitte rested a hand on Annie's wrist, and the warm fingers seemed to search beneath her skin, just as Margitte's eyes had searched her face. She didn't want to leave; there was something so peaceful about this gray and silver woman and her otherworldly grace.

"Yes, she's quite a sight, tramping the hills with her

gear in tow. Grainne is offering a workshop on landscape photography in June—she'll be roaming around the Beara and Kerry peninsulas with a small group, perhaps eight? If you are still in the area, you should join her. She's usually booked months in advance, but she slipped this week in with little fanfare, so you might be in luck. There's a brochure on the front counter—Seamus can help you."

The faint trilling of a mobile phone saved Annie from having to respond. Margitte mouthed her apology and stepped away, answering the call in a throaty language Annie guessed to be Danish.

Suddenly shy to be left with Daniel in the middle of this conversation and this room, she turned back to the photographs. "I wish I had a tenth of her talent," she said. "I could live inside every one of these photographs."

"You said that once before."

"I said what once before?"

"That you could live inside these views. Monday, on the Beara Way? I have a vision of you stepping over a frame into a tableau and waving good-bye to the rest of us stuck in the real world."

She wrapped her arms around her torso, to hug close the image of walking into this fantasy. "Wouldn't that be the dream?"

A faint humming interrupted the shared reverie. Daniel patted the front of his shirt, his jeans pockets, and finally retrieved his phone from a display table a short distance away. He thumbed the screen of his phone and grimaced.

"My niece," he muttered as he tapped out a text. "I dropped her and a friend off at the cinema a couple of hours ago and yes, I'm officially late picking them up, as six texts in the last fifteen minutes would attest." He tucked the phone into his front pocket as he came to her side again. Nodding at the photo of the storm that had so enchanted her, he said, "You don't have to dream it—the real thing isn't so far away."

"Yes, but I was hoping for an escape from the real world."

"You ask for a lot."

"No, I've learned not to ask for much of anything. But that doesn't stop me from dreaming." It was too late for more unguarded revelations. She had to let him go. Annie glanced at her watch. "I should be on my way, too—I want to be home before dark. Even with GPS, I'm bound to get lost on these roads."

"Follow me," he said. "The cinema is on the way."

30

The Kenmare Cineplex was housed in a strip mall, sharing space with a Vietnamese noodle joint, a dry cleaners, a nail and tanning salon, and a convenience store–petrol station that supplied cigarettes, beer, and deep-fried food kept warm under an orange light.

Daniel saw it now as Annie or any other outsider might and sighed at the depressing signs of development. If Eire-Evergreen were successful, it would surely add more commercial eyesores to the neighborhood. Was it arrogance, or regret born of an unrealistic romantic vision of rural Ireland that made these surroundings such a disappointment? Who were any of them to determine what the region needed and who could best meet those needs? The jobs these inelegant businesses offered—the store cashiers, the beauty technicians, the dishwashers, and the food servers—might pay a pittance, but that pittance could keep a family off public assistance or pay a son's tuition at a technical college or home care for an elderly parent.

Behind the tidy gardens set against houses painted in rainbow-bright colors, beyond the postcard fields of wildflowers and woolly sheep and the barren mountains, were families trying to hold together lives in a country that had gone from economic boom to bust in a decade. In those very fields lay the ruins of famine houses—homes abandoned during the Great Famine of the mid-1800s—left to crumble as a testament to the sorrows of the past.

In the years before he entered prison, the changes to his country had floored him. The wealth on display in the magnificent new housing estates, in the gleam and sparkle of Dublin's tony shops and restaurants, in the purr of sleek, late-model German sedans, and in the artfully landscaped gardens of hushed art galleries—it all belonged to a different world, not to the Ireland of his youth.

Now many of those housing estates were empty, their entry gates chained and patrolled by security companies to prevent looting and squatting; half-constructed home sites had been abandoned; For Let signs were posted in vacant shops; the headlines predicted continued gloom as the world recession ground on. The mine had the potential to change this grim scene, to be part of an investment in Ireland's recovery. But a copper mine on the Beara coast would be the equivalent to this strip mall on the outskirts of a beautiful village: a blight, a visual tragedy with longer-lasting consequences. The mine would do irrevocable harm.

His dreary reverie was stopped short by the appearance of Cat and Polly exiting the cinema lobby in a flurry of fabrics and colors—patterned tights under denim shorts, black leather high-top boots with loose laces, and bulky, vintage cardigan sweaters covering tight shirts cut far too low for the eyes not to be drawn to the girls' soft, pale curves. Daniel sighed. To be that young and vulnerable, yet so aware of your own power and possibility. The girls piled into the back, Cat's head bent over her phone, her fingers punching out a text with rapid dexterity.

"So, you wanted to meet Annie Crowe," Daniel said,

watching his niece through the rearview mirror. Her head snapped up. "She's parked just there, following us back to the village." Both girls whipped around.

"Why don't we ride with her?" said Catriona. "I mean, so I can give her directions if the cars get separated?"

"Not likely to happen. And she's got GPS. Stay put, Cat."

31

Annie had started the engine in anticipation but kept the gear in park when the girls popped out of the Range Rover and headed in her direction. She powered down the passenger window, and a young woman bent into the open space, her dark-brown hair falling straight and thick past her face.

"Hi Annie, I'm Catriona O'Connell, Daniel's niece." The girl, sweetly lush, flashed a bright smile. "This is my friend Polly." A petite blonde with a long ponytail pulled high on her head waved a shy hello.

"Hello, Catriona." Annie waved back at Polly. "Looks like I'm to follow you home so I don't get lost."

"Well, I thought that Pol and I would ride with you. I know the way, and in case you get separated from Daniel, we'd be along to get you sorted."

Annie looked toward the Range Rover and lifted a hand from the steering wheel in a brief wave at Daniel, who gave a half-smile and a shrug with his palms open, as if to say, *I didn't really have a choice.*

"Well, all right then," Annie said, amused, a little exasperated. Maybe curious. "Climb on in."

It took just a few minutes of Catriona's ("Call me Cat,

please!") high-spirited questioning for Annie to understand she was being vetted as a potential romantic interest for Daniel: *Wasn't Daniel the best guide? Didn't you just love his art?*

"He certainly knows the area. What little I've seen of his work, yes, it's beautiful," she managed to insert in between Cat's breathless wonderings.

Cat's declaration—"Uncle Danny hasn't had a girlfriend in simply ages, even though half the women on Beara are in love with him"—was followed by a snort from the backseat. Annie glanced into the rearview mirror and caught Polly's giant eye roll. The girl sat slumped with her arms crossed rigidly over her chest, staring out the window in sullen silence, biting her cheek. Of course. Polly had a crush on her friend's uncle. Oh, the tangled webs and heartbreaks of youth. *And it only gets worse, kiddo,* Annie thought.

"It's like a monastery around here. I mean, it's so not normal. My mom hasn't had a date in ages, and I don't know if Daniel, like, even wants a girlfriend."

"Catriona Margaret O'Connell." Polly piped up from the backseat, her voice mimicking an outraged schoolmarm. "What would possess you to say such a thing?" The girls giggled.

"So, are you married?"

At Catriona's blunt question, Annie reflexively curled her left hand to hide her bare ring finger. When had she taken off her wedding ring? She pictured it tucked away in a jewelry box in Seattle. One she hadn't taken with her to the extended-stay hotel.

"Yes," she replied. "Twelve years."

"Oh."

Another look at the rearview mirror to see Polly's secret smile at the window.

"Has your uncle ever been married?" The question was out

of her mouth before she could think better of it. Annie kept her eyes trained on the traffic as it merged into a roundabout. The answer Catriona gave was far more than she'd bargained for.

"No, not ever. I hardly knew him before he went to prison. I was so little, and Liam was just a wee thing. But he's lived with us since he got out, and he's never even been on a date. That I know of, anyway."

Prison.

"Jaysus, Cat. Maybe Daniel doesn't want his entire personal life splashed out to a total stranger." Polly spoke at last, indignant in her support.

"She's not a total stranger, Pol," Catriona snapped. "Besides, Uncle Daniel's never shied away from the truth of his past."

Polly leaned in between the two seats. "I've never heard you call him *uncle*. Not ever."

Catriona huffed and set her jaw in response. They passed a road sign for Ballycaróg. Another twenty minutes of this and then she'd be free.

"He doesn't like it when we call him *uncle*. But that doesn't change how I feel." To Annie, she said, "He's almost more like our dad."

"Well, you might as well tell her the whole story now." Polly sighed before dropping back to resume her crossed-arm sulk.

Catriona sat quietly, possibly chagrined by her indiscretion. She was a kind-hearted girl, if a bit naive.

"It's all right," Annie said. "I don't need to know any more."

"Well, if you spend much time in the village, you're going to find out anyway. Better you hear it from the family instead of in the pub."

Annie couldn't argue with that, or with her sad curiosity.

Catriona worried a piece of tissue in her lap, twisting it into a thin strip, unfurling it and twisting it up again. As she spoke, the tissue tore in two. She tucked her anxious hands underneath her thighs and hunched her shoulders.

"He was drink driving one night. Well, I think he probably did lots of nights. He was an alcoholic for a long time—since he was my age and quit school. I can't even imagine. Anyway, this was about ten years ago. He crossed the median on the highway between Cork and Portlaoise and hit a car coming the other way. It was a man and a woman and their two kids. The parents and the girl lived, but the little boy died a few days later. Daniel was sent to Cork Prison. He got out almost five years ago, and he's lived with us since."

The blood rushed into Annie's head like a dam breaking loose. Pinpricks of sweat needled under her arms, down her back, and into her cold hands. She wiped first one palm and then the other on her jeans and gripped the steering wheel. Now was not the time for a panic attack, not with such precious cargo on board. Daniel's Rover had rounded a bend and passed out of view.

Ryan. She cried out, but only in the rush and churning of her mind. *My sweet, sweet brother.* It was as if she were hearing the news for the first time. Her father sobbing into the phone, unable to speak, a neighbor coming on the line, bearing the awful burden of breaking her heart: *Your mom and your brother have been in an accident.*

But it wasn't an accident, not in the true sense. Her mother had gotten into that car, already intoxicated, in her normal state of half-lit, functionally drunk. She killed Ryan, as surely as if she'd put a gun to his head. Annie believed that. She would never forgive her mother for the destruction of that innocent, glowing life. Even though her mother had been dead for three years.

"Annie? Ms. Crowe? Are you okay?" Catriona placed a

warm, slightly damp hand on Annie's arm. Annie nodded quickly but dared not take her eyes off the road.

"Here." Catriona placed a tissue on her leg.

"Jesus." She grabbed the tissue to wipe at her wet cheeks. Polly leaned forward, pique subsumed by curiosity. Annie searched for an explanation for the girls, one that revealed nothing of her history. Nothing that would get back to Daniel.

"Sorry, you just caught me by surprise. I had no idea. It's a terrible story," she offered.

"When Daniel first came to live with us, he was totally dependent upon my mom. He wasn't allowed to drive; he didn't have a job. Mom had to take him into Castletownbere or Bantry for his AA meetings and to Skibbereen to his therapist's. Which wasn't that big of a deal, since she works all over Beara, but still. He renovated the old shed out back and moved in there. Sometimes days would go by and we wouldn't see him. Then, I don't know. He just got better. Nicer, too. Now I don't know what we'd do without him. He's practically raising Liam. Our dad's such an ass."

Annie let Catriona prattle on, grateful she didn't have to talk. But the resentment built. Hearing how Daniel "just got better" sent a wave of bitterness through her. Ryan never had a chance to get better. The little boy Daniel killed never did, either. His poor parents—to lose a baby like that, to be so helpless to save a child.

She recognized the approach to Ballycaróg, could see the few village lights twinkling in the dusk. This surreal interlude was nearly over. Annie circled around and dropped south, toward the coast. "Where is your dad?" she asked, to steer the subject away from Daniel and his post-prison healing.

"London. He and the step-monster live there with our half-brother." Cat shuddered.

"Cat, Mom says I can stay the night." Polly urgently tapped on her phone. "Think it'll be okay with yours?"

"I'm sure. Turn here, Annie." Catriona pointed to the road that broke away to the left. Annie crested the slight rise, driving past her bungalow. Fiana's place sat on a precipice, the land more open and flatter than where the Moyle house was situated. It was a breathtaking spot. The point seemed to shear off to nothing to the south and east, dropping straight into the ocean. She slowed as the road turned to gravel and passed a plaster-and-stone building with clerestory windows all around.

"That's Uncle Daniel's place. His studio. He lives there, too."

Annie pulled up behind his SUV, where Bannon twirled in circles beside the driver's door. A tan terrier raced over, yelping.

Polly was already out of the car, and Catriona had pulled up the door handle before Annie found her voice. "Thank you for seeing me home," she said softly.

"Thanks for letting us ride with you. Would you like to come in?"

"No, I'm pretty tired. I'd better just get home."

"Okay, well. Here comes Daniel." She nodded, and Annie looked out the windshield. He walked toward them, in conversation with the dogs leaping at his legs.

"It was great to meet you! I'm sure we'll see you around!" Catriona's phone was already out of her pocket before she'd slammed shut the car door behind her.

Annie longed to back down the driveway without a second glance. Instead, she lowered her window halfway.

"You survived," he joked.

"They are sweet. Your niece is a great girl." That much she could be honest about.

169

"Come on in for tea. I think there's apple pie, too."

Her *no* rushed out the second Daniel had finished speaking. He flinched. "I'm really tired," she continued, unable to meet his eyes. "I've got some work to do tonight and meetings all day tomorrow," she lied.

"Sure, okay. Well. How about dinner tomorrow night? Just here, with the family?"

"I don't think so. I can't. I'm sure I'll be working. The licenses are progressing for Eire-Evergreen." In her nervousness, she blurted what she shouldn't have. "Or at least, we've got word they're still being considered. Anyway, time is of the essence!" With a short, barking laugh, she shifted the gear into reverse. "I'll see you. Thanks again for the escort." She powered up the window.

One last glance in the rearview mirror showed Daniel standing with his arms at his sides. "Goddammit." She breathed. "Goddammit!" This time it came out as a shout.

~

The evening was still and warm enough to sit outside on the back patio. Annie changed into capris and a sweater, brewed a pot of chamomile tea, and curled up with a blanket on a cushioned lounger. The thump, whoosh, and sizzle of the waves meeting the shore provided a soothing soundtrack to the glow of the moon and starlight spilling into the ocean.

"I miss you, little brother. Oh my God, how I miss you," she said to the air. How could it be ten years already?

Annie waited a few moments, expecting the tears to flow again. But her heart beat steadily; her stomach didn't clench; her skin didn't pull against her bones and grow cold with sorrow. Whispering like wind through tall grass, the waves whumped against the sand as they landed and spread out, before pulling back with a crickle-hiss, grabbing at pebbles in their retreat.

"Ryan. What am I going to do?"

When Ryan died, everyone—Stephen, her colleagues, the friends she still had in the running community—had rallied around her, holding her up when she didn't have the strength to stand on her own. But they hadn't been enough. The slide started slowly in those early years; wine a few times a week became every night, earlier, and then more. Then Mom died. And soon she was stirring vodka into her morning cranberry juice. But it had always been there, within her, hadn't it? The need to take everything to the extreme. Once she lost running as a coping mechanism, she turned to something else she'd grown up with: alcohol. She'd pushed away the fear that she was becoming like her mother, certain she had control over the thing that had ruined her family.

"Here's the thing, little brother. I don't have the booze and the drinking buddies anymore. I don't have Stephen. And now my job. God. Ryan. Can I do this? Can I sell my soul, just to have a home to go back to?" She laid her head back and closed her eyes, listening.

Mise Éire: Uaigní mé ná an Chailleach Bhéarra.

She opened her eyes. The clear voice—throaty and rich, feminine and wise—could not be mistaken for a rush of wind. Not this time. Annie waited, the hair on her arms tingling as it rose in response to her alert mind.

Mise Éire: Uaigní mé ná an Chailleach Bhéarra.

The syllables were incomprehensible but distinct, flowing slowly and smoothly, like a river of cream. There was something ancient and otherworldly about the language. Mystical but comforting. Annie hardly dared raise her head to scan the darkness with her eyes, afraid of spooking the voice. A bubbling joy filled her, but it was tinged with longing and sweet sadness—recalling the lovely ache that had pulled at her heart as she stood on the mountain above Ballycaróg, or examined Grainne Petitt's photographs in Margitte's gallery.

Mise Éire: Uaigní mé ná an Chailleach Bhéarra.

Annie rose carefully, her bare feet whispering on the wood. She leaned into the railing and searched in the dark for the voice in the wind. Nothing moved, just a faint undulation of the sea, like a body shifting position under a thick blanket.

"I hear you," she answered back, seeking to match the soft and soothing tones. "I'm listening. But I don't understand what you're saying."

Mór mo bhrón was the reply.

She waited at the railing for many long minutes before retaking her post on the lounger, willing the voice to return.

Only silence followed in its wake. But the thoughts that rang through her mind, as clear as a ship's bell on a calm sea, belonged to her voice. What had been home belonged to an Annie who once was but who now floated free. The sweet-sharp longing she'd felt on the mountain returned, a torment of loneliness and grief mixed with wonder and joy. The exquisite agony of being alive.

32

He was drawn to her, drawn in by the vulnerability and pain that he knew so well, had worked so hard to slough off his own soul, like a snake shedding tired, used skin.

The rawness he'd seen on her face as she walked alone in Kenmare had softened as they spoke in the pub, then resolved itself into a different sort of exposed emotion in Margitte's gallery—longing. Wonder. Hope. At that moment, Daniel knew he'd connected with an artist. He recognized a different kind of need, a hunger to enter a different kind of world. Grainne's photography had reached Annie through the thirst, the emptiness that was left after the drink had been taken away. He'd wanted to linger with her there, to be the one to show her how art had redeemed him, how it could be the same for her. And watching her react to his art ... had he moved her in a different way? When he made his decision in the gallery—that his art would be his way to speak out against the mine—it was because of what he'd seen in Annie's face.

But the Annie who had driven away a short time ago was a different woman than the one who had appeared so vulnerable in the pub and the gallery. Her face closed, her eyes unable to meet his. What had changed in the scant hour's drive to Ballycaróg? She had shut down, turned away, become unreachable. She'd had time to reflect, he imagined, to realize she had gotten too close to the heart of the fight ahead.

He could have taken the coast path away from the house, toward the beach, but of course his heart led his feet down the drive, directly past the Moyle cottage. Annie was steps away, behind stone and plaster and wood—a knock on the door, and she would stand before him; he could read her face, hold her, embrace the ache, convince her they weren't on opposite sides, that she didn't have to fight so hard.

He dropped away from the drive, descending to the footpath that ran alongside the cottage, the same route he'd taken when he'd come across Annie screaming.

Mise Éire: Uaigní mé ná an Chailleach Bhéarra.

For a moment, he wondered if it was Annie speaking, if she'd kept hidden some extraordinary fluency in Irish Gaelic. But the voice wasn't hers. It was deeper and stronger. It emanated from his blood. Of course, the meaning of the words was no longer a mystery to him: *I am Ireland: I am lonelier than the Old Woman of Beara.*

Ignoring the clamoring of his thigh and calf muscles as they cramped in the crouched position, barely noticing the gripping ache, he let the voice sink into his mind until it seemed to come from inside him, only to dissolve in the salt sea air.

33

The sky lightened from blue-gray to pale rose in the time it took Annie to rinse her coffee cup and change into her running clothes. She'd managed a couple of late morning and afternoon runs since she'd arrived in Ireland a week ago, but she was freshest and strongest at dawn, when she had the roads, trails, and her thoughts to herself.

Normally she ran with headphones pouring out a random selection of tunes from her iPod, but on unfamiliar roads where dogs and drivers could happen upon her at any bend, she chose the sound of her pounding feet and heart. There was music in the ocean when she came to a clearing that gave a view of the sea, in the stirring of sheep that bleated in agitation when she ran by, in the finches and larks that rustled and chattered in the hedgerows and bushes. She searched the black bodies that sat on fence posts and telephone wires for red beaks and legs, but saw only the basic black crow—her adopted namesake.

Her left leg was always grumpy at the start of a morning run; the scar tissue—even after subsequent surgeries to clean it out—gummed up the fluid motion of her knee. Annie settled into a slow, even pace in the early miles on the undulating terrain to warm up her stiff joints.

She considered the up-and-over hill route into Ballycaróg but worried the slick grass and rocks would stilt her gait and ruin the easy rhythm she'd found. She kept straight, dropping into a silent and shuttered village, and ran to the cove road.

She reasoned she could follow the road and eventually end up not far from her bungalow. She'd prepared mentally for at least ten miles, tucking energy chews into the small backpack that also held a water bladder and a thin, water-resistant jacket, gloves, and hat in case the weather took a sudden turn.

The miles slipped under her feet, the patch of sweat on her back grew, and her legs, now warm and relaxed, picked up their pace, carrying her easily over the steep inclines. She encountered not a single car, though tractors rumbled toward her on side roads, and once a black-and-white sheepdog raced with her along his side of the fence, barking with delirious joy to find a human as eager to run as he.

The tarmac on Ballycaróg Cove Road petered out to packed sand and gravel. The sound of the ocean filled the narrow lane as hills rose to one side and stone cliffs to the other. Then the cathedral-like walls dropped away, and the bay opened into an expanse of gently rolling aquamarine. Annie ran as far as the cobbled surface of the boat launch could take her, and then continued on the packed, wet sand. Low tide presented her with acres of beach to traverse. Homesteads dotted the green fields that spread before the bay. A cluster of giant boulders, survivors of eons of water erosion that destroyed their brothers, pushed back against a cavalcade of waves.

She felt the whisk of sand against her calves as she kicked up a low spray behind her. Her face ached with a grin that stretched her mouth so wide, she could swallow the ocean. Endorphins coursed in her bloodstream, and she tore up the sand as she sprinted, lifting her knees higher and higher—feeling no pain, no fatigue, nothing other than the sensation of pure flight.

She came to a panting halt as the strip of sand gave way to small boulders and patches of driftwood. The sensation of being inside a cathedral grew as she entered the shelter of the cove. The cliff walls rose high, and the rush of waves reverberated in the vast but protected space. The aroma of rotting sea life swelled.

Above the sound of water, and more immediate than the scream of seagulls, were the percussive squawks and caws of hundreds of lean black birds. Their rapier beaks and delicate feet were scarlet ribbons in motion against the brown-black, pockmarked cliffs. As an ensemble, they sounded like a video arcade—a glorious, bustling, black-feathered chorus emitting pneumatic, high-pitched bloops and bleeps and squeaks.

"*Pyrrhocorax pyrrhocorax*," Annie announced, her hands on her hips, her head tilted back. She recognized their chatter from YouTube videos posted by bird enthusiasts from sightings in Spain and Morocco—where the Red-billed Chough continued to thrive. There were several clips from Ballycaróg Cove, Country Cork, Ireland, too, filmed in the spot where she now stood, grinning at the busy, noisy, charming birds.

She found a solid, dry expanse of driftwood and sat to watch the choughs. The social rules the birds had built into their habitat were too complex for her to ascertain, but their constant takeoffs and landings, squabbles, preening, and chatter were fascinating.

Once again, Daniel's words came to her: *nature as a cultural artifact*. The choughs, these vibrant, living artifacts of Beara, were survivors, but even they wouldn't stand a chance against heavy machinery, explosions, and drilling equipment. Their habitat would be blasted apart. As she watched them go about the busy dance of their small, vital lives, Annie understood how an artist could use her camera lens to help preserve this place instead of using her professional acumen to see it destroyed.

She watched until her damp shirt began to cool against her skin and her legs began to stiffen. Waving a reluctant farewell to the choughs, she ran back toward the small stretch of land where her cottage balanced above the ocean.

A switchback trail of sand and packed earth wound up and out of the bay until it merged with a small, crumbling road. Nothing was familiar, but, keeping the ocean to her right, Annie followed along until the road turned toward the village of Ballycaróg, far in the distance. She was close to home—about four miles from the choughs' town in the cliffs.

The road home would take her straight to Fiana O'Connell's. Her only choice was to skirt along Fiana's property, past the large picture windows that glowered with black irises along the front and sides of the house.

She would have made it but for Bannon, who nosed around the flowerbeds along one sheltered wall. The heeler lifted her head, spied Annie, and barreled down the slope to meet her. Annie halted, uncertain, and lowered her head and eyes, holding out curled fingers. But Bannon knew her scent and was delighted to see a friend. Annie rubbed the heeler's wiry fur until it stood on end, filling her fingers with the scent of damp dog and dirt. Then she moved along, hoping she'd pass unnoticed. But when Fiana's house fell away behind her, she saw Daniel in the threshold of his studio doorway, wiping his hands on a chamois. A surgical mask hung around his neck, and an eye shield perched on top of his head.

"The mad scientist at work?" she asked.

"Trying not to blow the place apart," he answered.

"I was just out for a run."

"I see that. Where'd you go?"

"Into the village, then down to the bay."

Daniel nodded. "That's a fair way."

Annie checked the Garmin on her wrist. "Ten point six eight miles. I'd hoped for eleven." His eyebrows furrowed. "I'm joking," she said.

"Ah." He hesitated into the thickness of anticipation. Annie carried the weight of what she knew about his past, wanting an explanation somehow, yet not wanting to allow any more of his vulnerability into her life. She'd known selling the mine wouldn't be without its complications, that she'd have to maneuver the politics of nature vs. development. But it seemed almost simple compared to the politics of emotion she hadn't prepared for.

"Do you always run without a jacket? Beara isn't the Bahamas."

"I should get back."

They spoke at the same time, her words running on top of his. Each motioned for the other to continue.

"You look cold. I'll fix you a cup of tea."

"Daniel." But he'd already turned and walked back inside. Exhaling deeply, she planted one foot in front of the other until she stood on the landing, peering inside his work and living space.

34

Maybe she was just cold. But even after Annie shrugged on the quilted flannel shirt Daniel offered, she stood with her arms crossed high and tight over her chest and avoided his eyes. Her posture, closed face, and terse replies mirrored the way she'd pulled out of the driveway last night—uncomfortable and distant.

He watched as she stepped softly and slowly around his studio to study his work, propped against the walls, placed on tables or windowsills, hung by wire from hooks buried in the wood picture rail.

Oh, she was pretty. Cat hadn't told him anything he wasn't acutely aware of the moment he'd seen her lift her slender frame from MacKenna's Mercedes. Even now, with her face clean of makeup, slightly flushed from her exertion and the cool morning air, her torso wrapped in his shirt, the solid ridges and curves of her bare legs impossible not to look at as she moved. Especially now.

His stomach flipped at the sight of the thick, white, puckered scar that ran the length of her left tibia and pulled at the skin of her knee. She leaned in for a closer look at the watercolor sketches he'd taped to the wall, favoring her uninjured leg, her hand massaging the scar tissue.

Daniel handed her a steaming mug of tea, and she smiled with gratitude, wrapping her hands around the warm ceramic. The shirt cuffs covered all but the tips of her fingers. She turned away from him, again not meeting his eyes. Annie tilted her head. He imagined closing the distance between them in three strides, taking her fine-boned face in his hands and covering her mouth, drawing the breath from her. No, not her breath. Her pain. Her sadness. Whatever sent her out the door and into the night, alone. He wanted to crush her against his chest, feel her warm, damp limbs wrap around his own. So close to this troubled, beautiful soul, yet he felt more alone than he'd allowed himself to feel in ten years.

"Your work is beautiful. I don't know anything about metal art, but the colors you achieve on the copper and chrome … it's like they've absorbed a sunset or the ocean. How do you do that?"

Sensing she'd rather he keep his distance, he moved to the other side of the long worktable. "I make up different patinas—that's what I was doing when you came in." He motioned to a covered steel bucket in the industrial sink. "It's a lot like working with watercolors, actually. I combine various chemicals to make different colors of patina. Then I paint or etch the patina onto the metal, where it creates shades and nuances of tones. These sculptures"—he pointed to a cluster of pieces perched on risers—"I patinized before I cut and hammered or soldered them together."

She wound slowly around the room. "The watercolors—they're so delicate, such a contrast to the solidity of the metal. Do you sell these, too?"

"Mostly they're just studies for what I want to etch into the copper sheets. Like this one." He motioned to the tilted artist's desk that sat adjacent to the worktable.

Annie turned to peer at the sketchpad. "A Red-billed Chough," she said softly.

"Yes, it is. I'm working through a series of studies for this panel." He came to stand beside her and lifted his chin to indicate the large rectangle of copper lying flat on the table. "Most of these sketches came from time I spent in the Channel Islands, working at an animal sanctuary where the choughs were being rehabilitated." Daniel told her of the Durrell Wildlife Park on Jersey and the success it had in bringing the Red-billed Chough back from the brink of extinction on the island.

"I went to the cove this morning," she said. "Just to watch them. It's like a little city. The birds are amazing. So busy, noisy, smart. It's hard to think of them as just crows."

"Crows are remarkable creatures," he said. "They get short shrift because they're scavengers. But they know how to work any system to get what they need. The Red-billed Chough isn't as robust as our *Corvus corax* or your North American *Corvus brachyrhynchos*," he said, naming two common species of black crow, "but they have been a part of southwest Ireland since time's memory. They're wrapped up in my memories of childhood. Choughs in the pastures, along the coast."

"I know," she whispered. She pressed a palm to her cheek. "I've stepped into something bigger than me, haven't I?" She spoke softly to his sketch of the chough, not to him. "I don't know what I'm doing here."

He took the open door in hand and walked through. "*Mise Éire*," he said, watching her face carefully. Her reaction was immediate.

"What did you say?"

"*Mise Éire: Uaigní mé ná an Chailleach Bhéarra.*"

Annie backed away, one foot trailing the other. She seemed

to shrink in the oversized shirt.

"You've been hearing it, too, haven't you?" he said. She shook her head as her face flushed pink then drained to white.

The ring and buzz of a cell phone echoed through the space. It was the ringtone he'd assigned to Liam; not a chance he'd put off answering his nephew's call. The phone sounded inches away and Daniel shuffled through papers next to the sink, but the acoustics of his studio were tricky. Then he remembered flipping through his e-mail while he drank coffee in bed.

"Hang on, let me grab that." He strode to the back of the studio and edged around the screen. When he returned moments later, phone to his ear, his flannel shirt was hanging on its peg. Annie had gone.

35

"Here it is. Listen to this." James was reading to her from an e-mail sent at six on Sunday morning from the home account of a contact in the Exploration and Mining division who worked with the deputy minister.

Annie hadn't spoken with James since she'd slipped away from their awkward meeting Friday morning. They'd exchanged several texts and e-mails, and no further mention was made of the tension. If he'd truly let go of his annoyance, perhaps she'd be able to persuade him that connecting with the community was vital.

Of course, he had no idea she was letting go, too. Letting go of this project, even if that meant losing her job. Especially if letting go meant losing her job. Beara's beauty had pulled her in. Yet it was more than the haunting landscapes or the healing power of this place that held her fast. It was that voice that seemed to be guiding her, searing her soul with incomprehensible syllables.

It was Daniel.

But this morning, a call while she'd been out for her run—the clipped tone in James's voice, requesting she phone as soon as possible. Two more calls followed, without messages.

She could feel his tension and exasperation coming through the line. Wondering what she'd done now, or what she'd be asked to do later, hoping, yes, hoping it was a crisis that spelled trouble for Eire-Evergreen, something that would call a halt to the exploration, anything to release her from her obligation.

While the voice mail played on speakerphone, she traced in her mind the words Daniel had spoken the day before, the words she'd heard in the wind Friday evening: *"Mise Éire: Uaigní mé ná an Chailleach Bhéarra."*

Her hands trembled slightly, but it wasn't James and the urgent phone call that made her fingers quiver. It was Daniel. These Gaelic words that she knew connected them somehow, the voices bringing them together.

"He says," James continued, snapping her back to the present, "and I quote, 'word got around that a coalition of environmental groups filed a motion to halt further development of the Eire-Evergreen copper mine. They're pursuing legislation under the Special Protection Area Act to declare the Ballycaróg Cove a protected habitat for the endangered Red-billed Chough.'" An exhale of irritation and James was back to his own words. "It appears they filed the motion late Friday afternoon, and they've requested an immediate injunction against all Eire-Evergreen activity—even the exploration that's already been cleared."

Annie's fist closed and pumped the air. Her skin tingled, as if her body responded to a part of her mind she'd shut the door on. Thank God they were having this conversation over the phone. If James had seen her reaction, involuntary though it was, he'd have every reason to call Serena, and Annie would be on the first plane home.

"How soon do you think you can get to Dublin?" James asked. Annie heard the staccato rhythm of a pen clicking; his nerves spilled out through his fingers.

"Dublin? Why?"

"Hugh Doyle will meet us at nine tomorrow," he said. "I want you there to discuss the community relations angle."

She nearly laughed out loud at the irony. Community relations, indeed. Of course she had to go. But Annie grimaced and mouthed a curse at the phone all the same. "It'll be faster if I drive to Cork and take the train from there." She scanned the timetable attached to the refrigerator. "I'll be at Heuston by six. If I recall, there's a hotel right across the street."

"You can stay with me. I've got a spare room." The statement was offhand, delivered along with the sound of furious tapping at a computer keyboard.

A practical solution, yes. *But perhaps hopelessly stupid,* Annie considered as she packed a bag. Yet she'd readily agreed. To see if she could trust herself. To see if she was really able to change. She'd had a number of conversations in rehab about her risk-taking behaviors, her therapist pointing out how she had to push everything to the limit, forcing a confrontation with a colleague or an argument with Stephen; pushing an opponent to kick hard near the end of a race, as a way to control a situation, to see how far her anger would carry her. It's what she was doing now, wasn't it—with James, with her job?

How far can you go this time, Annie? Staying at a client's apartment, a client whom you quite possibly slept with—the very definition of taking it to the edge.

"I'll meet you at Heuston," James had said just before they rang off. "We can go straight for an early dinner and discuss plans for tomorrow."

She was on the road to Cork twenty minutes later.

~

The clatter of dishes and the buzz of conversation bounced from the high ceiling and shot around the dining room of The Winding Stair. Tall rectangular windows set in trios along the restaurant's front façade were open at the top to let in the breeze that floated from the Liffey three stories below. Dark wood floors, original to the restored warehouse built at the turn of the twentieth century, stretched in patched and scuffed contrast beneath tables laid with starched white linens. Annie and James were seated at a table in the far corner with a bird's-eye view of Dublin.

She ordered the golden beet salad with a bleu cheese made in County Louth and seared plaice caught in waters north of Dublin; James, the lamb shanks dry-aged at a farm outside Belfast. He suggested they share a bottle of Nuits-St-Georges, and Annie died a little inside as she demurred. She could smell the flint and flora and taste the tart cranberry and raspberry of one of her favorite Burgundy wines. She asked for a Pellegrino and lemon. James handed his menu to the waiter, requesting a pint of stout. Annie excused herself to find the tiny restroom on the first-floor landing, and when she returned, their drinks waited on the table.

"I know you want to get ahead of this thing." Annie dropped them right back to the morning's e-mail and the injunction filed against Eire-Evergreen. "Unfortunately, no one bothered to consider the outcry by environmental groups over this little bird, so we're late to the conversation."

James paused with his beer glass halfway to his mouth, searching her face with narrowed eyes. "What's your plan?"

"I suggest Eire-Evergreen set up a fund to relocate the chough population and make the fund the center of your publicity campaign. You've got to show that you're just as concerned for Beara and the chough as any environmental group. More, in fact, because you're willing to put some money behind it."

Annie spread her linen napkin across her lap and folded her hands on the table. "There's a group on Jersey that's reintroduced the Red-billed Chough to the island—we can take a page from them, contact their team. Your materials—those glossy brochures, the presentations, everything—must feature the wild beauty of Beara. The public has to associate Eire-Evergreen with nature and conservation. You could redesign the mine logo to feature the bird somehow. The message is: Eire-Evergreen will not only bring jobs, they will save an endangered little bird. You stand for the best of what science and industry can offer—progress and preservation."

James's face remained unreadable, but he gave the waiter who deposited a breadbasket an absent smile before saying, "What makes you think this conservation group on Jersey would be willing to assist a mining company?"

"I know someone who's worked at the site." Searching for something to do with her hands while she talked about Daniel, Annie picked out a sourdough roll and tore it in half. "I don't know if the organization would be willing to help, but it's worth asking."

"Wouldn't they be more likely to join the fight against the mine?"

"Maybe if you promised to support their cause, they'd see benefits to lending their expertise." The words poured out of her mouth before she'd even considered what she was suggesting. *Quid pro quo*, with a quirky little bird in the middle?

He took a long swallow of the stout. "Are you trying to turn me into an environmentalist?" The flash of a smile quickly disappeared.

"I'm trying to help you get what you want. Which you don't make easy, by the way."

"Before we pour money into glossy brochures and bird conservation programs, let's see how things play out in Dublin," said James, his voice just audible over the dining room din. "Even if the injunction is successful, we'll counter file. I say we ride out this storm."

Their starters arrived, and James steered the conversation away from Beara to describe his life in Saudi the past two years. Although wondering when they'd continue to plan for tomorrow's meeting, Annie let him lead the way. She reasoned the quieter she was, the less she'd risk and the more she could learn about this man and his motives. She noticed that as detailed as he was about his life and work in the Middle East, he never once mentioned the French girlfriend.

Outside the restaurant, pale green-and-blue light rippled along the River Liffey as the cool spring evening fell toward night. "It's early. How about a drink? The Temple Bar is just over the bridge. Or we can find something quieter."

Annie groaned inside. "To tell you the truth, my legs are stiff as boards from sitting all day. I'd like to shake them loose with a walk." She tried to sound nonchalant, but hadn't she known that coming up here, staying in his flat, would be implicit approval of something more between them? Had she wanted it? "I need some time in my own head to sort out our next steps," she added. On the train, she'd located an evening AA meeting on Molesworth Street, which she reasoned couldn't be far. An hour of safety and she thought she could manage to stay overnight in a flat with this man who so unnerved her.

"It's just a drink, Annie."

Did he know? Was he testing her? Her palms prickled with sweat. "And we just had dinner. You're my client. Let's not confuse things. I'll take a cab back to your place."

She watched as he turned the corner on Liffey Street, toward the car park.

Before losing the restaurant's Wi-Fi connection, Annie punched her destination into Google Maps. Molesworth Street was just a kilometer from The Winding Stair, around the corner from the National Gallery. She'd be there with minutes to spare.

She hurried across Ha'Penny Bridge toward Wellington Quay. Once on Molesworth Street, she passed into a small street behind St. Ann's Church, coming to a stop in front of a red brick building fronted by a cruel-looking wrought iron fence. Others entered the building, singly or in groups of two and three. Annie approached a pair of women. One put her hand on Annie's elbow, and she was led up a ramp and inside.

~

She sat up in bed with the lights off, gazing at the Dublin city skyline. Radio and cell towers blinked red and white, and the canal reflected white and yellow lights from the surrounding office buildings and high-end flats. It wasn't a surprise that James had found a flat in one of the city's most coveted neighborhoods—a mid-rise glass-and-brick apartment building on Ringsend Road, overlooking the Grand Canal.

His apartment was a Scandinavian vision of wood, glass, and stainless steel. Sparsely furnished, the open front room contained little more than a leather sofa, an Eames chair, a blond fir dining set. The en suite guest room, where she'd found her overnight bag just inside the door after she'd arrived from her "walk," boasted the same view of the Grand Canal Quay, the River Liffey, and Dublin. She thought of the lights glowing from the high windows in Daniel's studio, where he worked perched high above the Atlantic, and a feeling of desperate loneliness swept through her. She exhaled in a hitching sigh.

Low voices murmured from the television in the living room, and she pictured James sitting on the squared-off sofa, pristine in its minimalist leather and chrome, his hand wrapped around a short tumbler of neat whiskey, flipping through the stations. Was he thinking of her, too, only steps away?

"This really was a bad idea, wasn't it, Crowe?" she murmured. "Staying here. What did you think would happen?"

Annie swung her legs off the bed. She pushed her cotton tank above her stomach and ran her hand over her belly, checking her body's profile in the mirror that made up the sliding doors of the closet. She pulled in her stomach, tucked her hips, and lengthened her spine. She tugged at the band holding a low ponytail and let her hair cascade around her shoulders. Then she looked at her face.

She longed for the oblivion of sex. In it would be the reassurance that even for a short while someone wouldn't care how badly her mind was messed up. Only how well her body fit into his. It would ease the unwelcome thoughts of Daniel, thoughts that left her feeling so vulnerable.

"You're going to do it, aren't you?" she mumbled. "For fuck's sake." She pulled on her pajama bottoms and opened the bedroom door.

The back of his head rested against the arm of the sofa, and one hand was propped on the coffee table, fingers curled loosely around a glass of amber liquid. But the hand remained still, and he did not sit up at her approach. Then she could hear the soft intake, pause, and release of breath. He was asleep. A grainy film in low orange hues played out on the TV screen at a low volume; with a quick glance, Annie recognized a young and golden Steve McQueen.

Her knees nearly buckled as it hit her what she was doing,

followed by relief that she'd come to awareness before it was too late. Standing half-dressed, only steps from her client, all intentions to join him on the sofa, curl herself around his body, fucking up once again. Annie backed away, placing one foot carefully behind the other.

The hand that held the whiskey jerked, and she backed into the corner of a wall in surprise. "Annie?" James raised his head; in a heartbeat he would turn her way.

"Just a sec," she called and whipped around. Two quick steps into the guest room and she grabbed the knitted cream cardigan that hung loose and long around her body.

"I just came in search of water," she said as she reentered the front room from the hallway. Of course, there was a water glass next to the sink in the guest room's adjoining bath. "Sparkling water, if you have any? My stomach's a little upset."

"Of course." James passed a hand over his face, and she saw his jaw stretch in a yawn. "Cold, in the fridge. Help yourself."

When she returned, he'd opened a small panel in the built-in wall unit, revealing a well-stocked bar. "Can I get you anything?" James motioned to the array of liquor.

Annie held up her glass of water. "I'm good, thanks." She took a seat in the white leather Eames lounge chair, tucking her legs underneath her and securing the sweater closed in the front, just as James returned to the sofa.

"We didn't finish our conversation about tomorrow," she said. "I still have some concerns before we meet with the deputy minister."

"Such as?"

"Such as the determination to proceed with no regard for the citizen's group that's formed, this Beara Chough Coalition? Or the larger group that's banded together to fight the mine? I state emphatically, as your communications strategist, that would be a mistake."

"Normally, I might be inclined to agree with you. But we may have a few tricks up our sleeve yet."

"Can you be more specific?"

"I'd rather wait until we meet with Doyle tomorrow. There's no sense in speculating until we're clear where we sit with the DCENR."

"So, I'm just along for the ride?"

"You've never been just 'along for the ride.' But I do wonder if your heart is really in this project." James set his perspiring glass carefully on a ceramic coaster, allowing his words to sink in. He looked around the room. Taking his time. Playing with her. "It's just a feeling I've had," he said, answering her unvoiced question. "A sense of distraction, that your attention isn't completely on the work."

"I've had to fight every step of the way for the information I need to get this PR operation under way." Annie's words were measured, her voice low. "Who was there Thursday night, making a case for this mine, connecting with the community?"

"Right. Fair enough. Your speech made quite an impression. The Dublin office has received several calls from locals keen to get information about potential jobs, even at this early stage. You did a fine job selling the mine. People take to you. They believe you. Frankly, you soften the blow."

"Yet you question my commitment?"

"You've backed out of or refused to have dinner every night Colm and I have been in Ballycaróg. Yet I don't see much evidence that you're burning the midnight oil to assemble a campaign we can immediately put into place. I expected the perfect spin that made the Seattle viaduct replacement campaign such a success. In fact, I thought you'd come to Ireland prepared with the bulk of this project ready to roll out. Now it seems this time in Ireland has been little more than a holiday in the country."

He seemed so casual, as if they were discussing their airline preferences, but she dared not move her head or shift her eyes for fear that he would see her shrink under the barrage of his words.

Do not cry, Crowe. Whatever you do, Do. Not. Cry. The confession nearly tumbled out of her. In a flash of horror, she saw herself leaping to her feet shouting, *I'm an addict! I run away to AA meetings every night because I can't face my pain alone. If I'm not thinking about alcohol, I'm thinking about not thinking about it. Can't you see how lost I am?*

The voice came, instinctive and inevitable. Or was it two voices? A sweet soprano, something new, laced over the top of the faceless contralto that had been following her around Beara. A smile tugged at Annie's lips, and she swallowed a giggle.

"Is something funny?"

"No. Not in the slightest." She composed her face. "Speaking of the Seattle viaduct ... I've reflected on that campaign quite a bit this past week. Most significantly on the person I was when I worked on it. The difference between then and now is that I truly believed tearing down the Alaskan Way Viaduct and replacing it with a highway tunnel was the best thing for the city I loved. I believed in that project, no matter how messy and costly. I am not anti-development or anti-industry, not by a long shot.

"But I will admit to feeling ambivalence with this mine. I believe that ambivalence is healthy. It keeps me on my toes, gives me a clarity of perspective that I might not possess if I were one hundred percent in one camp or the other.

"As for seeming distracted? I have no response to that.

My private life is just that—it is private. If you feel that I am somehow not up the standards you need to get this mine into Beara, then we should come to some sort of decision soon. I am here on your dime. Or euro. Whatever. I certainly don't want to waste your time or money."

James nodded slowly, swirling the remaining finger of whiskey in his glass. "Where do we go from here?" he asked, without looking up.

"That's a question you'll have to answer for yourself. You're my client, but you can pick up the phone and call Serena at any time. I'm expendable, don't you think? I'd be happy to recommend any of my colleagues. They are first-rate." Annie felt giddy as she spoke, as if strings attaching her to the earth had been cut loose and she was floating. She braced herself for what was to come.

"I don't have any intention of calling Serena," he said, now meeting her gaze.

"Was this some sort of a test?" she asked. "Push Annie's buttons and see which ones really get her going?"

She rose from the chair to signal an end to the conversation, but James said, "I'd like you to stay."

"Stay. Here? Now? Or with the campaign?"

"What do you think?"

"I think I'm going to bed. I'll see you in the morning."

36

After Annie had walked out of his studio without a word on Saturday, Daniel had traded the thin, pointed metals, harsh chemicals, and sharp tools for pliable canvas, tubes of paint, and soft-bristled brushes. He'd told Annie the watercolors displayed here and there around the studio were studies for his metalwork. True, yes. But the deeper truth was the solace and pleasure he found in painting. These pieces, not intended for sale, allowed him to retain a deeper connection to his art, like a poet scribbling a poem on a bar napkin and leaving it behind, or a dancer twirling with abandon in an empty dance studio to the music in her head. The pure satisfaction of the process, when it wasn't for any purpose other than the joy of creation. Rarely did he share his watercolors with anyone, not even Margitte. And this painting would surely be his alone. The one indulgence of longing he would allow himself before it turned into regret.

It began, as all his work did, from a sense of place, grounded in the land where he'd been restored and sustained. But this painting was not a landscape; it was a portrait. After the shades and contours of sky, sea, mountains, and the gorse and grass of fields came the cream of skin and hair and delicate dress. The sharp edge of rock and the soft curve of cheek and thigh. A gaze into the distance that was meant to capture the longing Annie had expressed to stay and his longing that she never leave.

As Daniel gave shape to his desire in the form of a woman he barely knew perched on a slip of land that formed his very soul, he drifted to other memories, an earlier time of abandonment and regret.

He'd never painted his mother, although he could still see the thick wave of her dark hair, the shade she'd given to Fiana, and her cool and distant blue eyes, eyes that looked back from the mirror at Daniel every morning as he shaved. But his lasting image of her was not one he wanted to commit to canvas. There he'd been, a ten-year-old boy standing still as stone between his mother's hands as she clutched his shoulders and kissed his cheek. A mother who laughed as she jumped into the back of a Volkswagen van, waving good-bye to her young son and daughter. She was on her way to England for just a fortnight to see some old friends and take in a few concerts at the festival in Glastonbury.

Decades later she resurfaced as a letter addressed to Fiana at the Ballycaróg Bayview Hotel, married, with another family, raising sheep in New Zealand's Waipara Valley. She'd been searching for her first children on the Internet, she wrote. It wasn't until Daniel's manslaughter conviction that she'd finally tracked down her son, then a resident of Cork Prison, and his sister, a social worker living in Ballycaróg. Neither Fiana nor Daniel had ever responded to that letter.

Daniel had yet to form a long-term attachment to a woman. He and Fiana had worked through the psychobabble a long time ago; they both had issues with trust. Of course he hadn't lived a monastic existence. He was away enough—overnight hikes, guide trips, scouting scrap metal—wandering from Beara to sketch or hike. There were the return visits to the Durrell Wildlife Park, where he'd first become enchanted with the Red-billed Chough; he'd sought out women who didn't know or care about his past. Even Fiana had been pestered for years by acquaintances who looked beyond Daniel's crime and conviction and saw only a somber, handsome man in need of saving.

But if his head had ever been turned, if he'd let go of his self-hatred long enough to care for anyone, he'd never admitted it to himself. Until this one. This troubled, flawed, vulnerable American who'd burst into their lives just a week ago. Whose presence would be extinguished as soon as she flew away from Ireland. He painted to capture and preserve what he accepted would never be his. Another layer of regret as thick as the scar on Annie's leg.

37

Colm, James, and Annie filed into the office of the deputy minister for Exploration and Mining—a subdivision of the Department of Communications, Energy and Natural Resources—promptly at nine.

"Hugh Doyle." A trim man of indeterminate middle age, with thinning blond hair and narrow black-rimmed glasses that seemed to close his face behind glass gates, stood and extended a hand to Annie. He knew Colm and James, of course. They each took a chair, sitting in a semi-circle in front of Hugh's desk.

"Well, it's a wrinkle, but not an unexpected one," the deputy minister began as soon as they were settled.

"What kind of delay are we talking about?" James opened his jacket and crossed his legs.

"Hard to say. We've got our team assembling the data on mining companies that have won exceptions to the SPA ruling—that's Special Protection Area," he explained to Annie.

She hoped the slight lift of an eyebrow was enough to indicate that she knew what SPA stood for. "It's curious that the data weren't prepared in advance," she replied. "You must have anticipated the need to support Eire-Evergreen's case, in light of Beara's SPA situation. For reasons of the Environmental Impact Statement alone, you'd have needed this information." Confused about why a government agency would do Eire-Evergreen's legwork, she directed this last bit to James and Colm.

"As you know, Annie, the reason I came to Ireland and Colm was pulled off the job in Lisheen is the unfortunate way things were handled in Beara," James said. "You're right, we've got a lot of backtracking to do." His reply was addressed to her, but his eyes were on Hugh Doyle. An unspoken message passed between them. The *as you know* was enough to tell her further mention of Eire-Evergreen's shortcomings would be unwelcome.

"How long until we find out if the injunction is successful?" she asked the deputy minister.

"We should hear something by the end of the week. We'll file a separate motion to make certain offshore exploration is allowed to continue, since it is not under the SPA jurisdiction."

"If it's anything like the States, these battles can take years."

Again, glances passed between the men. Even Colm's muddy green eyes flinched and hardened. Hugh Doyle folded his hands and tapped his thumbs. "Ms. Crowe, I don't think we need to worry about that. Copper is one of the world's most highly prized minerals. The Irish government is fully supportive of Eire-Evergreen's plans to extract copper from these mines, and I'm confident we will find a way to do so, safely and to the benefit of all. That's your job, isn't it? To convey to the community that this is not just about their backyard; it's about what's best for Ireland." He spoke slowly, enunciating each word as if she were a child.

The condescension floored her. She fought to keep the pink from rising past her neck to her hairline. *Breathe*, she cautioned herself. *Just breathe.* "How will you protect the chough?" she asked.

"Excuse me?" The deputy minister blinked once and pushed his glasses tight against the bridge of his nose.

"The Red-billed Chough. You will have an epic public relations battle on your hands unless you know exactly how to respond to the claims that this mine will drive an endangered bird from its nesting grounds and destroy its habitat."

"I hardly think I need to be told how to respond to outraged environmentalists. I've been at this business longer than you've been alive."

Annie suppressed a snort of laughter. "Thank you for the compliment, but that isn't the point, Mr. Doyle. You don't seem to understand. I'm not the enemy. If you get upset with me and can't answer my questions here, behind closed doors, how do you think you will manage in front of a crowd of protesters, all waving banners emblazoned with a little black crow with a bright red beak and shouting, 'Save the choughs! Save Beara!'? I've been doing my job a long time, too. I know you have to be more than one step ahead of the opposition. You have to write their business plan for them and then crush it with your own."

The deputy minister's pupils tightened and his nostrils flared, but his voice remained even. "Point taken. I'm not an environmental expert, and I admit to knowing very little about our red-billed friend. I imagine we all have our jobs to do."

The needled implication wasn't lost on Annie, and she grabbed at it. "Well, my job is to take your plans and sell them to the people of Beara. I have asked James and Colm to participate in a community meeting to outline the mine's benefits and to address concerns. It would send a powerful message if someone from the DCENR were there." *But not you.*

They'll eat your career civil servant ass alive. "What if someone from the Environmental Protection Agency office in Cork attended? A gesture of unity from government departments that would seem to have opposing positions would be powerful. If the Irish government is completely supportive of the mine, that is."

Hugh Doyle's eyes bulged, and he looked to Colm and James, as if expecting one of them to start laughing and assure him Annie's speeches were part of some grand, belated April Fool's gag.

"Community meeting?" he choked out. "What's this about a community meeting?"

"It's a scheme of Annie's." Colm stepped in to smooth things over, throwing Annie a warning look. She could hear the curse in his rich brogue, and she nearly provided the outburst of laughter that could have broken the tension in the room. "But nothing's been arranged."

"Well, thank God for that," said the deputy minister, wiping a hand across his desk blotter. He glanced at his watch. "If this injunction is successful, we'd only appear like idiots trying to sell the community a project that's been stalled due to environmental reasons."

"Wouldn't that be the ideal time to rally the peninsula?" When James finally spoke up, even Annie stared at him as if he'd lost his senses.

"Look," he continued, sitting forward in his chair, "if we come in with a clear statement of how many jobs these mines could bring, with euro amounts attached, and let people know the project is in jeopardy because outsiders are protesting and deciding what's right for Beara, the community could do our jobs for us. The government would have to respond to the pressure from its people, and Eire-Evergreen could rise above the controversy."

Annie had to admit this could work—but it could also backfire, depending on which symbol appealed more to people's sense of standing up for the little guy: the beleaguered Irish blue-collar worker or the defenseless little crow.

All eyes were on her.

"It's a possibility, but I don't think we can take the troops rallying around the cause of big business for granted. The meetings aren't a 'scheme' of mine. They are a required part of the confirmation process. As deputy minister, I expect you'd know this." She glanced away before he could react. "We need to arrive with clear answers of what will happen to this bird and its habitat and have a plan that everyone can live with."

Discussion moved to the offshore site and to the motion that would be filed that very day by Eire-Evergreen's attorneys to separate the undersea work from the proposed mine at the cove. The deputy minister ceased to look in Annie's direction, and after a few minutes, it was if she were no longer in the room.

There was a soft tap at the door. The DM's assistant poked her head inside. "Eire-Evergreen's attorneys are here. Should I show them to the conference room?"

"Thank you. We'll be along in a minute." Hugh's eyes, focused on James, moved ever so slightly to his left. In Annie's direction. She was dismissed.

"Right." James smoothed his palms over his trousers and turned to her. "Annie, you'll have to excuse us while we meet with the attorneys. I'm not certain how long we'll be, so how about I text you and we can meet for lunch?"

~

Annie drifted down a tree-lined avenue, passing a somber Gothic church, her thoughts carried on Gaelic words recited by a man who had broken so easily through her defenses. She turned right onto Earlsfort Terrace and headed toward the campus of Trinity College.

She entered the university green by way of Nassau Street. A fine April day, and the grounds were full of tourists. She walked toward the Old Library, where the magnificent, barrel-vaulted Long Room housed thousands of priceless volumes, and the climate-controlled treasury guarded the ancient Book of Kells. Standing before the massive gray stone Georgian building, she took in the line of tourists snaking along the sidewalk and around the shorn green grounds of Library Square.

No, not here. She wended her way between buildings of stone and brick, retracing her steps and dodging the crowds, not certain what she was looking for, why she'd wandered into this space that held ancient wisdoms and yet burst with modern life, young life …

"Can I help you?" A woman with long black hair, pale blue eyes, and creamy skin with a pepper-mill dash of tiny brown freckles across her nose stood with her toes turned out like a ballet dancer's. She held a black, soft-sided instrument case over one shoulder and clutched a black portfolio in her other hand. Her dress of sky-blue matched her eyes and flowed over thin leather boots. "Are you lost?"

"Not yet, I don't think." And then she knew why she'd come. "I was looking for the central library. Other than the Old Library, I mean. I'm hoping to find a translation of some Gaelic words."

"Ah, what you want is the Berkeley. It's just there, to the left of the Old Library. But I speak Gaelic. Could I possibly help?"

"You do? Of course you do." Annie laughed, scrabbling around in her leather satchel for her Moleskine journal, in which she written the few words she could remember. Once again, fate trumped coincidence.

"Sure. I'm from Ballinskelligs on the Kerry Peninsula, so. It's Gaeltacht—a Gaelic-speaking community."

"I've been there," Annie said, fully under the young woman's spell. "My husband and I hiked the Kerry Way a few years ago. It's beautiful."

"Yes, I miss it terribly. It feels impossibly far away from the city sometimes. I'm not really built for city life. But the master violinist I most wanted to study under is here, so ... " She nodded to the blue, bound volume Annie had retrieved from her bag.

"Oh, I'm so sorry. Here. I was hoping to find a translation for this." She held out the journal where it opened like a hymnal to the desired page. "I think it's a poem. Or a song? I've written it phonetically. I have no idea what it would look like in Gaelic."

The young woman scanned the handwritten words, her lips moving as she worked to make sense of Annie's contorted spelling. "This is an easy one." She closed the journal and returned it to Annie. "It's a poem most Irish children learn in their primary days. The first line, *Mise Éire*, is the poem's title. It means *I am Ireland*."

"Yes, *misha aira*—those are the words, but I had no idea what they meant."

"Have you heard the legend of the Hag of Beara?"

"Hag? No, I—"

"The Hag is the symbol of the Irish woman," she said, laughing at Annie's bewildered expression. "Look, this is getting heavy." Her head tilted to her shoulder, and her dark hair spilled across the instrument case strap pulling at her neck. "Do you have a few minutes? I could tell you about the legend."

"I'm so sorry. I must be keeping you from class."

"Not at all. Let's just sit for a moment." She walked toward a maple tree, and Annie followed, enchanted. The woman sank onto a bench beneath the tree.

"I'm Caoimhe, by the way. Caoimhe Burke."

"This is pronounced *kee-va*?" Annie asked, pointing to the string of letters, the young woman's name, sewn onto the fabric of the music case.

"Yes." Caoimhe giggled. "Irish Gaelic is so different from English. It's really impossible to sound things out by the way they look. 'Ao' is a long 'e,' like *tree*. 'Mh' is usually a 'v' sound, but it can be 'w' as well. It also depends which dialect you're speaking. Of course, I use Munster." Eyelids fluttering closed. A secret smile. Then her bright blue eyes again searched Annie's face. "But I promised to tell you about the Hag of Beara. Do you know the Beara Peninsula, in Cork?"

Where else? "I'm staying just outside Ballycaróg."

"Well, then. The Old Woman is your neighbor. Along the Beara Way, between Eyeries and Ardgroom, is the Kilcatherine Peninsula. Not far from Kilcatherine Church is a small strip of land that extends into Coulagh Bay. The Hag rests there, turned to stone by a priest millennia ago. Her profile gazes out to the bay. She is *an Chailleach Bhéarra*, the Old Woman of Beara, who shaped our land. It's said she lived seven lives, each representing a different stage of a woman's life, from childhood to crone. Her many children have carried her name and legend throughout Ireland and Scotland." Caoimhe's voice slowed and deepened, the retelling of the Hag's legend bringing her into a calm, almost meditative state.

"That's walking distance from Ballycaróg. A fair hike, but ... what does *an ... kha-yukh* Beara have to do with this poem?"

Caoimhe grinned at Annie's butchered pronunciation but did not correct her. "It's all woven together. This poem was written by the Irish patriot Patrick Henry Pearse, who was executed in 1916 because of his role in the Easter Rising. His poem uses the symbolism of the Old Woman of Beara as a symbol of Ireland itself. *An Chailleach Bhéarra* represents fertility and the power and resilience of the Irish woman, but she is also our mother, our protector, the true embodiment of the Irish people and our land."

"So this poem should be easy to find?"

"Of course. But I know it by heart." She closed her eyes and began to recite each line in a soft, singsong voice, one line in Irish, followed by the English translation. As her voice slowed, it deepened until it sounded to Annie like the voice that followed her on Beara—rich and full of weight and texture.

Mise Éire:
Sine mé ná an Chailleach Bhéarra.
I am Ireland:
I am older than the Old Woman of Beara.

Mór mo ghlóir:
Mé a rug Cú Chulainn cróga.
Great my glory:
I who bore Cuchulainn, the brave.

Mór mo náir:
Mo chlann féin a dhíol a máthair.
Great my shame:
My own children who sold their mother.

Mór mo phian:
Bithnaimhde do mo shíorchiapadh.

Great my pain:
My irreconcilable enemy who harasses me continually.

Mór mo bhrón:
D'éag an dream inar chuireas dóchas.
Great my sorrow:
That crowd, in whom I placed my trust, died.

Mise Éire:
Uaigní mé ná an Chailleach Bhéarra.
I am Ireland:
I am lonelier than the Old Woman of Beara.

Caoimhe opened her eyes. Her irises were almost invisible in the sunlight that shot through the tender young foliage. Her hands rested in her lap, knitted together loosely, and her back was straight. Annie thought again of a dancer, her lithe body leaping across a stage.

"That was beautiful. Thank you." She smoothed her palm over the cover of her journal. "I don't understand what it means. I understand the words now, of course," she hastened to add. "But I wish I knew why this poem has appeared in my life."

"How did you find it?"

How to explain the voices without sounding as though she'd lost her mind? Yet if anyone would understand about voices carried in the wind, it would be this beguiling musician.

"A friend. Well. Not a friend exactly. A walking guide in Ballycaróg. I meant to ask him what it meant, but—"

"A walking guide?" Caoimhe interrupted. Her soft voice carried an edge.

"Daniel Savage. He's an artist, but he leads hikes on the Beara and Kerry peninsulas."

A shadow passed across the young woman's face. The air rippled with a sudden chill, and it smelled like rain. Annie blinked, and the shadow was gone.

"I've got a class in a few minutes." Caoimhe touched the straps of the portfolio and instrument cases that were draped across her feet. "I really need to be on my way."

"Of course. You have been unbelievably sweet to sit here with me. I can't thank you enough."

They stared at each other for a heartbeat, and then Caoimhe sighed. She leaned in and pressed her cheek against Annie's. "If your friend truly is a guide, Annie, let him," she whispered in Annie's hair.

Annie watched her cross the green. As Caoimhe passed the spot where they'd met, Annie was jolted by a thought.

She rushed forward to catch up with Caoimhe. But the paved walkways filled with chattering, gesticulating, singing, shouting tourists and university students who rushed from one building to the next or into the surrounding city streets. Annie lost sight of the raven-haired woman who had, inexplicably, known her name.

She felt bereft, yet elated—that strange sensation of bittersweet yearning that had coursed through her since she'd arrived in Ireland. She left the university grounds and retraced her steps south. She wanted to go home. Back to Beara. Her phone, which she'd dropped into the pocket of her jacket, vibrated against her hip. The screen showed James's mobile number. She sent the call to voice mail.

She could have walked back to James's apartment, but suddenly time felt of the essence. She flagged a taxi, and in less than an hour—after grabbing her things and leaving James's key card with the concierge—she was back on the street, hailing another. There were several daily trains to Cork, and she made the two o'clock with minutes to spare. Ignoring a handful of calls, Annie switched off her phone and watched the scenery flow past. Leaving Eire-Evergreen's Opel in the long-term lot at the Cork station, she rented another car from a local service.

~

After Bantry Bay, the road curved to the west, and the incoming tide spit the North Atlantic over stone barriers and onto the highway. Annie pulled into a turnout, slammed the car door shut, and opened her arms wide, embracing the rocks, the hills, the rush of wind and water, the scent of soil, animal, rain, and sea.

She hitched herself onto the hood of the car and tapped her heels against a tire, watching as the evening sun tipped over the bay, shooting rays of copper and gold across the hilltops of bare rock. Her career had ended today. And she'd never felt so free.

Arriving at the Moyle cottage just before seven, she showered and ate. Only then did she turn on her phone. After several quiet hours on her own, she'd gathered a small reserve of calm strength to place the calls she had to make.

The first was to the small hotel in Ballycaróg. She planned to be out of the cottage in the morning, but she wasn't ready to leave Ireland, not just yet. Her plane ticket had an open return, and she trusted she would know when it was time to book the flight home.

The second was to Serena. Annie calculated the time difference and took a chance that Serena would be back in her office after lunch. It was early Monday afternoon. She'd catch her before the weekly finance meeting got underway at three.

"Funny, I was just about to call you," Serena said, her voice tight. Of course, she must have heard from James by now.

"My reputation precedes me, I take it."

"This was a bad choice, wasn't it? You weren't ready to take on something of this magnitude, and it's my fault for believing you were." Serena's voice flattened, disappointed but resigned. Annie pictured her scanning e-mails or editing a document by hand as she spoke, distancing herself from the conversation and her employee's plight.

"I was ready. I am ready. I've done good work here. Work I'm proud of. In theory," she added. Then cursed herself, silently.

"What exactly does 'in theory' mean, Annie?" The sharp tone returned. "No. Never mind. It can hardly matter now. I spoke with James MacKenna a few hours ago. He brought me up to speed, including how you left Dublin without a word to anyone."

"How much do you really know of what's going on here?" Annie blurted, frustration overwhelming caution. She winced. Her question pointed at territory to which she wasn't ready to lead Serena just yet. If ever. She had too much to find out first.

"What are you talking about?" Serena's voice snapped from detached to flashing fury.

Annie pulled her Moleskine notebook toward her. "Thank goodness I took good notes. I asked James MacKenna why Magnuson + Associates had been contracted, when Eire-Evergreen had their own in-house PR team. He informed me he'd asked for me personally, based on the pitch I'd made to him last year at the SME conference."

There was silence on the other end. Annie sensed the tension, felt Serena, waiting, motionless. "But apparently it was more than just my killer pitch that won him over. It seems I slept with our client last year at that same conference. I'm pretty hazy on the details—I was blacking out regularly at that point. Vodka in my water bottle, you know. But let's see. Here's what I've got—and I quote—'You know how to win people's hearts. That's what we're after here. You're terrific at your job. Or at least you were.'

"That last bit caught me off guard, Serena. Well, I was pretty floored already, but you let slip that I was in some sort of trouble."

"No, I did not." Serena's voice was low and controlled, a steel spring of anger held in place by dignity. "I merely said you'd been on leave and wouldn't be up to the demands of a complicated, extended campaign."

"Yes, well. I guess that sounds about right."

"Yes, Annie. As a matter of fact, it does. It doesn't sound as if you were up for this at all. Despite whatever good work you've done *in theory*"—the emphasis was delivered with a bite of sarcasm—"it appears that in reality, it's time for you to back out and leave this campaign in someone else's hands. Given the obvious personal conflicts, I have to insist."

"Whatever I say to you now will sound like an excuse. But I will not be manipulated or insulted by a client, and I will not be intimidated into leaving the firm."

"Did you sleep with him again?"

"The offer was made." Annie heard an intake of breath on the other line. "But no. I declined."

There was silence. Annie held a hand in front of her face. It shook. Cold sweat dampened her armpits and beaded around her hairline.

"When are you returning to Seattle?" Serena's voice had lost its edge but not the chill.

"I'm not sure. I'm moving out of this house tomorrow, and I'll purchase my own ticket home. I'll be in touch in the coming days."

"There's no need to purchase another plane ticket. Don't play the martyr. Just use the one you have. Take as long as you need. Maybe you should have just taken a true vacation instead of returning to work. Who knows?"

"Yes, who knows? If there is a playbook for addiction recovery, they didn't hand it out at rehab. Or maybe I slept through that session."

"What are you doing?" Serena softened. But Annie's heart didn't. She couldn't let it.

"I'm trying to do the right thing. Which isn't working in support of this mine."

"How can you say that? You've seen the data. The impact on the community will be minimal."

"How can *you* say that? This mine will destroy the habitat of a bird. Ruin a fragile ecology."

"Eire-Evergreen will work to ameliorate that. You are more aware than anyone what can be done."

"What I'm aware of, what I believe in my heart, is that this is the wrong thing to do."

"If I take you off this assignment, I will have no choice but to recommend to the board that you be put on administrative leave, and your role in this firm will have to be reevaluated. You recall the deal we made, Annie. This was one last chance."

"I would expect nothing less from you, Serena. I will seek counsel of my own. Trust me on that."

After their terse good-byes, the phone sat in Annie's palm, no larger or heavier than a deck of cards and holding the same element of chance. Confronting Serena took what little she'd had in reserve, and she wondered if she'd really accomplished anything. Perhaps she had called hoping Serena would fire her, so she wouldn't be faced with the decision to quit. So she could turn her termination over to an attorney and say, "Look, I'm in recovery; they gave me too big of a job, and now they're firing me."

Serena was too smart to fall into that trap and Annie too stubborn to quit. She'd lose any legal claim if she did. So they were at a draw, giving Annie a precious few hours, maybe even a day or two, to continue finding out what she could about Eire-Evergreen and what was looking more like their own Special Protection Area within the Irish government.

She let the phone slide from her hand and fall onto the sofa beside her. It hit a pillow and bounced to the floor, and Annie flipped it away with her toe, filled with disgust at the way the thing carried with it connections to her past, insisting she respond, listen, call, defend the person she was trying to leave behind. Bill's voice echoed in her head: *Ain't no leaving yourself behind, Annie. There's only facing who you are.*

Bill. AA. She hadn't gone to a meeting today, another she'd missed since arriving in Ireland. She didn't want to talk to her sponsor. She didn't want to go to another meeting. She wanted out of her own skin, away from The Addict who had taken over her life and seemed hell-bent on destroying every good thing she'd built. Just when she had found some peace.

The fatigue she'd felt moments after hanging up the phone with Serena was replaced by a restlessness, and that by a sudden need for the muscle-and-mind-dulling effects of a drink, the momentary alleviation of pain and shame. Something strong, fast, and burning: whiskey that smelled of peat and stone, the butterscotch warmth of cognac, the sweet rush of bourbon.

Annie's hand formed a cup in the air, and she swirled her imaginary tumbler and inhaled, her nose wrinkling at the rich burn. She missed it. The liquor. Annie lifted the glass to her lips, where the embers burned, the flames trickled down her throat.

The bar at the hotel would still be open. She could leave the cottage now, check in tonight, and sit in the amber dark of the wood-paneled bar and let the booze bury her thoughts. No one would know. No one would miss her. No one would expect her to show up for work tomorrow.

She drained the imaginary liquid and set the imaginary glass on the coffee table in front of her. Her Moleskine had opened to the page she turned to the most: the words from *Mise Éire*. Her lips moved with effort over her phonetic translation, trying to remember the way those strange syllables had formed in Caoimhe's throat and passed through her lips.

Her hands shook even more as she pulled on a pair of running tights and zipped her running jacket over a cotton-poly shirt. In the foyer, she laced her shoes tight, turned on the porch light, and shut the door behind her.

38

Bannon skirted the table, her toenails clicking with purpose. She whined. Her high-pitched yelp sent the small offset shears shooting from his hand and clattering to the floor.

"Sweet Jesus!" he shouted, and the blue heeler barked, but she stood her ground, staring at him with her eyes of liquid coal. The last light of evening had faded—the high windows to the west retained a golden glow, but those facing north and east had darkened to thick blue. Chilled air pushed through the door he'd left open as he worked. The spotlight from his headlamp allowed him to focus on the fine detail before him, and the daylight hours had passed unnoticed. He'd skipped dinner, and now Bannon clamored for hers.

"You're right, girl. It's time to call it quits." He picked up the snips from the floor, removed the headlamp, and arranged his workspace with the same precise attention he displayed while creating. Bannon sat at attention, following Daniel's every motion, the tiny black patches of her eyebrows shifting up and down as her tail swept the ground in hopeful anticipation.

At last, Daniel pulled the tab on a can of dog food and forked the contents into a bowl. He sat on the front step and placed the bowl at his feet. As Bannon inhaled her dinner, he rubbed her back and craned his head down the driveway. He could see the roof of the Moyle house. In his hand was a key Gary Moyle had given him a couple of years ago after Daniel had readily agreed to keep an eye out and tend to simple maintenance between tenants. It was the least he could do to repay the Moyles, who directed so many tourists to West Ireland Excursions.

He turned the Moyle house key over and under his fingers. He hadn't seen Annie since Saturday, when she'd simply up and walked away from his studio. She seemed to have vanished. He'd twice passed the Moyles' driveway, and the Opel was gone.

"What am I doing, sis?" The heeler leaned heavily into his bent legs, her tail thumping. "Who is she to me?" A fellow survivor. A fellow addict for whom he felt a sense of responsibility.

"Dammit." He sprang up, and Bannon barked at the sudden movement. In two minutes he'd grabbed his jacket, his phone, and the guide pack he kept readied with supplies and set off down the lane toward the cottage.

A VW Polo sat in the Moyles' driveway. Daniel sagged with relief. Yet his knock on the front door went unanswered. He climbed the back patio steps and peered through the large glass doors. A small lamp next to the sofa glowed. Annie's laptop sat on the kitchen counter, closed but plugged in. He tried the door handle. Locked. He went back around front and tried the handle there. Then Daniel inserted the key.

A slow, heavy drumbeat of fear at finding Annie collapsed on the floor, passed out in a puddle of vomit. Or worse. This gave way to a warm rush of relief as he searched the small cottage, seeing evidence of Annie's presence but no signs of distress. Shoving aside his guilt over invading this private space, Daniel snooped. He opened the refrigerator, kitchen cupboards, and trash. Beyond some fruit and vegetable peelings, the rubbish bins were empty. The recycling held plastic and glass water bottles, yogurt containers, a copy of *The Irish Times*. No beer or wine bottles, corks, wrappers, receipts. Clothing hung in the closets or lay neatly folded in the drawers. Her camera bag sat on the kitchen table, and there was a novel on the nightstand. Annie wasn't here, but the things that seemed to hold her essence were.

"Where are you?" He imagined Annie at the door, her shock at his intrusion, and his own voice stuttering out an explanation: *I was worried. Afraid you'd gone over the edge. I had to make certain you were all right.*

He left the way he'd entered.

Night had deepened to black, but the skies were clear and the moon was a hard, gleaming coin that bounced countless reflections off the sea. Too restless to return home, Daniel buckled the backpack strap across his chest and strode up the hill across the road from the Moyle house. He'd take the long way around and eventually end up in town, where there would be pan-fried trout and creamed potatoes at Tich Na Leigh. And bad but hot coffee. Bannon raced ahead, thrilled to be on an adventure after dark, when creatures might emerge from their hidey-holes in the thick shrubs or from under stone walls.

"Bannon. Hey, girl. I'm so glad to see you."

Daniel stopped and stilled his breath, listening past the breeze that ruffled the short grass. The bowl shaped by the hills made a perfect amphitheater, carrying the woman's voice across a hectare or more, but it sounded as if she stood only steps away. He wondered for a moment if it was the voice of the spirit that had brought him to *Mise Éire*. Then he heard his name.

"Daniel?"

He followed the voice, rounding one side of the bowl. His headlamp illuminated the scene before him: Annie lay just off the side of the road. Bare skin flashed white through her running tights and the arm of her jacket. She breathed heavily, through the tendrils of hair clinging to her face. The heeler sat by her side, whining, tail swishing the gravel; it began to thump as Daniel approached. Bannon circled and sniffed Annie, her snout worrying over the torn strips of fabric along Annie's right side.

39

In the split second before her toe snagged on the rock and she went flying, Annie's stomach dropped and her mind screamed, *Not again!* Her body had a premonition of the impending calamity except for her hapless foot, which moved forward of its own will. The moment froze in time, and then shattered in a million pieces, each crying *Noooo* as she flew through the air.

Her instinct was to protect that vulnerable, damaged left leg, and she fell heavily on her right hip. The sharp points of a rock bed ground into the muscle of her glute and into her bicep and shoulder as she angled her body away from her knees and tucked her head. Then all motion stopped. Her breath rasped loud and hot against her sternum.

She lay half on the dirt shoulder of the road, half in the shallow ditch where she'd tripped, coming off the hill. She was afraid to move. These precious moments of shock hid whatever damage she'd done in that five-second tumble. But she had to get out of the road. She'd emerged from the trail along a blind curve, and oncoming cars wouldn't see her; there wouldn't be time to get out of the way.

As she raised her torso, the pain cascaded in a wave of nausea. She stopped, drew in a deep breath, and rolled onto her behind. Her palm stung as dozens of tiny stones spilled from her torn skin. But she could stretch and bend her left leg. She brushed her palm against her thigh, wincing as she dislodged more pebbles, and leaned onto her hand to push herself up to sitting.

The right side of her running tights was shredded from her waist to her calf. White skin shone through, but it was streaked with black. Her arm and shoulder hurt too much to move; a slight tilt of her head was enough to see that her jacket was torn.

"Okay, kiddo. Breathe. It's all right. Just breathe." The realization that she hadn't hit her head on the sharp edge of a rock or against the tarmac brought tears of relief, and she began to shake. Suddenly, she was very cold.

"This isn't good. Stay calm." Her hat lay in the middle of the road, but her headlamp was nowhere to be seen. She'd been going at a slow clip—maybe eight-minute miles—but she couldn't be more than a fifteen-minute walk from the village. If she could manage to walk, that is.

She needed to get out of this road. Rolling onto her left side, she scooted until she lay with her legs below her in the ditch, her back cushioned by the water pack still strapped across her chest. She maneuvered the tube into her mouth, and the deep swallows of water soothed her shaking insides.

A yip and scrabbling of feet. Annie barely had time to absorb the sound coming toward her from the trail when a low, blocky shadow burst out of the dark, off a small rise, and a warm body was suddenly at her side, whining, a rough tongue licking her ear.

"Bannon. Hey, girl. I'm so glad to see you." With her left hand, Annie rubbed the heeler under her jaw and scratched the knob of bone between her small ears, breathing in the moist breath that smelled like grass and toast. She wanted to draw the warm bulk into her, curl the cold ache of her body into that sweet dog and just rest. She was so tired.

Daniel. If there was Bannon, could he be far behind? "Daniel?" she ventured.

Bannon went rigid, her ears shot up, and her tail made a few tentative wags. Then, with a bark, she shot off, back along the trail the way she'd come. Within moments, the dog stood at her feet again, Daniel quickly closing the gap between them. Annie went limp with relief. The tears came unbidden.

"Ah, Jesus, Annie." He knelt beside her. "No, don't move." He touched her face and her head with the pads of his fingers.

"I didn't hit my head. I can feel everything. Trust me. My right side is one big world of pain."

Daniel shrugged off his backpack and unzipped a pocket in the front. He pulled out a small square and snapped it open. A plastic shock blanket unfurled like a silver sail and settled over Annie's body. He moved to her right side, lifted the blanket away, and sucked in air.

"It is bad?"

"It's hard to see in this light. How long have you been here?" He took her wrist and pressed two fingers into her skin, searching for her pulse.

"Five minutes?" Annie realized she didn't know, hadn't looked at her watch, had lost all sense of passing time. She knew only how fortunate she was now. And that it was Daniel who found her. How closely could she look at this coincidence without feeling as if she were losing her mind? "Ten maybe? I was able to move myself into this ditch."

"Are you cold?"

"No." She shivered involuntarily. "Okay. Yes."

He folded her hand between his warm palms. "Your pulse

is strong. Do you feel lightheaded?"

"A bit stunned, but I'm okay. I'd like to try and move."

"Nope. I'm calling 999."

"If that's an ambulance, don't. Daniel, please. I'm fine." He'd already pulled a phone from his pack. Annie heaved herself to her elbows, pushed against her palms, and scooted back on her bottom until she sat upright. She brushed off her palms, gritting her teeth against the pain.

"See? Good as gold."

Daniel lifted the blanket and moved his hand gently down her leg. She winced and huffed a quick breath as he neared her knee, but the anticipation of pain was worse than the reality. He ran tentative fingers over her kneecap, gently probing.

"You took a hell of a tumble, but your knee seems to be okay. If your leg were broken, you'd be babbling in pain by now." He sat back on his heels and flipped on a small flashlight she hadn't noticed. He lifted the blanket again and peered at her leg.

"Looks like you landed here?" He shifted up to her hip. She could feel stone under her right buttock and cold air against her bare skin. "And here?" He touched her upper arm and shoulder, where fabric had peeled away in a long panel.

"I'd like to stand up."

Daniel crouched behind her and wrapped his hands around her waist. "Is that okay? No pain?"

"You're good. Just don't let that right hand go any lower. I'm not sure I have any skin left."

"Lean into me. Let me take all of your weight."

Annie pushed up on her left leg, and as she felt her balance sway, she tried to relax into the wall of Daniel's body behind her. Her right leg straightened and her foot touched the earth without a jolt, but her upper body throbbed, and she became aware of the tender ache in her ribs. She'd be a mass of contusions, road burn, and pain tomorrow.

Daniel still held her by the waist, and she pushed his hands away, her humiliation nearly equal to her pain. She took a first tentative step and grabbed his wrist as an arrow of pain pierced the flesh of her thigh and glute.

"Son of a bitch." She sucked air through her teeth.

"We're five minutes from the village. I'll run in, get Mack's car from the pub, and we'll take you to Liz Farley's surgery. You'll stay here with Bannon. I'll be back in fifteen minutes, tops."

"No. I can make it. I just need get the blood flowing. Do you have a walking stick?"

He helped her ease into a rain slicker that hung almost to her knees. She felt like a child. The torn running tights stayed where they were—the blood was drying, and Annie cringed at the thought of tearing them away from her raw skin. Daniel wrapped the shock blanket around her waist and tied it at her hip, the plastic skirt crinkling in the wind. He extended a collapsible walking stick and slipped the strap over Annie's right hand; then he hitched his pack over his shoulders and took Annie's left hand in his right.

"We'll take it slow. It's less than a kilometer downhill."

Annie's body and mind felt divided in two. On the right side, pulsating pain and the sense that with each step, her skin tore and her muscles separated. On her left, the solidity of someone else's strength, gripping her and moving her forward. Fear and peace, vulnerability and trust.

They limped together in silence, and within minutes the lights of Ballycaróg appeared. He brought her to the inner foyer of the hotel and set her gently on a cushioned bench, leaving Bannon to sit beside her while he walked through the lobby and disappeared down a hallway. The dog rested her snout on Annie's knee while Annie stroked her soft, square head. Moments later the door to the lobby slid open, and a tall, thin woman entered, holding a mug, steam rising from inside.

"I've called for Doc Farley, but she's on an emergency obstetrics call in Adrigole." The woman knelt beside Annie, her black hair hanging in two long braids over her shoulder. "I'm Kate Ahern. My husband and I run this place. Here." She handed the ceramic mug to Annie.

"Thank you," she murmured and brought the warm drink to her mouth. At the first sip she choked and spat it back into the mug. The hot flush of embarrassment made her forget for an instant the pain in her body.

"I'm sorry," she said, seeing Kate's shocked face. "I don't drink alcohol. I can't." Every nerve and fiber pinged and pulsed with alarm and desire. She sucked the sweet burn of whiskey-laced tea from her lips. She thrust the cup back into Kate's hands while her head screamed, *Keep it! Drink it!*

"Oh, Annie, I'm so sorry. I should have told you there was a dram of whiskey in it. Stay here. I'll get some straight tea. Honey okay?"

"It's okay. I mean, I'm fine. I just want to go home." Her flushed face quivered, and to her deeper shame, she began to cry.

"Daniel went round back to get our car. He'll have you home in no time. You're staying at the Moyle cottage?"

Headlights shone into the foyer. Annie nodded, wiped her face with the back of her hand, and pushed herself upright, leaning heavily on the walking stick. Now, instead of feeling like a child, she felt a hundred years old. Kate and Daniel helped her into the front seat. They exchanged words on the driver's side, Kate shaking her head and Daniel placing a reassuring hand on her arm. She turned her face away as Daniel opened his car door.

"I'm taking you to my sister's," he said, starting the engine. "Yes, I am," he added as Annie began to protest. She gave him a hard stare, which he did not meet.

"Please thank Kate for me. For the tea and the ride."

"Not to worry, Annie. We look out for each other here."

Annie was grateful for Daniel's silence as they drove the few miles toward the cove and into the hills beyond. Fiana waited at the patio door, holding it wide as they mounted the back steps.

"Daniel, just set her at the kitchen table. Cat's putting the kettle on."

~

She asked to be shown to the bathroom. Her bladder pounded, but more than anything—now that she was safe—she wanted a moment alone. Daniel led her down a short hallway off the kitchen and flipped on the light.

"Should I wait outside?"

"I've got it. Thanks. I'll be out in a few minutes."

"Clean towels in the closet. Pain reliever's in the cabinet. Use whatever you need. Fi won't mind."

She nodded and waited for him to shut the door behind her. A bottle labeled *paracetamol* sat on the second shelf of the medicine cabinet. With the remaining battery power on her phone, Annie tapped into the unprotected Wi-Fi and did a quick search online to make certain an alcoholic could take whatever it was without fear of disrupting her tenuous grip on sobriety. There it was. On the safe list; also known as acetaminophen. Tylenol. She unscrewed the cap with shaking hands and shook out two pills. Leaning against the sink, she lifted her head to face her reflection.

Her eyes were black stones against her white skin, the green irises nearly swallowed by wide pupils. A band still held most of her ponytail together, but limp strands of hair stuck to her face. She unzipped Daniel's rain slicker and let it drop to the floor, then unzipped her running jacket. Her thin technical shirt clung damply to her skin, but she couldn't raise her right arm more than a few inches from her side. The shirt would have to be cut off. She pushed it up and turned her right side to the mirror. Red. In a few hours it would be blue and green.

There was a soft knock on the door. "Annie? It's Fiana. May I come in?"

She closed her eyes and drew in a deep breath. "Sure."

With silent concentration, Fiana dampened a washcloth with warm water and pressed softly against Annie's leg and shoulder, loosening the blood and fabric that had dried together. Once the skin was soft enough, she used her sewing shears to cut through the fabric of Annie's running tights and shirt. Annie stood trembling in her bra and panties, tensing at the sting of antiseptic as Fiana dabbed away the road grit.

Sitting on the edge of the claw-foot tub, Fiana worked in silence but for a few gentle instructions: "Turn just a bit for me," "Can you raise your arm, love?" and "This will hurt, I'm afraid." At last she looked up. "The mother in me would have insisted on taking you to the hospital. But I wouldn't have wanted to go, either, if I were you. You'll be right as rain. Sore, but all right. Have you eaten?"

Her matter-of-fact manner was a balm to Annie's frayed nerves. "I could use something."

Fiana pressed her palms against her thighs and rose to standing. "Why don't you stay here tonight? We've got a guest room just down the hall. You can have a proper soak in this tub." Annie's head was shaking no, but Fiana persisted. "You can accept help, Annie."

There was another knock on the door. "Ma?"

"That'd be Cat. I asked her to scrounge up some clothes for you. Is it all right if she comes in?"

Annie was too weary to care. "Of course."

Fiana opened the door just enough to let Catriona angle in, a bundle of clothing pressed against her chest. "Hi, Annie." She took in the scraped and bruised skin and whistled. "Jaysus. You took a tumble."

"Thanks much for that astute observation, daughter." Fiana took the clothing from her arms and handed Annie a T-shirt and cable knit pullover.

Annie looked up helplessly. "I can't raise my arm. I'm sorry. Any chance of a zip or button-up?"

"Of course." She took the tops from Annie and hastened out the door.

"You're gorgeous," Cat said, handing her a pair of pink cotton sweatpants with a drawstring waist. "I didn't think women could really look like that—I thought muscles were Photoshopped into the magazines."

She tried to laugh, but the ribs in her right side protested. "Thanks, Cat. Though I wish someone could Photoshop out the bruises and road rash I'll have tomorrow." She sat on the closed lid of the toilet and eased the pants over her thighs, standing to tug them to her waist. They were snug, but the brushed fabric was soft and warm.

"Oh, these, too." Catriona handed her a pair of wool socks.

Annie held on to them, not wanting to go through the painful sit-stand routine again.

"I wanted to say I'm sorry for blathering on about my uncle

the other night. I think I just wanted to impress you, and Polly said I probably really betrayed Daniel's confidence. So, I'm sorry." The young woman blushed, her wide face earnest, her eyes shining.

Annie pressed a hand on the girl's arm. "No worries. Just women talking, okay?"

Catriona nodded, still looking miserable.

"Have you said anything to your uncle? About what you shared with me?"

She shook her head, started to speak, but her mother entered, a hooded cardigan in one hand. "Let's leave you alone," said Fiana. "The guest room is next door, first on the right. Daniel is making tea and toast. You'll stay the night. No arguing." She and Catriona left before Annie could protest.

Not that she would have protested too strongly. Yes, there it was. The hope to see Daniel, one last time.

40

"Tea for the walking wounded." Daniel was in the hall, carrying a tea tray, just as Annie emerged from the bathroom. He followed as she limped into the bedroom and set a mug of tea on the nightstand beside the bed. "Chamomile."

Annie pressed her lips into a weak smile and murmured, "Thank you," before sinking gingerly onto the bed. She scooted herself over the duvet until she could brace her back with pillows and slowly brought her legs up, easing them straight in front of her.

He held out a small plate with two pieces of buttered toast. "Honey or raspberry jam?"

Annie shook her head and bit into a piece. Her eyes closed, as chewing was almost too much. She swallowed with effort. "This is perfect," she said, then sighed.

Daniel pulled out a straight-backed chair from the small desk under the window and allowed silence to fall between them. He sensed they both needed the moment to gather their thoughts and Annie, her breath.

"How do you feel?" he asked. She'd finished one slice of toast and got halfway through the other before setting down the plate and picking up the mug of tea from the nightstand. "Really."

"Like an idiot. Really," she said. "An idiot run over by a train. You'd think once would have been enough."

"Sorry?"

"I've done this before," she replied, with a half-smile that ended in a grimace. "The first time ended my running career. Fortunately this time around, I think my pride is more wounded than my leg."

"That scar on your knee," he said.

She halted her tentative shifting on the bed, where she seemed to be seeking the least uncomfortable position. "When did you—"

"When you were in my studio."

Annie nodded, then leaned her head back to rest against the wall and closed her eyes. "I'm not sure what I would have done if you hadn't come along."

"As stubborn as you are? You would have limped into town." He hesitated but decided to risk the question. "I noticed a different car at the cottage. Should we let someone know you're here?"

She raised her head to answer him with open eyes but an unreadable expression. "I returned from Dublin on my own. That's a rental."

A useless nod, as if he understood what she meant. He waited for her to elaborate, but she turned her focus to the mug, worrying her fingers around the warmth. As though answering a question only she could hear, Annie shook her head slowly and returned the mug to the small table beside her.

"Why did you take off from my studio the other day?" he asked, filling the silence. "What happened?"

She moved to wrap her arms around her body, shrinking back into the pillow behind her, as though to protect herself. Then she winced, as if anticipating the pain in her ribs. She held her hands loosely in her lap instead. "What do you mean?"

"Friday night," he began, "after you dropped off the girls, you were in such a hurry to get away. I chalked it up to a need to retreat after we'd met in the pub. I get that. You can only share so much, and then it's as though you need to regain your strength. But when you just vanished Saturday morning, I'll admit I was a little bewildered. Then worried."

"Have you appointed yourself my guardian angel?"

"Maybe in a way I have. I've been clean long enough to know that every single day is a battle against what I want—which is to give in—and what I need—which is not to drink. You are so raw, the hurt just seeps out of you. It's hard to watch that and not want to step in—"

"And save me," she finished.

"Save you from yourself, maybe," he agreed.

"Did you hone that savior complex in prison, or is this a more recent development?"

Daniel's jaw clenched, and his teeth clicked in a syncopated rhythm of irritation. "So, you've heard. Don't know why that surprises me. You switched off like a light after the return trip on Friday. I should have guessed my niece said something."

"Don't blame her," Annie said. "Ironically, she was showing you off. To your niece, it's ancient history. It's part of the legend of Uncle Daniel."

"Ha. The legend of Uncle Daniel. That's rich. A tragedy in three acts."

"But your tragedy is over. You're alive and with your family." As soon as the words were out of her mouth, Annie's eyes rounded in horror. "Daniel, I'm sorry. I didn't mean—"

"Yes. You did mean. You're right to think I've been trying to make up for living ever since I killed that boy. But I never will. We both know that."

"You don't understand."

"What's there to understand? It couldn't be more simple." He stood and pushed his chair against the desk. "I killed a child. I live a peaceful, productive life despite what I've done, and I don't deserve to. I'm aware of that every waking moment of my day and plenty of the sleeping ones as well."

He turned and left her sitting there. This woman who had pulled apart the scars he thought had closed.

41

The guest room overlooked the back gardens, and she heard Daniel trod heavily down the porch steps. She willed him to turn and walk back into house, but the sound of footsteps crunching on the gravel path faded, then disappeared. The door to his studio slammed, and Annie winced.

"No. You don't understand what it has to do with me," she said into the empty room.

~

Annie slept hard, burrowing in the down and cotton bedding inside a silent room. Sleep was so immediate she didn't even turn off the bedside lamp. She woke in the same position, curled in a tight ball on her left side.

A warm bath loosened her stiff muscles and soothed the raw road burn. She felt battered and sore, but the long hours of rest did more to ease her discomfort than even the pain reliever.

Emerging from the bathroom in the same clothes she'd been given the night before, she padded in stocking feet to the kitchen. Fiana and Catriona were outside, hanging laundry. The day was golden and green, a breeze snapped the sheets from the women's hands, and Fiana's dark hair streamed behind her like a sail; she looked young enough to be Catriona's sister. They were laughing—mother and teenage daughter in a moment of sweet communion. Annie's heart pulled with sudden affection and a bittersweet longing to be a part of their tight circle. At sixteen, she'd held her mother's head over a toilet so she could vomit up the dinner that had been stewing in a soup of vodka. Never could she imagine sharing these moments of affectionate intimacy between mother and daughter.

Watching this family settle into their secret rhythms and language had revealed the similarity between angled and edged brother and his soft and petite dark-haired sister. It was in the shape of their faces—the full mouths set into strong jaws—in their wide-set, expressive eyes, and in their gestures. Fiana also raised her left hand to punctuate a phrase, and she had the same shrug and laugh and tilt of head.

These family moments had also brought Ryan vividly to Annie's mind. He was there beside her as she stepped out onto the porch, pulling faces, trying to make her laugh. Her parents were present, too, her mother ignoring Annie to make herself another drink, her father distant and sad until he finally wandered away after Ryan's death. Now he was only a shadow in her life. Family: one filling this place with affection and empathy; the other haunting her with memories and regrets.

"Annie, how do you feel?" Fiana dropped a wet towel in the basket and took her by the arm as Annie made a tentative descent of the porch steps. "I hope we didn't wake you. I've kept the kids working outside so you could get some rest."

"I won't be doing the Hustle anytime soon, but I'm okay. I slept like the dead."

"You did. I peeked in on you a couple of times and had to wait to see those covers moving up and down with your breathing. I'm so glad you slept. But you must be starving."

Annie wanted to crawl inside Fiana's arms, to be embraced by this unconditional compassion. She struggled to understand how anyone could open her home not only to a stranger but to someone who threatened the very integrity and peace of her community. Yet here they stood, two women worlds apart but connected by some force of spirit. "I could eat something," she admitted. "But just tell me where things are. It's probably best that I keep moving a bit."

"Help yourself to whatever you find. If it's breakfast you're after, there's muesli in the big blue ceramic jar on the counter and yogurt or milk in the fridge. Oh, and Annie." She shaded her eyes to block the sun. "Just inside the door is a pair of walking sticks. Daniel wanted you to have those—he thought you might need the support in the next days."

Before Annie could respond, Catriona—her hands now free of linens and her mouth empty of clothing pins—offered a subdued, "Good morning."

Annie waved and pulled herself back into the kitchen. A few minutes later, she eased her bottom onto the top step of the back porch, a bowl of muesli topped with thick strawberry yogurt balanced in one hand. "Ahhh. Okay. I think I'll just stay here the rest of the day, if that's all right?" She leaned against the door frame and turned her face to the sun, letting her limbs sort out their aches as she soaked in the spring warmth.

"Just eat and rest. I'll be finished up here in a tick," Fiana answered. Catriona was nowhere to be seen.

There was a wheelbarrow full of clippings not far from the laundry lines, and a rake balanced across the leaves and branches. Flower beds bloomed in shades of heliotrope, maize, and delicate pinks. Just beyond the garden, windows of Daniel's studio were open to the fresh air. Annie wondered if he was inside but swallowed the question.

"Daniel's gone over to Kenmare to do some work at the gallery. His show opens this weekend." Fiana had followed her gaze across the yard to the studio. Annie nodded her understanding at what she saw written in Fiana's face and picked up her spoon.

Fiana finished hanging the laundry and disappeared around the back of the house. When she returned, she carried a basket full of cut daisies. She dropped onto the step beside Annie and began trimming the flower stems. They sat in comfortable silence until Bannon and Kennedy raced across the yard, followed by Liam. He stopped short at the sight of his mother and picked up the handles of the wheelbarrow. Fiana and Annie chuckled as he pushed the overloaded cart behind a shed.

"Do you have children?" Fiana asked.

Annie set her empty bowl on the step below. "No. We always thought we'd have the time, later, but now it's later and officially too late."

"Nonsense. You have plenty of time."

"My husband and I split up right before I left for Ireland."

"I noticed you don't wear a ring. But that's not what I meant. You don't need a husband to manage a family."

"You do an amazing job raising these two on your own."

Fiana laid her cheek in a palm and tilted her head to Annie. "Their dad left when Liam was four, but that was a blessing, really. His business failed, and he got mean. There were some scary years on my own, but since Danny's been around, the kids have settled down. They both worship him, and it's mutual. Liam and Cat give him direction. A reason to keep moving forward. For a while there, they were his only reason to get out of bed."

"Cat laid out Daniel's past for me the other night." Annie spoke with tenderness, touching her fingers to Fiana's knee. She found herself wanting to hear more, to be included, to be closer to Daniel, even though she'd never see him again. "It wasn't what I expected to hear."

"I don't think he'll ever recover. By choice, I suspect. Five years was the toughest sentence the judge could mete, but sometimes I think Danny wishes it'd been longer. I fear he'll never forgive himself. As long as he wraps up in that mantle of guilt, he'll remain alone, and being alone is the surest punishment he can exact."

"But he's not alone. He has you, the kids, this community, his job, his art. From where I sit, it seems he has a full, rich life."

Fiana pulled her thick hair from her shoulders and coiled it into a loose knot at the back of her neck. "Of course, you're right. Yet somehow he's the loneliest person I know. He keeps everyone at arm's length but us and Mort MacGeoghegan."

"Mort's that lovely man with the beard? From the meeting last week?"

She nodded. "Mort adopted us as his surrogate family after his wife died. Another one to whom I owe a debt for keeping these two in line." She lifted her chin toward the house.

"There's something I want to talk to you about," Annie said. "But first you need to know that I'm leaving the mining project."

Fiana's mouth dropped open.

"Yes, it's true. I came back from Dublin on my own yesterday, and I need to make plans to leave Ireland, soon." She flushed, remembering she'd intended to be out of the cottage first thing this morning. Now she wasn't certain she could lift a laptop, much less a suitcase. But she could still drive. First things first.

"I haven't been fired, and I refuse to quit—we're in a stalemate, and I need to get back to the States to seek some legal advice. So it goes without saying that I must proceed carefully. I can't afford to make any errors of professional judgment, no more than I've already made, at any rate. But this is a question of ethics."

"I don't understand."

"I think it would be worth your while to check on the original applications MacKenna Mining filed with the Department of Communication, Energy and Natural Resources. I would look in particular for the public notices that are required to accompany the initial request for exploration. Also for the names of those at the DCENR who signed off on the applications."

"Are you saying there's something suspicious about the application?"

"I'm saying it would be interesting to see what you find. It may be helpful to get a list of the shareholders or investors of Eire-Evergreen Metals and MacKenna Minings. Look into some of those companies and individuals, compare them with the names at the DCENR, and see if you don't find a matching name or two."

"The mine could bring so many jobs to this community," Fiana said. "You wouldn't believe the number of calls I've had this past week—or maybe you would. All wondering if we know what we're doing, trying to scare away this investment."

"Are you having second thoughts?"

"No, not about the big picture. This isn't the legacy I want for my kids, or this place I love. But I respect that there are other things to consider. It's not a black-and-white issue. Which makes our fight more difficult. We can't really argue the high moral ground, can we? Not when people's livelihoods are at stake."

"You have to see both sides clearly before you can stand firmly on your own ground."

Fiana was silent, and Annie wondered what she'd done, what the woman beside her could be thinking. She stared past the yard into the green hills that rose above their corner of the peninsula. Shadows of stone rose and sank as the sun filtered through clusters of clouds. Seagulls drifted on currents and then pumped white wings to backtrack their flight to the shore. A meadowlark warbled in the hedge, answered by another hidden in the field. Nothing bad could happen here. Or so it seemed.

"Any names in particular I should look for?" Fiana asked at last.

"Start with higher-ups in the Department of Exploration and Mining. That's all I can say for the moment. I've probably said more than I should. But let me know what you find. Perhaps I can help confirm."

"Annie." This time it was Fiana who extended a hand. She placed it on Annie's knee with the gentlest touch, as though aware of the bruising under the pink cover of Annie's drawstring bottoms. "Thank you. Whatever you've risked to share this with me, it means everything."

"Will you do me one favor, in case I don't have a chance to do it myself?"

"Of course."

"Daniel thinks I'm holding what he did against him. I really don't know anything about what happened, and I don't need to. But what he doesn't know is that I lost my brother the same way."

Fiana dropped her hand from Annie's knee. Her mouth formed an O of surprise, but she quickly closed it. "How terrible. Annie, I'm so sorry. When did this happen?"

"It will be ten years this Saturday. Ryan was eighteen."

Fiana pressed fingers to each temple, and her shoulders rose in a deep sigh. "And the person who did it? Did he serve time like Daniel?"

Annie stared into the sweet garden and the hills beyond. If she could just rise and walk into those hills and never stop, never look back, she would. She closed her eyes and moved her head back and forth. A small moan of pain escaped her lips, and she felt Fiana's warm palm on her back, smoothing her shirt, a mother's gesture of comfort and reassurance.

"She didn't serve any time, but she was punished. Our mother was driving the car. She drank herself to death three years ago. A heart attack. I'm terrified I'll end up just like her."

~

She made it back to the Moyle house supported by Daniel's trekking poles. The movement felt good. No. Not good. It hurt like hell, but the best way to heal was to keep her range of motion supple and her muscles strong. It was time to move on, to let go of whatever soft-focus expectations she'd created; she wanted to be clear of Fiana's before Daniel returned.

Annie sat at the kitchen table and contemplated the waterfall of events she needed to set in motion. In her hand, she held the black rectangle of her phone. The battery had run out during the night, but she'd be happy to remain ignorant of the calls that waited. Still, she plugged it in to recharge. She had calls of her own to make. Then, moving carefully, Annie packed her bags and straightened the cottage. Soon it looked as though she'd never been there.

Stepping onto the back patio, she listened for the throaty-sweet voice. Although she now knew the meaning behind the

mysterious words, she was no more enlightened. Why was
Mise Éire meant for her? What did it mean that someone else
had heard the same voice? Not just any someone else. *Daniel*.

At last, with the undulating ocean in front of her for
perspective, she gathered the courage to turn on her phone.
A call from Bill. Two calls from Bill. One last night, another
this morning. A voice mail from her hair stylist to remind her
of an appointment scheduled for Thursday.

She'd forgotten all about the upcoming appointment. But
she hadn't forgotten how it felt to be a barely functional shell,
counting the minutes before she could leave the stylist's chair
and return to her own office, where she could shake out her
hair and clear her mind with her next drink. Two days after
her last cut, whey-faced and defeated, she crossed the Puget
Sound on a ferry on her way to Salish Treatment Center in
Port Townsend. With Stephen's arm draped over her shoulders,
they'd stared through the salt-sprayed windows, not speaking.

Annie gave her tender shoulder a light massage. She
marveled at how something as mundane as a haircut would
cause her to realize how far she'd come. When she made the
return crossing six weeks later she was clean but not healed.
How quickly she had stumbled into more mistakes, caused
more pain. Never could she have imagined she'd be here, on
the edge of the earth, feeling this strange poignancy. She
wondered whether what she'd learned would be enough to
get her through what lay ahead in Seattle.

There were no other calls. Nothing from James to ask
where she'd gone, what her plans were. Annie imagined the
conversations that had occurred between Dublin and Seattle
since she'd simply left the city without a word. The ranks would
have closed; she'd be edged out of relevance. But she could still
do some good. Eire-Evergreen did not have to have the last word.

Her finger lingered over Bill's name in her contacts list. She would call him tonight, after whatever was bound to happen today. She'd need his sense of humor and rock-solid faith in her.

She tucked the key under the front mat and bid farewell to Moyle Lane. As she backed into the drive that led to Fiana's house, her gaze lingered in the rearview mirror. There was a chance their paths would cross again in the coming days. She ached for it to be true. She'd likely lost Serena, the only woman in her life who had offered a strong shoulder and straightforward guidance. She liked to think that in Fiana, she'd gained the respect and compassion of another.

42

He hoped never to see her again. At least that was the story Daniel told himself as he turned onto the R571, spinning gravel onto the road. There was no room in his life for someone as vulnerable and temporary as Annie Crowe. She was a windmill ready to fly apart, and he wasn't the one to pick up the pieces. She would return to her world; he would remain in his and try not to make the same mistake—attempting to salvage a life that wasn't his to save. It cost too much, this push-pull of opening and withdrawing, sharing and covering up. He'd worked too hard to create a life where the ebb and flow of his emotions were as steady as the tides.

He was heading for the Kilcatherine Peninsula. He'd promised Malcolm he'd walk this stretch of the Beara Way, making note of fence damage and trail washouts from the recent rains, while clearing the worst of the brush and debris. This maintenance was part of the unwritten contract between hiking tour companies and the farmers who allowed the national trail system to pass through their private lands. The farmers took pride in their breathtaking patch of Irish soil, but they were also acutely aware of the millions of dollars the trail system brought to the Irish economy.

Daniel slapped the steering wheel. Here was yet another argument against the copper mine. Those tourist dollars would be washed out in the tailings of scrap metal and wasted rock and soil. Who would want to amble past the open sore of a mining pit or stay in a B&B just off the road, within range of the rumble of trucks and clash of machinery? What brought people to explore and invest in this wild land was the hunger for untouched places within easy reach of airports and ferries, where hikers could tramp in solitude for hours all day and drift into the comfort of a hot meal and a soft bed every night.

The arguments circled through his thoughts and distracted him from admitting why he steered the Rover along the contours of the narrow road as it dipped and wound to Ballycrovane Harbor. Margitte was anxious to finish the installation of his pieces in advance of Friday's show, but he wasn't expected at the gallery until the late afternoon. He had time.

He told himself another story as he strode toward *an Chailleach Bhéarra*—the Old Woman—where he'd taken hundreds of hikers on their way to Glenbeg Lough. It could be rough walking on boggy ground, exposed to the winds sweeping in from the bay, but the views of the Slieve Miskish mountains, the Kenmare River, and Ardgroom and Kilmakilloge harbors made it one of the most anticipated days of the multi-day excursions he led a few times each year.

He'd pause at the Hag and share the legends that surrounded this curious, jagged, animated rock face while the hikers rested, took photos, nibbled at biscuits. Now he could add *Mise Éire* to his storyteller's repertoire. Perhaps even throw in the detail that he'd heard the woman's voice from across the sea, carried on the wind from Ballycrovane to Ballycaróg, a poem that belonged to all of Ireland, inspired by the woman who had given birth to this fierce and beautiful country.

The path was dry, and there was little evidence anyone had hiked this way in recent days. It was the hush before the storm of hill walkers who would soon arrive from every corner of the world and walk well into September. But never so many that you lost the sense of isolation and peace.

The Old Woman sat alone on her perch above the harbor. The wonder of the changing light on the Slieve Miskish to the east or the sheet of sparkling blue that tipped over the horizon and disappeared into the white-blue of the sky never failed to exalt his soul. To the west, the land grasped the sea with fingers of green pasture and knuckles of gray stone mountains. The specks of white and black villages looked like pushpins on a map.

He braced his back against the Old Woman's neck of stone. For once the wind did not push against his skin or pull at his clothing—there was only a faint motion of air. The beeping of a tractor-trailer backing into a drive and the bleated complaints of sheep as they were chased from a pasture rose from behind him. From his pack, he pulled out a wax- and foil-wrapped scone with a thick slab of Irish white cheddar tucked into its sliced middle. He bit and chewed, resting his wrists on the top of his bent knees.

The crunch of gravel and the rhythmic clicking of sticks on dirt and stone caused him to sigh. Not even fifteen minutes alone. He swallowed the last of his late breakfast and shoved the wrapping in a side pocket. The pack was still in disarray after last night's hasty search for a flashlight, bandages, and the emergency blanket to cover Annie's trembling legs.

"I'm beginning to think there are dozens of you, spread around County Cork, just lying in wait for hapless me to come stumbling along."

Annie. Leaning heavily onto his trekking poles, faint lines of sweat running down the sides of her cheeks like tears. Her pallid face was pinched between her eyes and at her lovely mouth, which couldn't quite manage a smile.

43

The road started out easy enough, and the day was so soft and warm Annie felt bathed in a glow of gentle light. Then the base of her right pole slipped on a loose rock, jarring her shoulder and wrenching her tender knee. She stumbled, cursing, but stayed upright. The sun bore down. Sweat prickled her armpits and ran down her spine. Gritting her teeth, she called on the blind determination that had carried her around track ovals in spite of a hairline fracture in her left metatarsal, or a strained groin, or an IT band so tight it felt like guitar strings fused together. It pushed her toward the Old Woman.

Annie continued until she saw signs directing the way toward Kilcatherine Church. She was close, but her feet led her up the drive, onto the grounds of this seventh-century monastic ruin perched above Coulagh Bay. Gravestones topped with Celtic crosses leaned heavily toward the earth like old men bent by the weight of their years. The church itself was barely more than a jumbled collection of roofless walls, a patchwork of stones covered on top by mosses and ferns. Enchanted, Annie wended her way slowly among the gravestones and stood in the shelter of the church walls, smiling up at the tiny cat face carved into the stone above an archway, Kilcatherine's famous Cat Goddess.

"It's a fine day for walking, so."

She was greeted by a tall, thin woman of an indeterminate age, wrapped in a dark-green, knitted cardigan over a loose polyester dress, her salt-and-pepper hair piled at the back of her head, her sharp green eyes peering at Annie over cat-eye glasses.

"You're all alone? You're a little peaked."

Annie straightened her spine and tried to even out her stance. She couldn't help the wince as she put weight into her stiff right side. "It's been a long couple of days," she admitted.

"Well, you're headed to just the place." The woman's smile softened the sharp planes of her cheekbones and forehead. "The Old Woman will give you peace, and if you give her a chance, she might even heal some of those hurts."

"The Old Woman ... do you mean the Hag of Beara? How did you know I was on my way to see her?"

"You have that look about you. Searching for something deeper, something to make you whole."

Tears started in Annie's eyes as she looked into the piercing green ones that saw into her soul. "Who are you?" she whispered.

"Oh, I'm Róisín, but that's not important. *An Chailleach Bhéarra* is the name you'll be remembering. And you can't miss her. If you get to Kilcatherine Village, you'll know you've gone too far. Just turn around and try again. She'll find you."

"That's what I'm hoping," Annie said. "I'm hoping to be found."

"Who's to say you haven't been so already?" Róisín lifted her glasses from her nose and dropped them to her breastbone, where they hung from a chain like an old-fashioned schoolmarm's. "Ask the Old Woman," she said. "She'll tell you."

Annie left the church grounds and continued on the small

lane. Rounding a bend, she came upon a Range Rover tucked into a turnout beside a stone wall. Annie recognized the West Ireland Excursions sticker on the back bumper. Around a bend, a brown, arrow-shaped sign pointed west and proclaimed in white block lettering: AN CHAILLEACH BHÉARRA—HAG OF BEARA—500 M.

She stopped to contemplate the obvious choice: to go back the way she'd come and save the Old Woman for another day, or accept fate, with all its aggravating tendencies.

His tanned legs, covered in fine golden-red hair, were stretched out toward the sea. She couldn't see anything else, but those legs were unmistakable; so was her sense of relief. From the moment she'd seen Daniel's car parked off the road, she'd willed him to be here waiting for her, called to this place by the same force that had brought her up the mountain. The Old Woman was in control now.

44

"I'd call you a fool for making the walk out here, but I can see from your face that the pain is punishment enough."

"The more it hurt, the more determined I was to get here." Annie grimaced and made one last step up to lean against the Old Woman, taking the weight off her sore right leg. "I hope it's not sacrilege to touch the stone. I guess it was too much to hope for a picnic table to sit at. A bench, even?"

"*An Chailleach Bhéarra* would be honored to be your support. But no. No picnic tables. Not even a bench."

Annie lifted her face to the sun, Daniel turned his toward the sea, and silence fell over them.

"Daniel, here's the thing—"

"I'm sorry I walked out last night—"

Their words burst into the air, bumped into each other, and tumbled to the ground. Daniel pushed himself to standing and walked around the Hag until he stood in front of Annie.

"She's smaller than I imagined," Annie said.

Daniel blocked the sun from her face, and she tilted her head to look at him. Her eyes were dark green, with a golden cast at the edge of her irises that he'd never been close enough to see until now. Her hair was tied in two braids, and loose strands fluttered over her ears. Smooth, round studs of jade were pressed into her lobes, and high in her left ear a tiny silver hoop pierced the shell-like cartilage.

Her hair was parted down the middle, and her scalp was tinged lightly pink. He would dig out a billed cap for her. It might not be the warmest, but the Irish sun could burn just like any other. Her skin was free of makeup, and the downy feathers of blond hair swept her lower cheeks and turned golden above her top lip.

Standing so close, he caught a whiff of something soft and delicate—lilies and an oriental spice he was far too removed from the world of women to name. There was the musk of her sweat, an aroma that made him want to pull Annie into his arms, crush her body to his, and bury his face in her hair, her neck, press his lips to the soft skin of her breasts and trace the hard points of her hip bones. Remembering the patches of bruised skin just underneath the thin rayon shirt stopped him from bringing her up and into the core of him.

She was silent, her eyes wide and wary. Daniel realized she was pressed into the stone, unable to edge away. He should step back, pull his shadow away from her body, but he couldn't, not just yet. The sight and feel of her last night hadn't registered with him when it happened—he'd been in guide mode, thinking only of the crisis at hand—a circumstance he faced numerous times each season with hikers who twisted ankles, melted with sunburn, or met the bad end of a raw oyster.

But later, alone in his studio, the vision of her thigh as it met the curve of her bottom had risen, unbidden but not unwelcome. His hands remembered the feel of her waist, the hard planes of her back and shoulders as she pressed into him to gather her strength and find her balance, and, finally, the way the muscles of her abdomen tensed as she pulled away.

He'd allowed his imagination, only for a moment, to hold on to that waist, to feel that body in his hands.

His hand floated to her face. His rough fingers—their skin broken and split by chemicals, metal shavings, and wind—spread across her pale cheek. His thumb landed on the fluttery beat of the pulse in her neck. She closed her eyes, and her lips parted. She exhaled a small, private sigh that hung in the air between them.

He kept his eyes open as he bent his neck to kiss her. Her lips were cool and tasted of the sweet mint of her lip balm. All he wanted was to taste her for one moment. One moment, to forget all the moments that had come before and all the rest that would follow. His hand dropped from her face, and there was a clatter of plastic and aluminum as Annie dropped the trekking poles and caught his hand in her own. She wove her fingers between his and pressed back with her mouth.

No. This is no good. Not for either of us.

Why? was the whispered reply, her mouth opening, her teeth skimming his.

Had he spoken? Had she? Would it be so wrong to be vulnerable, just this once? She was leaving, after all.

45

No. This is no good. Not for either of us. She shrank slightly, not so much that he'd think she was afraid or resisting him, just enough to release the connection of their lips.

Why? he responded.

Annie had no answer. There didn't seem to be a single good reason why she couldn't stand there forever, folded into Daniel's arms, protected from the elements, sheltered from reality. But he released her. Perhaps it was she who shifted away from him. Who blinked, who released whom?

As their bodies separated, she readied herself to erect a shaky wall of defense by turning the encounter into a joke. She dreaded the awkwardness that would inevitably follow.

"Annie." He beat her to the first word, stealing her chance to break the tension with self-deprecation or irony. "What I did, destroying that family, made it impossible for me to believe I'd be allowed to love someone again."

She realized they were still connected. Her hand clasped his, her fingers lost in his warm grasp. His eyes held a journey of pain that gripped at her heart.

"There's someone in my life who would call bullshit when he hears it, Daniel." She felt his fingers tense, and she squeezed hers even harder, refusing to let him go. "My sponsor would tell you right now to cut the crap and stop feeling sorry for yourself. You're not the same person who was behind the wheel of that car. You can't bring that child back, but you have done good in this world. You have to admit that people need you, and that being needed feels good."

"But none of it's necessary. I vowed in prison I'd live only with what's necessary. I've taken too much. I'm trying to tell you that I've nothing to give."

"Listen to yourself. *Necessary*? How are any of us necessary? We get only one shot at this. You and I have messed it up pretty badly, but we're hanging in there. Look at you—what you've been given. These hands and this brain." She shook their still-fused fists, and with her right arm she tried to stretch, forgetting the spear of pain that would accompany any motion above her waist. She winced and gasped but continued. "These legs that carry people through the hills and bogs, making them fall in love with this place. Your art shows them why they love the world, in all its terrible beauty. Your family, this peninsula, your art. They're as necessary to you as food, water, and shelter."

He pulled his fingers from her grasp and took a step back, but she wouldn't be deterred. "And what about love? Does love fit your definition of *necessary*? Or do you plan to spend the rest of your life alone?" She mocked his word, but her tone was gentle.

"Yes."

His simple answer shut her down. She, who had yet to exist alone in her new, tender skin, who had not been truly alone in years, could offer no further argument. In one word, Daniel said everything about their kiss that she dreaded he'd say: *It was a mistake, and it won't happen again.*

"I need to sit," she said at last, slumping against the Old Woman.

Daniel took her by the elbow and led her to a faint depression in the ground, where she folded herself down to rest her back against the rock. She took a long swallow of water from the bottle tucked in the side pocket of her backpack and accepted a wrapped chocolate from Daniel's extended hand. He settled in next to her, on her good side, and Annie fought the urge to curl into his arms.

"I'm leaving Ballycaróg. I'll be gone by the end of the week," she said and popped the candy into her mouth. In her peripheral vision, she caught Daniel's eyebrows raised in surprise.

"What about the mine?"

She considered how much to tell him now, knowing Fiana would fill him in later. Annie was so weary of talking about it. And raising the specter of Eire-Evergreen only seemed to sully this sacred space. "I plan to wrap up my part in this before I leave. Eire-Evergreen doesn't agree that reaching out to the community is all that necessary now, so there doesn't seem to be much need for my skills."

"They're that confident of success? Even with the injunction we've filed?"

"It would appear so."

"Would you consider switching sides?" he asked. "Working to save our little bird?"

Now it was her turn to raise her eyebrows. She flashed Daniel a grin. "I have to admit, I like the sound of that. *Our* little bird." Annie folded the crinkly chocolate wrapper into a tiny square and tucked it into a side pocket of her hiking pants. She left it at that, let a silence fall between them that still seemed like an ongoing conversation.

When the quiet became too heavy, she asked aloud, "How long were you in prison?"

"From the time of my arrest, through the trial, and after I was convicted of manslaughter: five years, eight months, and twenty days."

She watched his profile as she asked her next question. "What is your relationship with the boy's family?"

His jaw tightened, and a faint pulsing began where his teeth gripped and ground together. He met her eyes. "We have no *relationship*." He spat out his answer and bit the final word short. "The boy's name was Daniel. Isn't that rich?

"Will you tell me what happened?" Annie prodded gently.

Daniel's explanation was succinct. He spoke to the sea, not to her, as he recited merciless facts neither time nor punishment could diminish.

Stoned, drunk, behind the wheel of an ancient Volvo and speeding the wrong way down a highway, he had plowed into a car carrying a family named Burke. The young mother and father escaped with broken ribs from the airbag, and the father, Patrick, suffered a crushed left wrist. Their twelve-year-old daughter, Caoimhe, sustained a broken nose and collarbone. Five-year-old Daniel, strapped in his car seat in the back, was pulled unconscious from the wreckage without a scratch on his body. Yet he never woke up. *Diffuse axonal injury*, the coroner had declared. The boy's fragile brain had suffered such trauma that his parents were faced with the horror of a son alive but existing in a permanent vegetative state.

Five days later, while Daniel Savage shivered and vomited in a hospital bed with acute alcohol and methamphetamine withdrawal, Daniel Burke died. For his parents, the child's death was perhaps merciful. For Daniel, it meant the charges against him were amended from assault to vehicular manslaughter.

Within weeks, his system was cleared of years of substance abuse, and the cast was removed from his broken arm. It took months for his case to go to trial, but in the end, he was sentenced to five years in Cork Prison, the maximum sentence.

Annie offered no words of comfort or anger, nothing to indicate she could forgive him or reviled him. But she stayed by his side as the sun warmed their skin and the wind whispered. "Have you ever spoken to Daniel's parents?" she asked.

"Yes." He continued to stare at the sea; whatever emotion his eyes could convey was hidden from her. "I addressed them at my conviction and apologized for what I'd done. Claire Burke began writing to me during my final two years in prison. They'd given birth to another daughter, and Claire let me know they'd forgiven me for killing their son. She and Patrick and their older daughter, Caoimhe, appeared at my first parole hearing and asked that I be released. Parole was denied, and they appeared again a year later and pleaded on my behalf. But I served my full sentence."

"You should contact them, tell them what you would be doing and why, and ask how they'd feel about you appearing on television on behalf of Beara, to save the Red-billed Chough. In case your past and their loss are dredged up."

"You've got to be kidding."

"I would never kid about something this serious. But there is nothing wrong with being part of this campaign. Your art is part of this land, and it tells the story of Beara and its creatures. You are a gorgeous, rugged creature yourself."

Daniel snorted, and Annie was relieved to have made him smile.

"It might never come out. You could simply be Daniel Savage, artist and crusader for the Red-billed Chough. But if it did, and the Burkes have truly forgiven you and give their blessing to put yourself out there, the story would be as compelling as the copper mine."

"I don't want to be a compelling story. Goddammit. I don't want the Burkes to be used like that. I can see why you aren't too torn up about your job. It's a nasty business you're in."

"My business has always been about telling people's stories, Daniel. I've never done anything I'm ashamed of."

"Until now?"

"I wouldn't be ashamed to use you to tell the story of Beara, if that's what you're asking."

"I'm not." He punched at the dirt with the heel of his boot. "You didn't come here to sell my story, or the Red-billed Chough's. You came to tell the story of the copper mine. You never answered my question. Why are you leaving now?"

"I can't tell you that. Not all of it, anyhow. What I could, I shared with Fiana this morning."

Daniel worried his lower lip between his teeth, and Annie took his silence as an indication that he understood. He straightened the watch face on his wrist. "I'm expected at the gallery in Kenmare soon. We should probably get back. It's nearly two."

"We?"

"You're not thinking you'll make it back on your own?"

"I'm not ready to leave here." She swept her hand across, taking in the scenery. "There are things I'd like to share with this Old Woman. Alone." Seeing the doubt on his face, she said, "Daniel, please. I'll be fine."

"I know you will be." He opened his pack and dug around. "But here's an extra bottle of water. And some biscuits."

Annie accepted the supplies, tucking the bottle in a side pocket of her backpack and dropping the McVitie's inside. Daniel planted his feet, as if getting ready to stand. "I wasn't certain I'd see you again," he said.

"I was certain you didn't want to."

A small shake of the head, a breath exhaled. Frustration in, resignation out. "Nothing could be further from the truth." Daniel spoke slowly, evenly. "I hoped you'd find some reason to stay."

If it were only that easy to listen to her heart. Annie had come up with a multitude of reasons to stay, each more emotional and selfish than the last, each built on a scaffolding of fantasy and longing. And what would be the point of explaining it all now? Caught in her own tongue-tied emotion, she remained silent.

Daniel tried one more time. "I'll be at the AA meeting in Kenmare this evening, if you fancy a bowl of Irish stew later," he said.

"I'd like that. I'll try to make it over," she lied. "Good luck with the installation." She'd come to the end of her courage. If she were going to leave, it had to be now.

"Annie." In that one word, an invitation to remain. How she longed to give in to the forgiveness and grace that might await her if she stayed.

"It just couldn't be any other way, Daniel. I have to go. There's just too much work to do."

He probably thought she meant work on the mine and the chough. Annie thought she probably meant work on herself. But the distinction hardly mattered now.

"I'll never forget that kiss." This was as much of a good-bye as she could say.

"I won't, either. Of course I won't."

He rose like a tower above her and slung his pack over one shoulder. There was a moment when the toes of his boots were inches from her hand. She could have stopped him with one touch. As if sensing the same possibility, he hesitated. Then his feet turned in the grass and rocks, the earth trembled slightly with his tread, and she was alone.

Annie folded her arms over her knees and let the tears flow. She cried until she began to laugh in great hiccupping giggles. At last, spent and hungry, she stood and gathered the trekking poles. *Damn.* Daniel's poles.

She cautiously put weight on each leg, bending and straightening her knees. Her bruised muscles protested, and Annie leaned into the Old Woman's solid, silent support. She drained the water from the bottle. "Thank you," she whispered and kissed the pockmarked stone. The Hag's face was immutable, her proud chin tilted up slightly as she stared with hard eyes toward the sea, hair streaming behind in her in the permanent wind of stone. Annie pressed her cheek to the Hag's. "*Mise Éire,*" she said, and her lips met rock warmed in the sun.

Then she listened. She heard the barks and yips of a sheepdog, the alarmed bleats of its fluffy charges, the growl of an engine, the *put-put* of a tractor motor. Carried through the short, green grass, whistling over the stones, came the reply: *Uaigní mé ná an Chailleach Bhéarra.*

I am lonelier than the Old Woman of Beara. Annie had memorized the strange syllables until they'd become fused with the English translation. She listened for more, but the breeze carried no other sounds that didn't belong to the valley below. She ran a hand along the Old Woman's ridged spine and stepped away. As she joined the paved road, her stride became more confident, and the trekking poles clicked and tapped against the rocks in playful strokes.

She tossed the poles in the backseat of the car without noticing the eyes like sea glass that watched her from several yards up the road, the only part of the man that didn't blend into the green, black, and brown turnstile where he sat, making certain she was safe.

~

As she approached Faunkill, every sense ached, urging her to turn the steering wheel left and follow the road to Kenmare, to Daniel. After a few miles, Annie snapped off the Mozart aria trilling from a Cork station and rolled down the window. She pulled off the North Road just outside Castletownbere and popped open the glove box, where she'd stashed her phone before hiking to meet the Old Woman. She hadn't spoken to Stephen since she'd left for Ireland. Less than two weeks ago, yet her marriage felt like part of another person's life.

It was early morning in Seattle. The phone rang several times, and her heart fell with disappointment. She'd finally been ready to make this call and wasn't certain when she'd have the strength again. She waited for the inevitable voice mail. Then she heard Stephen's muffled, "Annie?"

"Did I wake you?"

"Of course not. It's after six. I'm running." She could hear it now, the rhythmic puffs of his words, the distant whoosh of traffic. He must be at Green Lake, headed toward Aurora Avenue.

"Where are you?" he asked.

"In Ireland still. I just wanted to talk to you."

"Now? Now's not the greatest time, Annie. I've got a training session at eight-thirty, and I'd planned for ten miles this morning."

"I just wanted to let you know I'm coming back sometime this weekend. I'm finished here."

"That was quick. You haven't even been gone a week, have you?"

"Ten days, actually." As though he'd already dismissed her, the way he dismissed a lost race or a thwarted personal best. Stephen picked up and moved on better than anyone. They were opposites in this regard. She brooded, reliving every sling and arrow until she pricked her hide raw.

"Sorry." He exhaled in a huff, and Annie imagined him coming to a quick and irritated halt on the trail. "Are you okay?"

Just like that, he tugged at her heart. She got out of the car. She'd parked across the road from a bridge spanning a long canal that fed out to the sea. The water was tranquil, reflecting the bright green tendrils of willows that dripped into the canal and swirled in eddies. A leaden bank of clouds hung over the ocean to the south, but around her the air was still and golden, and the pavement cast a faint warmth.

"It's just as pretty here as I remembered, Stephen. Maybe prettier. I feel like I'm seeing it for the first time."

"It sounds like getting away was the right thing to do. I'm glad you went."

She pictured him running a hand through his damp hair, blond like hers but thinning on top. He would have stopped the timer on his Garmin, calculating how he could still get in the miles he'd planned for this morning's run. She wouldn't keep him. But she wouldn't let him go just yet.

"I've had some time to clear my head. I hope we can talk when I get back."

"Annie."

We're not getting back together was what she heard in his cautious tone. She cut off his thought. "I know it's a cliché, but I want us to be friends. We can't go on to this next phase of our lives, whatever is in store for us, hating each other."

His relief that she hadn't called to beg a place back in his life came through the line as clearly as if she stood next to him, seeing the dread drain from his face. "I never hated you," he said. "Angry at you? Sad and disappointed? Of course. But I could never hate you."

"You deserve so much more than what I could give you. That's why I called. Just to say I'm sorry."

"We tried. We really did. I think things were over even before your drinking became a problem."

She didn't have the heart to argue. At one time, she would have picked him apart, pointing out instance after instance when her efforts exceeded his, when he had clearly given up long before she. "Maybe you're right. If you want to talk things through when I get home, we can. But if you don't, if you just want to get on with the legalities, I'm okay with that too. I just want to start over."

He didn't respond right away. In Seattle a police siren flew by, and then another. She was right—he was somewhere off Aurora. If it were a clear morning, he'd just be able to see the dome of Mount Rainier to the south, like the rounded top of an ice cream cone.

"I'd like to think we can work things out between us, without lawyers." His voice softened. Stephen sounded resigned, almost sad. "I've gathered the divorce paperwork. It seems pretty simple—just checking the boxes and signing off."

She nodded her assent, even as her eyes filled with tears. "Okay." She let a breath out. "That's good."

"We can talk about all the rest—the house, whatever—when you get back."

"Of course. I should let you go."

"You know this isn't about not loving you anymore, Annie. I do. I always will."

There were stones piled up on the ledge of the bridge. As if someone had collected them, intending to return on another day. "I love you, too." She picked a stone out of the pile and dropped it over the side. It hit the water with a cheerful plop. The ripples shifted a paddling drake, and he squawked at his mate. "I'll be going back to the Rainier Suites. I'll call you after I get in."

She drove to Bantry in silence and pulled into the car park outside the Anglican church. Leaving the car, she walked the half mile back into town, in search of a grocery store where she could buy supplies for a picnic dinner. The AA meeting wasn't until six-thirty—she had a few hours to kill.

~

The meeting drew to a close, and Annie joined the queue at the refreshments table, hoping for a Styrofoam cup of hot tea before taking to the road to Ballycaróg. She closed her eyes and pressed her fingers against her right hip and outer thigh, where the flesh knitted together in tender ridges.

"Well, hello there. I'm Bea Moriarty. Welcome to Bantry."

An old woman beamed up at her. She was like a wren, tiny and round with spindly limbs, bundled in soft browns. Annie could see her pink scalp, mottled with age spots, through the fleecy curls wound tightly against her head. She wanted to scoop up this tiny creature and tuck her into a pocket.

"Hello, Bea Moriarty. I'm Annie Crowe." She extended a hand, and the brown sprite pressed a cool, frail claw into her palm.

"Well, now, that's an Irish name if ever there was one, but yours is an American voice I'm hearing. One never knows if suggesting someone might be American is the right thing to do, just in case you are Canadian."

Annie laughed out loud, and Bea giggled. Their turn came at the tea and coffee. Annie dunked a Lipton tea bag into a cup of steaming hot water and held up her palm at Bea's offer of the milk pitcher. "More's the pity. If my grandfather really had been Irish, I could use that to find a way to stay."

Bea peered up at her through faded blue eyes. "So, this is just a short visit then. I wasn't sure, after seeing you here last week. I wondered if you were a friend of Daniel's. West Cork is a small world," she finished, responding to Annie's sharp glance. They'd moved back toward the center of the room, and Bea responded briefly to the many hands pressed to her shoulder with kind but not inclusive greetings. Those who passed gave Annie an inquisitive look but moved on without joining their conversation.

"Some of these souls I've known for most of their adult lives," Bea said. "And some, their parents before them." She placed a feathery hand on Annie's wrist. Despite the ridges of blue veins on the back of her hand, her palm was soft as down. "But you'll be wondering why it is I asked about Daniel."

"I've encountered so many strange things this past week. I've learned to stop asking and just wait for the inevitable sign."

Bea tilted back her head, and laughter warbled forth. "You're Irish, even if your ancestry says not. Come, let's sit. My feet are ready to burst out of these cursed shoes." She wore badly polished brown heels, and her scrawny legs ended in puffy ankles that strained at the tops of her pumps.

Annie took her hand and led her to a pair of folding chairs, the only ones that had not been scooped up as the room was cleared. They sat down, younger woman and old. Bea kept hold of her hand, and Annie felt something like love in the current that ran between the women's skin.

"Signs. Well, yes. I've gone through many years of training to recognize all kinds of signs," Bea said. "But before I was a counselor, even before I was an alcoholic, I was a woman. Didn't I have walking them down the lane and knocking on my front door!" She grinned, showing tiny teeth flecked with red lipstick. "I've seen lots of women enter this church basement and others just like it across the county and set their sights on our Danny. You're the first I've seen him look at with that same sort of hunger."

Annie was floored. Perhaps less by Bea's declaration than by the thrill the words gave her. *Oh, Annie,* she warned herself.

"I'm no different than any other woman who's crossed the thresholds of these church basements. I fell madly for Daniel the moment I laid eyes on him." Annie smiled to indicate she was joking, but her words were the truth. Bea knew it, too. "But I'm leaving Cork in three days. I'm the last person Daniel needs in his life."

Bea clucked and shook her head. "The Addict doesn't have to control everything you do. She doesn't have to define you or decide your life. I know it might seem like that now, when this new world is so raw and unfamiliar, but someday soon, you'll be in charge of your life again."

"How did you know?" Annie leaned in, searching the crimpled pink face.

"How did I know what, dearest?"

"How did you know about The Addict?"

Bea touched Annie's cheek and then pulled her close. Annie smelled the rose lotion her grandmother used to wear and the biscuity scent of ironed linens and something fainter but richer—the scent of peat and brine. Bea kissed the tender skin in front of her ear, whispering, *"Mise Éire: Sine mé ná an Chailleach Bhéarra."*

She sat back with her hands cupping Annie's cheeks. "She lives inside me, too. The Addict. But the Old Woman is stronger. Let her in, Annie. She has enough lives for us all."

"I feel something here," Annie said. "Something in West Cork that I've never felt anywhere else—a sense of being alive, free, strong. I don't want to lose this feeling. I'm terrified to go home."

"Go home you must, dearest," said Bea.

Annie nodded, and the tears spilled hot from her tired eyes.

"But of course, Ireland's not going anywhere."

46

Daniel stood on the window bay, scowling in concentration as he held one of his copper canvas abstracts by the outer edges while Margitte's assistant, Seamus, connected the hanging wires to the hooks above.

"Got it. I'm good, Daniel," Seamus said from his perch on a ladder. "Let her go and see how she hangs."

Daniel eased his grasp and then let go completely. The painting swayed slightly and then stopped, held fast by galvanized steel wire and hooks.

"Perfect," Margitte declared and gave a thumbs-up. The men inhaled and relaxed.

Seamus maneuvered the folded ladder through the gallery to the back storeroom while Daniel stepped out of the window bay and joined Margitte outside. He unconsciously mirrored her stance, crossing his arms over his chest and tilting his head slightly to the right, contemplating the piece as it floated in the window.

The late-afternoon sun shot across the rooftops behind them and through the gallery's plate glass. It struck Daniel's painting, setting fire to the Glengarriff woodlands that shimmered on a panel of copper sheeting. Over a layer of brushed-on patina, he'd painted a patch of downy birch and rowan arching over a carpet of foxglove and buckler fern. He'd created the fine detail of trees and blossoms using oils crafted just for metal canvases, and with the verdigris patina he'd brought out the shifting colors of the sky. As the sun danced with the copper, the painting glimmered like a dream.

"There, you see?" Margitte said, not moving her eyes from the window. "I said this piece would be perfect in this precise spot."

Daniel tapped his elbow against hers and responded to her soft snort of laughter with a chuckle of his own. She'd envisioned a display of his copper sculptures in this large, light-drenched spot, and it had been a battle of wills to convince her otherwise. But as Daniel worked on the painting over the winter, he'd tracked the sun as it angled through his studio and knew this piece had to be where the rays would caress it just so.

"Your friend, Annie. Are you bringing her to the opening?" Margitte's tone was casual, but Daniel caught the impish hint in her voice.

"Why do you ask?"

"I'd like to see her again. There's something alive in her, trying so hard to break through. The woman is like an uncertain moth, searching for her creativity like a flame to send her into flight."

Margitte had described Annie perfectly. An uncertain moth, fragile but determined, searching for light to show her the way. Daniel wondered if he'd ever find out the path she'd choose. If he'd see her work in a gallery someday. Or if she'd just fade from his memory. He hoped for the former, doubted the latter. "She's leaving Cork at the end of the week."

"I'm sorry to hear that." Margitte placed her long, beringed fingers on his arm. "You seemed very attached to her."

"Did I? I hardly know her."

"So why do you smell like her lotion?" Margitte arched an eyebrow and stepped past Daniel, her heels tapping a rapid staccato as she returned to the gallery's bright white interior.

Daniel raised his hands to his face and breathed in. Underneath the scent of paint and copper, he could just detect lilies and the sagey musk of sweat—Annie's scent.

47

Rain pelting against the window roused her from a deep sleep. As Annie drowsed, the crisp patter turned to the sound of water dashed against the glass by the bucketful. She padded to the window and rolled back the curtain. Water sluiced the panes. In the distance the sea was a blanket of gunmetal disturbed only by a wave breaking against the riptide. She cracked open the window so the wind could howl through and returned to bed to watch the grim day begin. She'd gone running in Seattle in weather this ridiculous, when gusts forced even the seagulls into chaotic trajectories, but this morning she would curl up in one of those deep, low sofas downstairs, flip the lid on her laptop, and continue following her hunches.

She probed her hip and thigh, flexed her muscles, and stretched. Her injured side was tight, the skin rough to the touch, and there were pings of pain when she pressed too hard, but it was nothing compared to how raw she'd felt yesterday morning. The healing mystified her.

Lingering in the glassed-in breakfast room, she watched the storm roll over Ballycaróg. Rose, the hotel staffer who replenished the breakfast bar, assured her that the forecast called for gradual clearing and a fine, bright day. As she folded the last bite of smoked salmon into her mouth, Annie vowed to go for a gentle run in the afternoon. She felt that good.

She accepted Rose's offer of a fresh pot of coffee and was flipping through *The Irish Times* when the swinging door that led from the lobby to the breakfast room opened and a silver-haired man in golf togs entered. Annie caught his double take at the sight of her, and she trained her eyes back on the newspaper, resisting the obvious discourtesy of snapping it open in front of her face. Maybe if she pretended she didn't speak English ...

"Well, I'll be damned. We thought we'd never see you again." He was tall, deeply tanned, trim, and he glinted—his wristwatch, the sunglasses perched in his carefully groomed hair, the large platinum-and-diamond wedding band on his left hand, and the thick, braided gold ring on his right. Annie pushed back a giggle. If she were attracted to this manicured, moneyed sort of man, she'd be just like her namesake, a crow pecking at pretty, shiny things.

She composed her face into a vague smile. "Should I know you?"

"You were in the lobby last week when we arrived."

Annie groaned inwardly. Of course. The American golfers who'd piled into the lobby while she was meeting with James and Colm. And this was the one who had watched her so closely from behind his sunglasses. Annie folded the newspaper and ran her finger down the crease, preparing herself to get rid of him with firm grace.

"I'm sorry, I didn't catch your name?"

"Paul. Paul Webster, Las Vegas." He extended a hand, which Annie looked at for a long moment before raising her eyes to meet his.

"Paul. Paul Webster, Las Vegas. Do me a favor. Piss off."

His grin faltered, and his white brows knitted over pale blue eyes.

"It's a dreary morning, so. But she'll clear up before noon, mark my word. Your coffee is brewing, Mr. Webster. Full Irish breakfast?" Rose bustled into the breakfast room with a press pot of coffee, which she set down on Annie's small table, unaware of the bubble of tension she'd popped with her cheery greeting.

Paul and Annie remained silent, locked in a battle of wills. At last, he dropped his hand and his eyes. "I guess you're from the place where they don't teach manners" was his parting shot as he puffed out his chest and strode to his table.

"Everything all right here, miss?" Rose asked in a low voice.

"Just a little peg knocking-down."

"Well, good for you." She leaned in, and Annie caught the scent of scones and butter and lilac soap. "Those lads he's with have come in drunk every night they've been here. Rich American golfers. You watch yourself." Rose angled herself around so she could speak without being overheard and fussed with the jams on Annie's table. "They're leaving tomorrow, off in the morning. Thank God. But I thought you might know them? Or this one, at least?" She lifted her chin in Paul's direction.

"Why on earth would I know them?" she whispered back.

"Well, I've seen that one talking with your man James. They had dinner here together just last night." Rose excused herself to greet another couple who'd wandered in weary-eyed, dressed in full hiking regalia.

Annie considered the rain and wind that pushed against the breakfast room windows. A few minutes later she rose with her mug of coffee and approached Paul's table.

"Hi," she said, resting a hand on the back of an empty

chair. "Please let me apologize for my earlier prickliness. A woman traveling alone has to always be on her guard. There are a lot of assholes wandering around. I'm Annie."

He stood, smoothing his ironed Ralph Lauren polo, and offered her a manicured hand. She accepted it, but her belly lurched at the cold slate of his eyes. Something familiar there chilled her, that fleeting feeling of unease that had pulled at her in the hotel lobby last week. Still, she sat in the chair across from him.

"I understand you know my colleague, James MacKenna?"

A slight tilt of the head, the tiniest shift of his brow—bemusement, swiftly covered. He nodded. "I've known James for years. Longtime associate of his father's."

"So you're in mining?"

"Me? Mining? Oh, no. Mergers and acquisitions. I bring together like-minded companies that could be stronger unified than as competitors." Again the half-smile, polished teeth just visible, a white flash against tanned skin. He raised himself off his seat slightly, retrieved his wallet, and offered her his business card. CEO of Las Vegas–based ...

An icy current vibrated through her. ARC GROUP: MERGERS AND ACQUISITIONS SINCE 1992. Of course she'd heard of them. This same business card was in a pile she'd sifted through before leaving for Ireland. Contacts she'd made at the SME conference, few of which she could actually remember. *Keep going, Annie. Play this out.*

"But then, neither are you," he said. "In mining, that is."

Rose returned carrying another pot of coffee. Her eyebrows shot up under her bangs when she saw Annie at the American's table. Annie winked as Rose placed the pot on the table.

"And you know that how?" she asked Paul when they were alone again. Now there was a smirk. And she knew.

A heartbeat pause. "MacKenna told me. You're the PR."

She nodded. "And it's not a coincidence you're here."

He shrugged, replacing his wallet. "It's serendipitous timing. I've been coming to southwest Ireland every spring for nearly ten years to golf. Kerry, Cork, some of the best courses around. Headed to Waterville today as soon as this squall clears. But sure. ARC has worked with mining and manufacturing companies for years. I've known Redmond MacKenna since he bought his first company in Ireland in 1985."

The dining room door opened again, and three men trundled in, their faces ruddy with sunburns and swollen with sleep—the rest of the American golfing party. It was time to cut her conversation short, before her tentative memory and the connections she was struggling to make tripped her up. The men paused at the oak buffet, which was laden with bowls of cereal and fruit, yogurt, and sliced breads.

Annie rose from the table, hoping to avoid introductions. Pointing out the window, she said to Paul by way of parting, "Behold blue sky and sunshine. Looks like it's tee time."

The eastern horizon still glowered, but Ballycaróg was bathed in sunlight. The pavement gleamed, and droplets clung to petals and leaves, glinting like diamonds. The wind flung an occasional spray of rain from a treetop, but the clouds had skittered off. Before Paul could reply, she collected her bag and sweater and slipped away.

On her way out the door, she glanced over a shoulder. Her parting image was of three men in various states of movement, pulling out chairs, pouring coffee. Only Paul was still, his pale eyes fixed on Annie.

~

Half an hour later, she emerged from her room with her laptop bag and crept downstairs. Rose was in the lobby, talking with the front desk clerk.

"Have they gone?" Annie asked in a stage whisper from the bottom of the stairwell.

"Their driver collected them just five minutes ago. They're headed to the far side of Dingle, so they won't be back until after dinner, we hope. And gone tomorrow."

The desk clerk pulled a face, and Rose huffed. "I love Americans, don't get me wrong. I've got family in Milwaukee, Wisconsin, myself. You're all the loveliest people. But this lot. You should see the state of their rooms. Poor Maggie and Cliff, who have to clean up after them. I shudder to think what their wives must go through."

"I'm sure their wives are glad to have the houses to themselves right now."

Annie settled herself in a deep wing chair tucked into a window bay. She'd checked the tide charts earlier. Low tide at Ballycaróg was just after three. She'd work through lunch and leave for that run at two. She had to say good-bye to the cove. Good-bye to the choughs.

~

"So, tell me." Annie inched forward on her seat and tilted her head toward Paul Webster, drawing him in. "Being in mergers and acquisitions, you must spend a lot of time in Ireland."

He moved his hand closer until their fingers were nearly touching. "Look, are you sure you don't want an adult beverage?" he said, nodding to her tall, slim glass of sparkling water and lime and tapped his own cut-crystal glass filled with two fingers of Bushmills.

That afternoon, the front desk clerk had handed her a folded slip a paper when she returned from her run, drenched from another sudden squall, yet exhilarated by being out in the driving rain.

Annie,
Chased in early by the storm. Our conversation this morning seemed to have ended prematurely. Would love to meet for drinks this evening and talk more shop. Or not, if you prefer. Text me. Up in my room, napping off the rain.
Paul

Annie had crumpled the note and tossed it into the wicker trash basket next to the small writing desk in her room. She showered and settled at the desk in front of her laptop to continue weaving the various threads among ARC, MacKenna Mining and their many investors, and lobbying groups with ties to the DCENR. Dinner was a swiftly inhaled energy bar and a banana she didn't taste, eating only to silence the occasional grumbling sounds from her belly.

But early in the evening, she'd plucked the note from the basket and smoothed it out on the desk. With a sigh and curse, Annie admitted that a chat with the CEO of a mergers and acquisitions company tied to the Ballycaróg mine could be a valuable shortcut through the muddy backwaters of corporate lobbying and finance. Her text to Paul suggesting they could meet downstairs was answered immediately: *Sounds great. Hotel bar, 20 mns.* Annie changed and dashed on some makeup, hardly able to meet her own gaze in the mirror.

And now, as Paul leaned close to her at the bar, she thought: *Just one. I can handle this.* Just one to loosen *his* tongue, to let him think she was relaxed and available; one drink to suggest that the evening may promise more than a chat in a bar lit by the glow of the long spring sunset, the sun at last winning its daylong skirmish with the clouds.

Blackout. The single word came in a chorus of voices. Bill. Stephen. Ryan. Dr. Lamott, her counselor. Serena. Her mother. Daniel. *Daniel.*

She'd never know how many times she'd functioned in public—present, communicative, but so intoxicated her long-term memory held nothing but white noise. Those waking blackouts left no clues telling her in whose room she had awakened or what she'd compromised—her physical safety, her professional integrity, her soul—by drinking herself into oblivion.

I'll stop in time, she told herself. *It's not that I want a drink. There's a greater good …*

And she closed her mind against the protests, signaling the bartender by pointing at Paul's glass and then waggling two fingers. Moments later she took her first sip of alcohol in nearly four months. Smoked honey and vanilla spread across her tongue and coated her throat, and the fiery alcohol warmed her chest as it spilled down the waiting cavity of her body.

"So, you haven't answered my question." Annie inched forward on her seat and tilted her head toward Paul. "About how much time you spend in Ireland."

He leaned in, his cologne grabbing at her with thick and cloying fingers. She drew back slightly, covering her aversion with another swallow of whiskey. "Let me cut to the chase," she said, allowing a coy lilt to temper her words. "Double Irish?"

Paul dropped his head back, his laughter large and loud. "What, did you spend the afternoon reading back issues of *Forbes?*"

She ignored the condescension. Let him think she was

fishing without a hook. "I just didn't realize until I began working on this campaign how attractive Ireland is to offshore companies. Those low corporate tax rates are pretty compelling. But somehow I missed the news that MacKenna Mining had set up two subsidiaries. Eire-Evergreen here in Ireland. And what is the other?" She snapped her fingers, pretending to struggle for the name. Or was she pretending? Her limbs suddenly felt loose and heavy in their joint sockets, harder to move. "In the Bahamas? No, Bermuda. No corporate taxes there. It's like a shell corporation, isn't it? But legal somehow. How does that work, exactly?"

Paul coughed into his palm. "Hypothetically? You could set up a shell corporation." His glance around the room was swift but unmistakable. But the few patrons in the bar were focused on the hurling match playing out on the television mounted over the bar's far end. No one could hear the conversation unfolding beside glasses of whiskey. "Ireland is notorious for being a great place to legally launder money—just look at the Google case."

Annie shook her head to express ignorance, but of course she'd read up on the recent raid of Google's Dublin offices, the company suspected of evading taxes by not declaring the full extent of its business activities within Ireland and beyond. Paul warmed up to his topic, and she let him pour out the scenarios, hoping she'd be able to sort out later what could possibly fit Eire-Evergreen's structure and Ireland's regulations.

Another whiskey, *or was it two*, and Paul's fellow golfers joined them at the bar. Introductions were made, and, like Paul, they were executives from corporate America. Holding on to their names was more than Annie could manage. Holding on to the barstool was difficult enough. The warm, loose-limbed pleasure of that first drink was curdling into shame as she drained the second. Her brain seemed to rattle inside her skull. The nausea felt less tied to the liquid she'd consumed and more to the molten contempt and remorse that churned hotly in her belly. Would she be able to stop before it was too late? Was it too late already?

48

A small reading lamp attached to the wall above his bed etched humped and angled shadows throughout Daniel's studio. He lay on top of the duvet, his hand clamped around a collection of Colm Tóibín short stories. His eyes scanned the words, but his brain took nothing in. When his phone buzzed somewhere in the dark of the studio, it pulled him out of a space deep inside that clanged with the echoes of loneliness.

Cursing, he slapped shut the book and shoved his feet into flip-flops. To wander in bare feet was to gamble with pain. The detritus of his art—metal shavings, tiny nails, wood slivers—escaped his careful sweep each night. Bannon was forever worrying the rough pads of her paws, sucking out the odd injustice.

The dog raised her head, her tail ticktocking hesitantly, and then jumped off the end of the bed to follow Daniel. He skirted the aisle between his worktable and the counters mounted along one wall, hoping he'd see the phone's screen flashing amidst the works in progress. The buzzing stopped just as he spied the phone on the far side of the sink. After a minute or two, another brief drone signaled a voice mail.

"Danny, hiya, it's Kate Ahern. So sorry to bother you, but

I didn't know who else to call. It's your friend, Annie? Danny, you should come down to the hotel. She could use your help. I'll try Fi's number, too, just in case you're up at the house."

His shoulders sagged and his stomach dropped. In his gut, he knew exactly what had happened. He replied to Kate via text: *I'm on my way.*

~

Fiana ran one hand through her thick brown hair; the other pressed a phone to her ear. "Kate, he's just leaving. Annie may not want him there, if she's in any sort of condition to care. God knows she'll care tomorrow. I'm on my way, too. We'll take separate cars, just in case."

"Mom?"

Daniel turned away from the window to see Catriona hanging back in the doorway, listening. She stepped into the room as Fiana tossed her cell phone onto the bed.

"Kitty-Cat, Daniel and I are running into the village. Please make certain your brother turns his light off before eleven. I don't know how long we'll be." She brushed her daughter's bangs out of her eyes and pushed up on tiptoes to kiss her cheek.

"It's Annie, isn't it?"

Fiana shot Daniel a glance and pressed her lips to stifle a grimace. "It's nothing you need worry about. She'll be fine. We're just off to the hotel to see if there's anything she needs."

"Why can't Annie stay here?"

The memory of his first raw and angry years as an addict slammed into Daniel with Catriona's question. Fiana had tried to shield her children from the worst their uncle had inflicted on others. She didn't want that ugliness and helplessness in her home again. Neither did he.

283

"She'll be fine where she is, Cat," Daniel said. "I'm off," he said to Fiana. "I'll meet you there."

Moments later, the Rover's tires spit out gravel as it tore down the drive, Bannon running alongside, barking in fury at being left behind.

~

Daniel met Kate in the lobby. He could hear shouts and laughter from the pub next door. Nothing out of the ordinary, though perhaps more exuberant than usual for a chilly Wednesday night.

"She's at the bar," Kate said in a low voice laced with anxiety. "There's a group of American golfers with her. It's their last night, and they're in high spirits, to say the least. I wouldn't have called, but after what happened Monday night, I knew she shouldn't be drinking."

Daniel squeezed her arm. "Thanks. Which room is hers, so I can get her upstairs?"

"Twelve. I'll meet you up there with some water and tea. Mack is just parking the van, but he'll be in to help in two shakes."

Daniel entered the breezeway between the hotel lobby and the attached pub. His heart sank. He tamped down his despair and took quick stock of the scene.

Annie sat on a stool at the bar, her hair a jumble of shining blond curls. She wore a sheer silk wrap blouse in a green that matched her eyes, and a long leg painted in denim extended to the floor for balance; manicured toes peeked from heels. Two men sat to her left, one stood before her, and a fourth had swiveled his chair so he could rest a hand on her thigh. He handed her a tumbler of whiskey, which Annie accepted in a burst of laughter. She knocked it against the glasses around her circle of revelers. Daniel willed the tumbler to break—less he'd have to wrestle from her—but the commercial-strength glass held firm.

Just as she brought the drink to her lips, her roaming eyes landed on Daniel. She grinned and jerked the glass toward him. Amber liquid sloshed over the rim and onto the rolled cuff of her blouse.

"Well, if it isn't a real live Irishman," she called. "Make room, lads."

Daniel caught looks exchanged between the man who had handed Annie her drink and another who stood just off to her side, his hand on the back of her barstool. Those two were the most sober and, potentially, the most trouble. He ignored Annie and peered into the shadows of the dining area. The few booths and tables were occupied by tourists; most of Ballycaróg's locals found their way to Conor's pub down the road. Daniel walked to the end of the bar, where Luc, the French barkeep who played bohdrán for a Bantry-based ceilidh band, was wiping the counter.

"What's the story, lad?" he asked.

"Daniel, man, I didn't know. She met this guy in the bar earlier and ordered only water with lime at first." Luc's accent was thickly, stubbornly French. "This other American is ordering whiskies. She has maybe two." He grimaces and slaps the bar with a damp towel. "Three? Then Kate tells me cut her off. That she shouldn't be drinking."

"And the guys? Know anybody's name?"

"In the blue tie is Paul. The one with his hand on her leg, he is Vince." *Veence.* "The others won't give you trouble; I think they're embarrassed. But Paul and Vince—arrogant pricks." *Preeks.* "I'm sorry, Danny. I didn't know."

"No worries, lad. No one will hold you responsible. It wouldn't take much to crash her system." He slapped the bar and walked over to the small group.

"So you're not going to play hard to get after all!" Annie popped off her stool, and her knees wobbled.

Daniel's hands shot out and grasped her by the elbows as she tilted into him. The American in the blue tie—Paul, remembered Daniel—grabbed her by the belt looped around her thin waist, and for an odd moment, she was caught in a tug of war between the two men. Annie righted herself, still holding her glass, though most of the liquid had ended up on the front of Daniel's shirt. The acrid, smoky scent of whiskey burned in his nose.

"Whoops!" she exclaimed and slapped his chest where the liquid had soaked through. "Now you're baptized in the waters of Ireland."

"I had that anointing many times over, a long time ago, Annie," Daniel muttered. "Now, it's time to go."

"What's your problem, pal?" Vince set his drink on the bar with a smack and laid a hand on Annie's shoulder. "The lady is with us. Why don't you buzz off?"

"I'm not your pal. And in Ireland, it's bugger off, which is what you need to do. Take your hand off the lady. You too, lad." He nodded to Paul.

The others rose from their barstools. Daniel shot a quick glance to Luc, who was on the phone. Annie had fallen silent, and Daniel felt her trembling.

"Look, Paddy. You can bugger off or buzz off or whatever the hell you want. Don't tell me what to do."

Paul tugged on Annie's belt in an attempt to draw her toward him, but with Annie between them, Daniel dared not force the hand away. Luc slammed down the phone, yanked off his round, rimless glasses, and in three strides he cleared the bar, his scarecrow body taut, fists clenched at his sides. The pub's customers had turned in their chairs or leaned out of their booths, with mouths agape in anticipation of a brawl.

"Gentlemen, looks like there's been a misunderstanding." The voice came from behind Daniel. Annie came to life at the sound. Her head shot up and her bleary eyes widened. "Oh my God," she moaned. She tried to slap away the hand that still grasped her by the belt.

With Annie's squirming, Daniel found his opening and pulled her in a half spin out of the circle. His momentum carried her around, and she collided with James MacKenna. Behind James, Mack Ahern, Kate's husband, came running through the breezeway. He stopped short, taking in the scene and the tension singeing the air.

Free of Annie, Daniel turned with knees loose and slightly bent, his forearms raised to block incoming fists or the barrel of a skull aimed at his face. Instead, the Americans were already shrinking back against the bar with their hands raised, conceding defeat.

"She's all yours, *Paddy.*" Paul smirked. The others edged away, blinking, as if they'd just woken from a dream to find themselves in an unfamiliar place. "Good luck cleaning up the mess. She looks a little green around the gills." The men chuckled.

Daniel felt a hand on his shoulder. "You all right, Danny?" Mack muttered in his ear. "It's over, relax. Go on into the lobby. I'll take care of these bastards."

Daniel straightened and dropped his arms, but his hands remained bolted in fists.

"Luc, thanks. Get back to work, son," Mack continued. The bartender's bony shoulders sagged, and he stopped at a couple of tables to collect glasses.

"We won't be serving you any more alcohol this evening, lads." Mack addressed them in his smooth baritone. "I suggest you let us send up tea to your room, or we can offer you a table here in the restaurant if you're interested in dining this evening. In case you don't like either of those options, be aware the Guards have been called and are three minutes out. I'd hate to see your time in Ireland end on such a sour note." Emanating from Mack's barrel chest, the words carried authoritative weight.

To a man, the Americans stepped away from the bar.

"We've got an early flight. Let's just grab fish and chips across the way," said the beefy, balding one in a thick, drawling accent. Euros were left on the bar, jackets were grabbed, and in two minutes the hush in the pub was broken by the murmur of conversation and the chattering of commentators on Sky Sports from the television that hung above the bar.

Daniel turned, but Annie and James had gone.

49

She wanted the swirling to stop. She ached to slip past the oily nausea and pounding disgrace and hit the rewind button. Two hours, at the most. That's all she needed to reclaim. Two hours to pull back from the brink and erase the nightmare she'd created.

A sober Annie floated above the scene and flinched at her doppelgänger below, wilting against James. She felt his stiff-armed hold of her sloppy limbs, his tight grasp on her arms as he fought to keep her upright. The pads of his fingers dug into the tender spots on her bruised arm, and the echo of pain gave her one more connection to sobriety. She grasped at it, and her two selves reconnected.

The growling voices behind her assembled themselves into speech. She heard Paul call Daniel "Paddy" a second time, and she waited for the crunch of fist against bone. But none came, and her feet moved forward. James had wrapped an arm around her shoulders, steering her out of the pub, through the lobby, and to the stairs.

"No, wait." She grabbed onto the newel, jamming her bare toes against the bottom step with her abrupt halt. The soaked cuff of her silk blouse caught her woozy attention. She brought it up to her nose, and the rotted sweet scent of whiskey brought another wave of nausea. She swallowed hard against the rising bile in her throat. "We can't just leave him in there with those assholes. We have to go back and help."

"He has help, Annie. I wouldn't worry about your friend. He can handle himself in a bar brawl."

"What is your problem with Daniel anyway? You're jealous of him, you know that?"

"Christ. You've got to be joking."

"No, just admit it." Annie swayed and grabbed the carved top of the newel with both hands to steady herself. "You can't hold a candle to someone like Daniel Savage. He has more integrity in his little finger than you'll ever have. Lying and cheating, trying to trick these people into accepting this mine. Talk to me about Paul Webster and ARC Group, Las Vegas. Acquisitions and mergers, my ass. How about shell corporations?"

"Come on, let's get you upstairs." He moved up a step, but she resisted, slipping out from under his arm.

"What, so you can fuck me again while I'm drunk?"

James turned and grasped her elbow, holding fast to her arm. She returned his glare, willing herself not to sway. "The SME conference last year. Yours was the room I woke up in that last morning, wasn't it? You've been playing me for a fool from the moment Serena agreed to give me this campaign. This is all just a game to you. You're bored and spoiled. There was never a question you'd get your mine."

James looked past her shoulder, scanning the lobby for listening ears or watching eyes. "Keep your voice down," he hissed. "You're only making a bigger fool out of yourself."

"Ah-HA!" She yanked her arm away and waggled a finger at him. "See, I'm right, and you know it. You and that slimy minister trying to cover your tracks before everyone finds out what you're up to. Well, you haven't fooled me. Oh, no."

Annie danced on a fine wire. She was inebriated, no question. She thought she had about three minutes before her stomach and small intestine revolted, sending her meager dinner back up. But there was a filament of clear-headed focus, as crystalline and fragile as a glass bubble. She'd have plenty of time to regret her stupidity later. But now she had a chance.

"You don't know what you're talking about."

"I know you started the exploration without the proper permits. You didn't bother to follow protocol. You just shoved money into a shell company that Hugh Doyle's a part of, that Paul Webster set up, and the paperwork magically appeared— signed, sealed, and delivered." She threw out her theory with garbled laughter, fishing with accusations she could later claim to have no memory of.

James's face blanched under the shadow of his unshaven face. His pupils were wide in the low light of the stairwell, his irises hardened to chips of gray agate. His lips disappeared into a tense white line. And Annie knew.

He gripped her arm again, his fingers grinding into her sore, bruised muscles. "You stupid bitch." This made her grin through the fog. *Bull's-eye.* "One word of this to anyone, and Serena Magnuson will be the second call I make. The first will be to our attorneys. The cost of fighting a lawsuit will bury Magnuson + Associates. Either way, you are finished."

The nausea rolled through her in a thick, noxious wave. The odor of whiskey and beer penetrated her mouth, filling it with bitter saliva. "I'm going to be sick," she mumbled. She pulled herself up the stairs with surprising agility. The motion-controlled hall light clicked on as she ascended, and the glare shot blades of pain through her eyeballs.

Swallowing hard, she fumbled with the old-fashioned skeleton key, unable to connect the teeth with the warded gears. Hands closed over hers, stilling her frantic motions, and the key slipped into place and clicked. Annie shoved open the door and bolted into the tiny bathroom. The door slammed shut as she dropped to her knees in front of the toilet.

50

Daniel passed Kate on his way upstairs. She stopped, holding her cardigan closed at the neck with her long, tapered fingers. Her brow knitted under thick red bangs, and worry lines pulled at her chapped lips. "She's with MacKenna. I'm just after some soda water. She started throwing up, and I think she'll need the liquid once she's finished."

He patted her arm, muttered, "Ta," and took the remaining steps two at a time.

The door to Room Twelve was closed partway. He pushed against the wood and entered. James sat in a chair on the far side of the bed, hunched over a laptop open on the white down duvet. He sat up abruptly at Daniel's entrance, his eyes wide, his mouth pinched. He eased the laptop closed, but his hand rested proprietarily on the cover.

"Daniel."

"MacKenna." He wondered if that stricken look was concern for his colleague, if perhaps this man had feelings for Annie that were something like his own.

Their terse greeting was punctuated by the sound of the sink running in the bathroom. The sounds of a toilet flushing followed, and moments later Annie opened the door, clutching a white terrycloth towel.

Her skin was as pale as parchment and mottled with faint pink. With her hair pulled back and her face scrubbed clean, she looked not much older than Catriona. The green silk blouse was gone, and she wore a cream camisole. Daniel took in the patches of blue and yellow on Annie's shoulder, shaken by the sight of the vivid bruises. He felt her pain.

"So, here you are. Both of you. My humiliation is complete." Her voice was shaky as she enunciated each syllable. Even if she'd emptied out her stomach, the poison still coursed through her blood. Tomorrow would be rough.

Placing both hands on the armrests of a chair by the bed, Annie lowered herself gingerly. She sat rigidly, as if hanging on to the shards of her shattered dignity. The unspoken thoughts of three people slammed into each other and caromed off the walls, filling the small space with jangling silence.

"I'll be fine," Annie said into the space between the two men. "There's no reason for you to stay."

There was a soft tap on the door, and Kate poked her head inside. The door opened wider, and she entered with a large bottle of Ballygowan sparkling water.

"I'll just leave this here for you, Annie. Clean glasses are in the wee cabinet."

"Thank you, Kate," Annie replied.

James, now standing with his arms crossed and his feet set wide apart, responded with a slight twitch of his shoulders and eyebrows that Daniel took as a shrug. "I'll give you a call in the morning, Annie. Good luck," he said as he skirted around the bed. He turned sideways past Daniel and Kate and left the room without another word. Daniel noticed he'd left behind the laptop.

"Is there anything else I can get for you, love?" Kate asked.

"I'm good. Please tell your husband how sorry I am. I'll tell him myself in the morning, but I want him to know I'm aware of what an ass I was. I'm sorry I brought my mess into such a fine place."

"Ah, you're grand, Annie." Kate waved her away, brushing a hand through the air. "That was nothing compared to a Saturday night in August, with the Australians outshouting the Irish and the Brazilians trying to hug everyone. I'm just glad those golfers are leaving tomorrow. They've wandered in drunk every night." She sighed. "Get some rest."

Annie closed her eyes and gave a tiny nod, almost a breath. Kate held open the door, offering Daniel a small smile of what he hoped was approval. With one last glance at Annie, Kate closed the door quietly behind her.

Daniel moved to the window and watched as the four Americans spilled into the street, breaking the peace of the village with their hard, flat voices. They piled through the doors of the Fish Platter a few storefronts in the other direction, and silence fell again into place.

Moments later James MacKenna walked out the hotel's front doors. He crossed the street and climbed into his Mercedes but left the door open. His face, illuminated by the interior light, was turned toward the hotel, his gaze to the second floor. Daniel read the turmoil in his unguarded expression, the anger in his clenched jaw. He spoke something unintelligible into the night, slammed his door, and reversed into the street.

Daniel turned back at the sound of Annie blowing her nose. She exhaled a shuddering sigh. "I feel ancient. About as old as that Hag on the hill." She tried for a smile. Her skin was nearly translucent in the low light. "Thank you. I know what you're trying to do, and I'm grateful that you came to my rescue once again. But I'm too tired to sort through all of this now. I'm not the woman you thought I was."

"Can you tell me what happened?"

She dropped her head against the high back of the wing chair. "I met Paul at breakfast this morning. He works for a firm in Las Vegas that facilitates corporate mergers. He's involved in all of this. He knows James, James's father. I'm certain he's part of a scheme to help Eire-Evergreen channel its profits offshore. As soon as my head clears I'll be able to explain it, but right now ... " She waved a hand in front of her face.

Daniel nodded his understanding but hoped she'd keep talking.

"I thought if I could get him to loosen up a little bit ... oh, the irony." She dropped her face into her hands, and a low moan, barely more than a breath, filtered softly between her fingers. "I'm the one who loosened up, thanks to a whiskey, or three. Maybe I did get him to talk, but at what price?" She rested her hands in her lap and smiled weakly, her feline green eyes huge in her white face. "Why are you here?"

"Forgive yourself for the relapse, Annie. There is no shame in being vulnerable."

Annie curled her legs under her and clutched her ankles, shrinking into the chair. "Tonight I remembered that nothing feels as good as being high," she whispered, her eyes closed again, her face contorted in pain. "It's as if rehab never happened. All these months of being clean, wiped away—"

"That's shite. Utter, complete shite."

Annie looked up, startled. But he wasn't willing to listen to her wallow any longer. "You didn't go into that bar tonight to get drunk. I don't believe that for a second." He jabbed a finger toward her, his voice rising along with his frustration.

"You convinced yourself, yet?"

"We both know something happened on that mountain." Their kiss flashed in his mind. It wasn't the something that he meant, but he was helpless not to recall. "Some kind of healing. Your eyes carried a light I've never seen before. I knew then you'd make it, wherever your life carried you."

Tears trickled down her cheeks, and she swiped at them with the back of her hand, her eyes shining even though the fragile skin beneath them was smudged faint blue with fatigue. Daniel wanted nothing more than to scoop her up and cradle her. "I can stay. Tonight. Here. With you."

She blinked, and her body went still. Daniel was sure the thudding of blood in his ears could be heard outside. He'd gone too far. But it was too late to take it back.

"You could."

The thudding quickened.

"But you won't. Go home, Daniel. Good luck."

51

Stay. Please stay.

Just as she had at Ballycrovane Harbor, leaning against the Hag, Annie knew with one word, one touch, she could turn Daniel back instead of turning him away. Yet she sat, fused to the chair by her shame and humiliation, as if she might never move again, until she dissolved into nothingness.

Annie waited until she heard the door click shut before she looked toward it. *Come back. I didn't mean it. I don't want you to go.*

The phone trilled. It took all her effort to raise her hand to the bed, where her mobile sat beside her laptop.

"Annie, it's Fiana. I hope it's not too late to call."

"No." And suddenly it all became clear in her mind. The fatigue drained away, leaving her oddly empty but clear, like a glass bottle. "Your timing is perfect. I need to talk with you. Where are you? Can I come to you?"

"I'm just downstairs at Kate and Mack's. I'll meet you in the lobby."

~

"I heard it all, Annie." Fiana spoke as she crossed the parquet floor.

Annie sat on the sofa's edge, a notebook in her lap, a bottle of Ballygowan before her. She shook her head, not registering Fiana's meaning.

"I was coming through the back hallway when you and James stopped on the stairs."

Annie cringed inside. *Had she really heard it all?*

"Not to worry," Fiana said. "I'm not here to judge." She sat and took Annie's hands. "Do you remember what MacKenna said to you?"

Her own fingers felt like cold twigs, but they grasped Fiana's in a fierce clench. "Yes, I remember. I wasn't as drunk as I let on … " And then it hit her. "Fiana. My God. You were there! To have you as a witness. This is gold." Annie was almost giddy. "I'll write down what I recall, but you can fill in the rest. And there's more."

She handed Fiana a file folder that sat on the coffee table before them. "I made photocopies, but this is everything. I'm not sure what legal lines I'm crossing here, but if you can just help me put tonight's conversation together, it's all yours."

Fiana checked the time. "It's late, but let me make this call. We need to let Mort know what's happened."

From Fiana's grimace, Annie guessed she'd connected with Mort's voice mail. She left a cryptic message, saying only that she'd learned something about Eire-Evergreen and to please call her; it was urgent.

She disconnected and picked up Annie's notes. "I have notes at home of my own," Fiana said. "Mort and I did as you suggested and began connecting names in the DCENR with mining company shareholders. Are you staying tomorrow?"

"I'm leaving in the morning. But you can always reach me. You have my number and my private e-mail." She stood to release Fiana of any obligation or expectation of staying with her. "I should get some rest." The two women embraced.

"You are welcome in our home anytime," Fiana said as they broke apart. "Cat will be gutted not to have said good-bye."

"Please give her a hug for me. You have a wonderful family. I can't thank you enough for all that you've done."

Fiana leaned in once again. "Come back to Beara, Annie," she whispered. "We'll be waiting for you." She touched Annie's shoulder before leaving.

~

The alarm yanked her out of a muddled scene in which she and Daniel were drunk and she was behind the wheel. Or was her dream-self really her mother and the passenger her brother? The sheets were soaked in her sweat, and her throat was clamped in dryness. The anniversary of Ryan's death was Saturday. She had to be home with him, had to be at his graveside. Shaking, she dialed the Aer Lingus reservation line. Annie changed her ticket, wincing at the change fee. Whatever. She'd pay Serena back. Something to be dealt with later.

The room was too small for yoga. She'd bump her head into the nightstand pulling into upward-facing dog or smash her toes against the wall jumping back into *chaturanga*. But she managed a few gentle stretches. Her head was clear, despite a lingering ache between her eyes; her muscles tired but not sore; her knee just its normal twingy ache after yesterday's run. She was still in one piece. It was time to go.

Annie pulled on her suitcase and carry-on. They bumped down the stairs behind her, and she held her breath, hoping the momentum wouldn't send her sailing to the bottom. She'd never figured out where the elevator was, or if there even was one in the hotel. It was more of an oversized bed and breakfast, really.

When she'd come down to the bar the night before, she'd caught a glimpse of Mack and Kate's private living quarters through an open door in the hall. The sound of the evening news and the smell of fried onions wafted out, and inside a child bounced in a mobile swing, her thick pink legs pumping. An older child pulled a face at Annie and slammed the door. She marveled at the full lives behind the doors of this tiny, secluded place that seemed so vulnerable and yet ancient.

Kate herself was at the front desk when Annie pulled up. Her kind brown eyes were puffy with morning sleepiness. Annie realized they must be the same age, that if she lived here, she and Kate might be friends. Hell, Kate had already seen her at her worst. They could dispense with all the getting-to-know-you business and meet for walks, Kate pushing the baby's stroller, Annie holding the leash of a Golden Lab.

"How are you feeling this morning?" Kate's soft lilt eased her out of her reverie.

"Surprisingly well. Thank you so much for the tea and the TLC. Was it you who called Daniel?"

"It was. And Fiana O'Connell." Kate's assent was tentative, as if she feared Annie's reaction. "I hope you don't think I was interfering."

"That call saved my skin," Annie reassured her. "I'm not very good at asking for help; you and your husband were angels to recognize I needed some."

Kate smiled. "I thought we'd have you for another night. But here you are, packed and ready to be on your way."

"I'm sorry for the last-minute change of plans. I rebooked my flight this morning. After last night, I just want to get h—back." She stumbled over the word *home*.

"I understand completely."

"I'll take back far more of Beara than I ever expected to."

She squeezed one of Kate's hands.

"You'll always be welcome." Kate's warm fingers closed over hers. "I'm poking my nose in here, Annie, but I'm going to say it. As long as I've known Danny, he's never given a woman a second glance. We get a lot of hikers here, being right on the Beara Way, and I've heard conversations among some of the women who've been on his hikes that would make you blush. But it's all just admiration and longing from afar. He's the most closed-down man I know. And the loneliest. Until you came along."

Annie melted. Melted into yet another encounter with an open-hearted stranger, one of many that shone like sea glass on the shore, a rare and delightful find. Once, Kate's declaration would have sent prickles of irritation along her skin. But now, after feeling her heart held time and again in this verdant, ancient place, she was able to accept something she'd really wanted to hear. Even if it changed nothing.

"My life's a mess. My husband and I have just separated. It's a nice dream, but I'm the last thing Daniel needs. Then there's the little matter of logistics. I don't belong here."

"No, you don't *live* here. Belonging is quite another thing."

A commotion of voices and feet erupted on the floor above, carrying down the stairwell and into the lobby.

"Ah, Jaysus." Kate's eyes widened, and she pushed away from the counter. "The golfers. Their airport van is due any minute. Why don't you step down the hall to our place. Mack is feeding the kids their breakfast. I'll just text him you're coming." Her words rushed out.

"It's all right. I can handle this one."

"I'm calling Mack all the same. I don't want to deal with them alone." Kate's mobile phone was already at her ear. Her sharp, "They're coming down," was almost lost in the din of the men upstairs corralling their luggage.

"Just one question before they get down here," Annie said.

Kate nodded, her eyes on the stairs.

"Do you have any idea what James MacKenna was doing here last night?"

"He's the Aussie from the mining company?"

"Yes. He came into the pub just as everything started to get a little crazy."

Kate tilted her head in puzzlement. "I was here at the desk when he walked into the lobby. It was just a few minutes after Daniel went into the pub looking for you. He—James MacKenna, I mean—said he was meeting you for dinner."

"Really? How interesting."

"Not true?"

"Not in the slightest." The lie confounded Annie. But it mattered so little now. Eire-Evergreen no longer mattered. James MacKenna was one flight from becoming a memory.

The clatter of men and luggage and golf bags on the lobby's tile floors took Kate's attention away from her at last. Mack emerged from the passage that led to their private quarters with a toddler in tow and an infant pressed against a broad shoulder. He offered Annie a warm smile, transferred the toddler's hand to his wife's, and walked to the group, bouncing the baby in a footed yellow sleeper.

Annie realized she had this one moment to leave her key at the desk and slip away; the hotel had run her credit card when she checked in. She turned away from the commotion—the men hadn't noticed her yet—and gauged her route to the hotel's front door. A door that James MacKenna was just opening. She groaned and laughed. The fingers of fate were not to be trusted. One moment a caress, the next a slap.

"I keep hoping the last time I see you will be the last time I see you." She greeted him head-on, ready for the moment to be behind her.

To her surprise, he laughed. "I expected a far more humbled Annie Crowe today. But not much takes the fight out of you, does it? I admire that." As he spoke, James rested an elbow on the counter and moved closer, his voice sinking into her ear. His tone and the swelling aroma of his aftershave released the memory of a hissed, *You are finished*, and the feeling of fingers squeezed like steel bands around her arm.

Annie recoiled, stepping back into her large suitcase and knocking it off balance. The suitcase toppled to the floor. James leaned away with a smile and then pushed back from the counter, stepping past Annie with his arm extended. James and Paul grasped hands in a vigorous shake.

Annie yanked her suitcase upright. She should have known the world was too small to accommodate her scheme of saving Beara. All she'd done was tip off James that his machinations had been divined and given him time to cover his tracks. But she wouldn't run for cover. Not now.

"Well, if it isn't our favorite PR rep." Paul had grasped James by the upper arm in a show of masculine solidarity but turned the full force of his arrogance to Annie. "You're looking well today, Annie. Far better than I would have expected after your dramatic exit last night."

She weighed the dignity of silence with the satisfaction of a retort.

"You think you'll get away with it, don't you?" she replied. Her voice was low and smooth, with a hint of seductive irony. Years of making presentations allowed her to act the part, though her heart raced and her palms prickled with cold sweat.

"I've worked with men in positions of power for a long time.

Some of those men were truly powerful—they were leaders who steered others by showing respect and compassion. You may be in positions of power, both of you, but you are not powerful. Only the weak and stupid would try to take advantage of an intoxicated woman in a bar."

That was it. It was all she wanted to say. To let them both know she knew. She was done here. The lobby had fallen silent but for the cooing babble of Mack and Kate's baby.

Mack stood off to one side, still jiggling the baby on his shoulder. His wife stood abreast, the other child's hand in her own. The boy asked his mother a question, his Irish accent making his high-pitched words incomprehensible to Annie. Kate ruffled his hair and put her finger to her lips.

"Mack, could I get some help out to the car with this luggage?"

"Of course." He handed the baby to his wife as Annie spun her carry-on in place and walked past the stunned group. As she came alongside Kate, she stopped and kissed her cheek.

"Your children are beautiful," she said. "I hope to see them again before they get much bigger."

"I'd love that. You're welcome anytime, Annie."

Mack was already ahead of her, pulling her suitcase down the hallway toward the exit. Annie followed without looking back.

~

Mack situated her suitcase in the Polo's trunk while she settled her carry-on and laptop bag in the backseat. The doors shut with simultaneous thuds that echoed in the courtyard. The finality of the sound pinged at Annie's heart. It was a good-bye sound, the signal that something had ended.

She drove up Ballycaróg's main street just as the crayon-colored shops were coming to life. From the outside, it seemed that time had skipped over the tiny village, but behind the lace curtains, televisions and computers flickered and hummed just as they did in downtown Seattle. People here worried about climate change and war in the Middle East, whether their children would go to university, the results of their last mammogram, and whether there was enough money for a holiday someplace warm, just as they did in London and Minneapolis. Romanticizing the seemingly less-complicated life here was condescending to people who worked and worried, loved and dreamed as passionately as anyone.

Yet. The slower pace wasn't just an illusion or a tagline in a tourist brochure. This was a restful place, where the weather and tides dictated daily rhythms and moods, where the sounds of waves and wind, sheep and tractors formed the soundtrack; no one spoke of light or noise pollution on Beara. A traffic jam was three cars entering a roundabout at the same time.

It was a choice the residents of the community made, most of them, to live quieter lives, removed from the city and its constant thrum of activity. They weren't removed from the small and large problems, but there was less urgency, less reaching and grasping. But no less devotion.

Annie thought of the faces she'd seen at the Beara Chough Coalition meeting last week and the AA meetings she'd slipped into nearly every night. Wind and worry had etched lines into pale and dark faces alike; people whose families had known no home but Ireland sat beside others who strained to decipher a new language. They all fought to make secure, meaningful lives.

As the bright storefronts disappeared from the rearview

mirror, she sent a silent prayer of thanks for the moments of tender, sometimes painful, introspection the time in Ballycaróg had afforded her. She also prayed that the right thing would be done by the community and the peninsula.

The somber, overcast day weighed as heavy as her heart. It seemed as though she had to push through a thick, invisible barrier to make her way out of Beara. She imagined the elements at work on the peninsula—the sea, the rock, the wind, and the spirit of the community—conspiring to create an enchantment to prevent her from leaving.

She steered the wheel to the left, exiting the roundabout heading southeast, taking the road toward Cahermore. It was the opposite direction she'd intended to go, pushing her deeper into Beara instead of leading her away, but she'd still make Shannon by dinnertime.

She had to have one last look, make one last climb. Not to the Old Woman on the hill, the Hag who'd healed her; they'd had their moment together. No, this was to the first place that had stopped her heart and made her wonder about the direction of her life. The first place where she ached with longing for the home that Ireland called out to be. She drove from memory back toward Knockoura, grasping at the small roads she recognized, laughing with triumph at the brown markers that proved her instincts correct. She parked in the same lay-by Daniel had, beside the pasture of cows, where a laddered turnstile would take her up and over a post-and-wire fence.

It seemed as though one prick of a sharp stone would unleash a torrent of rain from the pregnant skies. The foolishness of climbing without the proper boots occurred to her as she searched for the top of Knockoura, hidden by a thick blanket of gray down. But she'd made it up once with her trail shoes, not to mention soaked socks. She could damn well do it again. Annie decided she'd make it a fast up-and-back, and if it got too wet or windy, she'd turn around.

She popped the trunk to dig out the shoes from her suitcase and saw the hiking poles. She'd meant to leave them at the hotel, but in the rush of leaving, they'd been forgotten. Now the mud-spattered aluminum sticks gave her comfort. They were something to hold on to, here where the silence was so vast.

The sweet-faced, lumbering cows were nowhere to be seen. Annie missed their pensive companionship, wishing they could bear witness to the fluid motion of her legs as she cleared the pasture and rose on the switchback trail. The fog swirled down to meet her, covering her hair in droplets and washing cool on her face. She was glad for the warmth and protection of her fleece pullover and waterproof jacket.

Higher she rose, into the fog, away from all sense of place, where sights and sounds were swallowed in a white wall of moisture. Just at the point where she considered turning back, for there would be nothing to see anyway, she felt a lessening of pressure on her head, a brightening of light above. She stopped and tilted her head toward the sky. The fog wasn't so dense—she could see it shifting and swirling, revealing thin streaks of blue sky before rushing to cover them up. Maybe if she got high enough. She climbed on.

The path leveled off and straightened. Annie felt as though she floated over a green carpet moving beneath her still feet. She slowed her pace, worried that she might take one step too many and walk right off the plateau of land. But she had her bearings; great stones emerged from the fog, and she recognized their faces. She stood inside a small circle of bare earth, imagining it to be the spot where thousands had stood before her, gazing into the valleys and sea below. Her camera bag hung unopened at her side.

The back of her head grew warm. She placed a palm against her skull, felt the heat soaking into her hair. With eyes closed, she tilted her face to the sun. Within minutes the rays encircled her. She faced the ocean again and opened her eyes.

Suffused by sunlight, the water was translucent aquamarine—more balmy Caribbean than frigid North Atlantic. The tans and grays of sand and rock at the shoreline gleamed and sparkled as if sprinkled by glass confetti. They formed a thin borderline between the ocean and the pulsing green of cliff-side pastures. The cloud cover retreated slowly with the force of the sun, but the valley was lost in the fog. Annie had the feeling she could take a running leap off the plateau and land in a soft pillow just above Ballycaróg, sinking layer by layer until she touched down.

"Hopeful, Annie. Be hopeful." She stood a few minutes longer, until the clouds pulled away from the village. Then she whispered, "Good-bye."

Her shoes were damp, the tread caked with mud and who knew what else. Tonight she would wash them off in the sink of her Shannon hotel, wrap them in newspaper, and tuck them in her suitcase.

Or she could leave them where they belonged.

The trunk remained closed, and her trail shoes remained in Ireland, propped against the stile, as if resting before making the climb up Knockoura one more time.

~

"What an unexpected pleasure!" Margitte approached Annie at the gallery's transaction counter and handed one of the two coffees she held to Seamus. She placed her free hand, silver rings adorning her thin fingers, on Annie's forearm.

She felt a faint trembling, a hum of blood and electricity, in her body. "I'm so glad you're here. I have a favor to ask." Annie held up the poles with a sheepish half-grin. "Could you see that Daniel gets these tomorrow? I managed to leave town with the pair stashed and forgotten in the trunk of my rental car."

Margitte tilted her head, searching Annie's face. "You won't be at Daniel's opening tomorrow night?"

Her tone was mild, but her words carried weight that settled heavily in the air between them. It held the burden of Annie's regret.

"No, I've got to get back to Seattle. I'm leaving tomorrow. In fact, I'm on my way to Shannon now, to stay the night." The brief flash in Margitte's eyes pierced Annie's defenses. She'd been read and her excuses found wanting.

"I understand," was the simple reply. And Annie thought she just might, despite the disappointment brimming in her eyes. "Seamus?"

Margitte's assistant looked up from the computer and stood with eyebrows raised, ready to do her bidding. "Just leave those with Seamus—he'll complete the handoff to Daniel tomorrow."

Annie placed the poles in the assistant's waiting palms. It seemed as if she were giving up her last connection to Daniel. Her last excuse to stay. Then she paused and brushed a stack of brochures sitting on the counter with the tips of her fingers. With a tiny shake of her head, she turned back to Margitte.

"Let me say how sorry I am to see you go. I'd hoped you'd be enticed by Grainne's photography retreat." Margitte nodded to the brochures, where Annie's fingers lingered.

"Oh, yes. This." Annie ran a finger down the crease of the brochure, let her hand linger on the cover, longing suffusing her. How easy it would be to stay ... "It's not the right time," she said. "But maybe someday."

Margitte steered her gently away from the desk, toward the adjoining gallery. "Someday," she echoed and let the word hang between them for a moment. "Would you come into the other gallery with me? There's something I'd like you to see before you go." She turned, and Annie followed. "It's so recent, we didn't have time to fit it with a frame, but I rather prefer it this way. It looks so clean and natural."

Margitte led her to a small, unframed watercolor on canvas. In the painting lived all the colors of Beara: the blues, greens, and shades of browns, the hard lines of black rock softened by strokes of creamy fog. The scene showed the profile of a woman in sitting on a low, flat rock on the edge of a high, green plateau. She wore a white tank top and a long white skirt, pulled up to reveal the curve of an outstretched leg. Her hands were folded on the bent knee of her other leg, and there she rested her chin, gazing over the valley that dipped into the ocean far below. Her long blond hair was swept back from her face on one side, cascading over her head to the opposite shoulder. The eye visible to the viewer was a dab of faded emerald.

"He brought this to me just yesterday, hoping I'd include it in the show. I told him I hoped he'd bring me more." Margitte turned from the woman on the canvas to the woman standing beside her. "Your profiles. They are two sides of the same face."

Annie recognized in the painting the blades of her own cheekbones; the long, straight slope of the nose; the cascade of hair; the same expression of longing.

"I so rarely see Daniel's sketches before they become paintings on metal or etched into glass," Margitte said. "This is his only traditional watercolor on canvas I've seen. He's never shown me any of his work with human subjects."

"It's beautiful," Annie whispered.

And it was. Light emanated from the canvas—the woman's skin glowed, and her hair seemed to shift like gossamer thread in the breeze. The ocean sparkled in a slow undulation toward shore, and she could smell the damp grass. She counted back the days. Only eleven since Daniel had taken her and James up to Knockoura, and he'd finished this watercolor.

Annie touched the stamped metal tag mounted to the side of painting. All the other works on display had a brief description under the title. This tag read simply: AISLING, APRIL. Underneath, a smaller, computer-generated tag read: NOT FOR SALE.

"What does this mean?" She pointed to the unfamiliar word. In her heart she meant, *Who is Aisling?*

Margitte said the word aloud, and Annie shivered at the sing-song, delicate pronunciation: *ash-ling.*

"Aisling comes from Irish poetry. I suppose it would be correct to say it's a vision poem, inspired by a feminine spirit. The aisling is the poetic form, and she is also the spirit of the poem."

"Like *an Chailleach Bhéarra?*"

"Well, yes, very much like the Hag of Beara. The Old Woman had seven lives, each in a different form of a girl or woman. She is the soul of Ireland."

Seven lives. Seven women. Annie ticked the names off in her mind: Fiana O'Connell, Bea Moriarty, Margitte Vaughan, Róisín—the woman at Kilcatherine Church—Caoimhe Burke …

Caoimhe Burke. The sister of Daniel Burke, killed by a drunk driver. Tears burned suddenly at her eyes. The beautiful girl at Trinity. It couldn't be …

"Daniel asked that there be no accompanying text,"

Margitte was saying. "It's in the eye of the beholder to interpret its meaning, isn't it?" Her voice touched Annie like a hand, gently steering her toward the right path. "But its subject has insights the rest of us can only guess at. Whatever you think it means, you are correct."

~

A week later, in Caffe Vita on Fremont Avenue, Annie shoved away her laptop, where she'd been customizing her résumé for a PR job in Portland, and picked up *The Seattle Times* she'd tucked underneath her bag.

A small blurb—two short paragraphs—on the front of the business page pulled her in: COPPER MINE YIELDS GOLD FOR IRISH POLITICIANS? Below that ran a subtitle: *Corruption Accusations Unearthed; DM Under Fire.* Annie read on, setting her coffee on the table without lifting her eyes from the page. What she read made her smile.

She folded the section and tucked it inside her laptop bag. She felt deeper inside for her journal and pulled out a thin trifold brochure. It was from the Vaughan Gallery in Kenmare, the brochure that advertised Grainne Petitt's summer photographer's retreat in Beara.

The retreat had never been more than a pipe dream, and Annie had resisted taking a brochure from the gallery. Yet one had somehow come home with her. She'd found it the day after she'd returned to Seattle, tucked in her Moleskine notebook with her airline boarding passes.

She opened the cover, lingered over the small squares of Grainne's mesmerizing photos, skimmed the text that promised the photographer's one-on-one attention and guidance, daylong hikes throughout the peninsula, and warm, dry evenings at carefully selected hotels and B&Bs, getting to know your fellow artists over dinner and ceilidh dancing.

It occurred to her then that she'd counted only five names at Margitte's gallery. Five *aislings*, five spirits, five guides. The sixth and seventh spirits of *an Chailleach Bhéarra* had eluded her.

She flipped to the back of the glossy trifold. With a fine-point pen someone had written, *Annie. Please come.* She ran her finger over the handwriting. From her seat, she looked out the vast wall of windows, past the busy city streets. She saw a green, rolling meadow, and through a thin veil of mist, an etch of brown mountains, and beyond, the vast stretch of blue. She knew, as she punched in the numbers that would connect her with a mobile phone somewhere in Beara, the voice that answered would be in the shadow of those hills.

Eighteen months later

The downy fledglings that broke through their shells of creamy brown or faded jade in May are now spirited juveniles in this waning October warmth. They will remain with their families for many months yet, part of an extended family that nests by the hundreds in the shelter of Ballycaróg Cove.

Sleek, blue-black bodies with crimson beaks prance on red feet, hustling and bustling in the crevices and cavities of the rocky precipice. Pairs at rest warble softly, while others in flight or feeding in the grassy pasture above chatter *kwee-ow* and *chee-a*. Not a one utters a *ker-ker-ker* or *karr* in warning, for their numbers are strong enough to face the rare intruder.

The birds seem unconcerned by the small group gazing at them from the shore below, their cameras clicking and binocular lenses glinting in the sun. The group is hushed, as though they understand they have entered a sacred place. They lean in to hear the low voice of their guide. Every few words, a slight *uh-i* slips into the guide's long *i* sounds, and her r's roll from the front of her mouth. She isn't Irish, they are certain, but on their own last night at the pub in Castletownbere, the group had decided she was Canadian. Either way, she won't say. But she is Grainne's assistant, knows her way around the

315

peninsula, and can hike them all under the table.

A statistician and amateur photographer from Berlin shyly proposes taking her for a drink after the week's photography retreat. Shaking her head, the guide says, "I don't drink," and then tosses a rubber ball along the path. The blue heeler that accompanies her everywhere bounds after it.

"Coffee, then?" He tries again.

"That's so kind, but no. I'm off to London at the end of the week for an art opening. My fiancé is showing at a gallery in Mayfair."

The small, secret smile tells a complete story. The German wonders who the lucky artist is and whether he's skilled enough to catch the light in this woman's eyes. Light that looks like the Atlantic at sunset. The Slieve Miskish at dawn.

"If you come down here at night," she is saying now, "when the moon is bright and the tide is low, you might hear *an Chailleach Bhéarra* speak."

"Who's that?" asks a graphic designer from Nashville.

"*An Chailleach Bhéarra* is the Old Woman of Beara, the symbol of Ireland's women."

Their guide closes her emerald eyes, tilts her head to the cliffs where the precious crows swoop and chirp, and recites:

Mise Éire: Sine mé ná an Chailleach Bhéarra.

Mór mo ghlóir: Mé a rug Cú Chulainn cróga.

Mór mo náir: Mo chlann féin a dhíol a máthair.

Mór mo phian: Bithnaimhde do mo shíorchiapadh.

Mór mo bhrón: D'éag an dream inar chuireas dóchas.

Mise Éire: Uaigní mé ná an Chailleach Bhéarra.

Author's Note

In May 2002 I traveled to Ireland for the first time, to hike portions of the Beara Way. I tramped through bogs, up rocky slopes, and down into villages for pints of Guinness and evenings of *craic*. At the end of my journey, as the Aer Lingus flight taxied down a Shannon runway, I dissolved into hitching sobs. I felt as though I were leaving a lover I'd never see again. Ireland, and in particular the Beara Peninsula, had changed me. I felt a terrible longing—what the Welsh call *hiraeth*—for this place that was not my home but where I felt my soul had found purchase and purpose.

I did return to Ireland—several times, in fact—to hike the Wicklow Way and the Dingle and Kerry peninsulas, each visit revelatory and treasured, but it was always Beara that held most fast to my imagination.

In January 2014 I began my second novel knowing only that it would be set in Ireland and that an Irish legend would be woven through the contemporary narrative. As I began crafting Annie and Daniel's characters, both artists with addictions, I researched various legends and tried out a number of locales. Nothing took my characters in the directions they seemed to be called, and the author couldn't tear her mind away from Ireland's Southwest.

Then one late winter's day I came across *An Chailleach Bhéarra*, the legend, and soon I was reading Beara poet Leanne O'Sullivan's collections *Chailleach: The Hag of Beara* (Bloodaxe Books, 2009) and *The Mining Road* (Bloodaxe Books, 2013). Leanne's poetry spoke to my heart, and within her themes, I found mine. *The Mining Road* tells of the Allihies copper mines that flourished and then faded in the mid-late nineteenth century, of miners and the land that was forever changed by famine, industry, and migration.

In June 2015 I had the pleasure of a writing residency at Anam Cara, a writer's and artist's retreat just a short walk outside Eyeries, Beara, County Cork, run by writer and editor Sue Booth-Forbes. I spent a solitary week working on copyedits of my first novel, followed by an astonishing and serendipitous week with a handful of writers in a poetry workshop led by Leanne O'Sullivan. It was there I wrote my first poems. And I hiked every day, retracing my steps of thirteen years prior along the Beara Way, visiting the places Annie discovers in *The Crows of Beara*.

The village of Ballycaróg and Ballycaróg Cove are imaginary places—exceptions in a novel that winds its way through the real towns and villages and trails of Beara and County Cork and Dublin city streets. Ballycaróg is of course based on Allihies, but don't search for similarities beyond the presence of the former copper mines—unless of course you are looking for the elusive Red-billed Chough. She's there, flitting between fields and cliff, claiming her space in this most beautiful place.

All gratitude for my agent, Shannon Hassan, whose belief in my writing never wavers, and for Midge Raymond and John Yunker, the visionary founders of Ashland Creek Press and my patient and gentle editors. My heart reaches for Sue Booth-Forbes and the extraordinary space she has created for artists in the peace and beauty of Beara—Anam Cara; for John Ahern, who guided me on the Beara Way, and over these many years has become a cherished friend; for Brendan Johnson, who walked so many miles with me, always and ever by my side; and for those friends who opened their hearts to me, sharing their most personal and painful stories of addiction and recovery. I learned from you, and from Maia Szalavitz's important work on addiction and treatment, including the value and the limitations of the 12-step recovery process and principles. To my friends and loved ones: Thank you for your honesty and your vulnerability. Your strength and integrity amaze and humble me.

Julie Christine Johnson

Port Townsend, December 2016

About the Author

Julie Christine Johnson's short stories and essays have appeared in journals including *Emerge Literary Journal, Mud Season Review, Cirque: A Literary Journal of the North Pacific Rim, Cobalt,* and *River Poets Journal;* in the print anthologies *Stories for Sendai; Up, Do: Flash Fiction by Women Writers;* and *Three Minus One: Stories of Love and Loss* and have been featured on the flash fiction podcast *No Extra Words.* She holds undergraduate degrees in French and psychology and a master's in international affairs.

Named a "standout debut" by *Library Journal,* "very highly recommended" by *Historical Novels Review,* and "delicate and haunting, romantic and mystical" by bestselling author Greer Macallister, Julie's debut novel *In Another Life* (Sourcebooks) went into a second printing three days after its February 2016 release. A hiker, yogi, and swimmer, Julie makes her home in northwest Washington state.

Ashland
Creek
Press

Ashland Creek Press is an independent publisher of ecofiction, which includes books in all genres about animals, the environment, and the planet we all call home. We are passionate about books that foster an appreciation for worlds outside our own, for nature and the animal kingdom, and for the ways in which we all connect. To keep up-to-date on new and forthcoming works, subscribe to our free newsletter by visiting www.AshlandCreekPress.com.

CPSIA information can be obtained
at www.ICGtesting.com
Printed in the USA
FSOW01n1208060218
44253FS